BUGHOUSE

JOSEPH H BASKIN

ISBN: 1534702563
ISBN 13: 9781534702561
Library of Congress Control Number: 2016909953
CreateSpace Independent Publishing Platform
North Charleston, South Carolina
Cover Illustration: Tamara Višković

During my employment in the Massachusetts Department of Corrections I encountered employees from every discipline dedicated to the highest standards of professionalism. Each instance in this novel where I detail deviations from that standard is in service to the story and in no way indicative of any behavior I witnessed. Depictions of inmates, too, are archetypes rather than specific examples. All scenarios involving the protagonist are products of my imagination. The only character with some basis in reality is that of Paul and to the extent I represent him in a positive light, I will have done him a modicum of justice.

For my wife

Bughouse: prison parlance for a hospital housing the criminally insane.

The degree of civilization in a society can be judged by entering its prisons.

—Fyodor Dostoevsky

CHAPTER 1

You should probably never attempt to break a criminal psychopath out of prison. Not that I'm trying to give you advice. I mean, we just met. But avoid it whenever possible. Shit, I loathe the idea of advising people. Worst business to be in, the advice one. When things go right, they don't give you credit, and when they go wrong, they don't give you peace. It wasn't my intention to become indebted to a white-supremacist gang leader. In my defense, I did it for a woman. Pathetic, right?

"Who the fuck are you talking to?" Manson was skittish. Understandable. He squeezed the back of my neck. "You need to shut the fuck up. Don't crack up on me now that I'm so close."

Behind me, I heard the sounds of a riot and the stateys and feds charged with putting it down. I closed my eyes and saw fresh images of beaten corrections officers and burning mattresses. The odor of burnt rubber remained in my nose. A command center stood lit up in the parking lot about a football field away to our left. Everything else was dark. I visualized where my car sat parked. To think I'd taken that stroll to my car so many times without fully appreciating the sheer joy of walking away from prison. My car was tantalizingly close. Maybe fifty meters—half the distance of an Olympic sprint. Those bastards did it in ten seconds. As scared as I was, with the possibility of bullets cutting me down, I figured I could do it in five flat.

A moment of reflection. A pause before the plunge. I didn't know if this qualified as a foxhole, but I would have prayed like the first theist if I had known how. Goddamned secular education. I couldn't even do a confession justice. To take my mind off my predicament, I reflected on my curiosity about prison psychiatry.

When my employment began with the Massachusetts Department of Corrections, I had to complete an all-day orientation on rules and procedures. Mostly bureaucratic stuff. To pass the time, I made my requisite jokes to those in close proximity. Wiseass stuff I'd done my whole life. It was mostly to entertain myself, but more's the better if I got chuckles from those around me. Toward the end of the day, a corrections officer gave us a lecture about inappropriately helping out the inmates. He provided examples. Bringing them innocuous things, such as cell phones or toiletries—or, you know, drugs. The CO's attitude wasn't pedantic or authoritarian. It was sympathetic. That was what caught my normally short attention. He said it wasn't that people had bad intentions, but they could be manipulated into doing things they wouldn't ordinarily dream of doing by superior criminal cunning. They would be drawn into schemes by hardened cons before they even realized they'd been duped. *What kind of dumb shit would you have to be to get caught up in that type of scheme? Never happen to me*, the naïf laughed to himself.

However, here I crouched at the mouth of a fence. Jagged edges jutted out toward me. I was as vulnerable to the rifle of a sharpshooting state trooper as any escaped convict. I looked down at my white jumpsuit. No get-out-of-jail-free card in my pocket that would shield me from a hail of bullets. I shook my head and marveled at the curveballs life served up.

I had pursued the job of prison psychiatrist with an equal mixture of idealism and curiosity; I liked the idea of serving the underserved, and it didn't get much more underserved than the prison populace. And I was attracted to the excitement of working in the joint. I'll admit that. Like most of my generation, though, I grew up watching movies and playing videogames, and I didn't think of my own life with enough realness to appreciate consequence. I took chances; stepped out on a proverbial ledge and dared life to make me pay. It didn't disappoint.

I'm getting ahead of myself, though. We'll get back to Manson and the prison break in due time. First, I want you to have the background stuff. Maybe you'll see things my way, or more likely it will confirm what a jackass I am.

CHAPTER 2

Several months earlier, I drove in the rain to my first day on the job. It was appropriate. When speeding to a prison complex, the weather should cooperate. Being disposed to some melancholia, I could never envision living in a place where the sun shone throughout the year. Sometimes I needed it gloomy. Central casting calls for overcast skies when the mood dictated.

The Wampanoag State Hospital. A hospital by name, it was run by the Massachusetts Department of Corrections. If you had doubts about the nature of the place, the serpentine road to the facility educated you about its purpose. The hospital sat on a corrections complex that housed several facilities. Each was decked out with razor-wire fencing. The first was a drug-rehab boot camp. Men could be court ordered to dry out there for thirty days. Then there was the sexual deviants' treatment center. That was where the most troubled sex offenders resided. Lastly, there was the cluster of permanent and semipermanent structures that made up the state hospital. It was easy to be intimidated by the layers of fencing interspersed with microwave dishes that detected the slightest movement. I thought of all the prison-break movies I had seen and worked on my own plan—should that prove necessary.

I parked. The rain had stopped, but the skies remained overcast. I walked to the front gate without a viable escape plan.

When I'd interviewed for the job, they'd taken me through the multitude of locked doors that served to separate and secure the inmates. The medical director had asked me how I felt after that first door locked behind me. He'd

4

said you could tell whether a person was going to take the job by his or her reaction to the slamming door. Some freaked out. They never got comfortable with the feeling of being trapped. Not being in control of their own movements. I didn't freak out, but it wasn't a comfortable feeling. Physicians are all fairly narcissistic, given the necessary trek through higher education, and we find it difficult to have our comings and goings tracked and limited so thoroughly. I didn't take the walls lightly, but they didn't dissuade me from the job.

I entered the prison's administration building. The superintendent (warden, if you like) and medical director had their offices there. A heavyset corrections officer sat in a glass booth. She wore the familiar navy-blue uniform with a nametag over the left side of the chest. Hers read "Jackson." I held up my identification. She didn't give me a glance. I shifted from foot to foot with a goofy grin on my face. No dice. Fed up, I gently rapped on the glass. That was a big no-no.

Without looking up, she said, "Sit down, and I will be with you shortly."

I looked around at an empty foyer without benches. A good first lesson for me. Corrections officers controlled all doors. Those officers sat perpetually in judgment in their glass-encased booths and decided who was going to be allowed access in a timely fashion and who was going to cool their heels. Any outward signs of frustration were only used as fuel for their passive-aggressive engines. I learned to become Doyle Brunson. After a couple of minutes, she looked up and asked if she could help me. There was no irony in her voice.

I could see my new boss, Paul, through the window. He was the head social worker and admissions unit director. He said a couple of words to Jackson, and she flashed a brilliant smile at him. When she turned to me, the smile vanished faster than a fart in a wind tunnel. She buzzed me in to a little antechamber that had a metal detector and a guard with a wand who didn't use either, but waved me through after checking my badge.

Paul greeted me warmly.

"So you found the place OK."

"I did."

We shook hands.

"I'll shepherd you to the unit," he said.

After several more locked doors, we got out to the yard. It was the length of several football fields. The grass was broken by crisscrossed concrete walkways that led to different destinations. The yard was full of inmate patients in their white prison-issued jumpsuits. The "DOC" labels on the backs confirmed each as the property of the Department of Corrections. They walked in formation. This was a reasonable facsimile to a military base. Here the tight formations were part of the strategy of controlled movement to maintain order. I learned more about that later.

Mixed in with the patients were cadre workers (regular prison inmates, or noncrazies, who volunteered to work at the psychiatric hospital in order to get their own rooms and time off their sentences) with their green uniforms displaying the same "DOC" labels. There were no trees in sight, but there were occasional stumps. It made it seem more barren.

Paul must have read my mind. "Used to be a time when there were trees everywhere. Big, old oaks. Beautiful in the spring and fall. Then some knucklehead climbed a tree, and they couldn't get him down. They kept us on lockdown for half a day. After they got him down, they chopped down every goddamned tree. Every last one." He shook his head. "That's the DOC. They would use a sledgehammer to kill a cockroach." We stopped, and he pointed out the different buildings that formed the boundary of the yard. "Each walkway leads to another two-story building that houses two units of men. One unit on each floor."

"No women, right?"

"Not here. Over there are the minimums." He pointed out two buildings. "Mostly the long-termers. Nonviolent guys who will spend their lives here and get buried in that shitty cemetery out back. Over there is the cafeteria. That doubles as a gym. And way over there are the maxes. That's where we keep the more hard-core guys.

"There's an interesting mix of patients here. Thrown in with convicted prisoners from other state corrections facilities are pretrial detainees—some right off the street. They've not been convicted of crimes, but they can be held here against their will due to their craziness.

"Behind us is the building with the infirmary. There's a regular doc who works there. He can handle most small things, but when it gets too serious, he sends the inmates out to a general hospital we contract with. That building also has the Shoe, the high-security unit. It's the prison within the prison. When we get transfers who are especially violent or out of control, they are housed there in isolation twenty-four seven. They can be restrained and treated against their will, if necessary. And there, necessary is quite frequent. If they cooperate, they can sometimes make it to general population. Usually the max units."

I pointed to a tower behind the gym and cafeteria building that dominated the rest of the two-story structures. "Is that a manned tower?"

"Hasn't been for many years. I suppose they could use it in a pinch, but I haven't seen that happen in my fifteen years. Let's move."

Paul and I walked toward the unit on which I was to work. All the admissions from any source were triaged there—sent to longer-term units, returned to the prisons from where they came, or sent back to court. On my interview tour, I knew right away this was the unit for me. The pace was quick, the patients were more acute, and the action was better. Most of the minimum-security units housed the chronic psychotic patients. Many of those patients were part of the great shuffling mass recognizable in any psychiatric hospital. This was the consequence of both mental illness and the drugs used for treatment. The pace on those units was the tortoise to the admissions unit's hare.

Lost in my thoughts, I casually took a shortcut across the lawn. The second my feet hit grass—and I mean the second—a shout tore through the air.

"Who's walking across my goddamned lawn?"

The corrections officer patrolling the yard came our way. I felt my face turn red as I scampered back onto the concrete.

"Sorry," I yelled.

Paul called out playfully to the officer. "C'mon, Jimmy. No reason to bust the kid's balls. It's his first day."

"You better potty train him quickly." The officer continued on his patrol.

"Don't let them intimidate you. They'll bust your hump, but once they know you and you earn some respect, they'll look after you. You'll come to rely on them." He stopped and held my arm. "In that vein, I should tell you there's been a change of plans in terms of your job."

"Oh?" I said.

"Yeah. You were hired to provide extra support to Jack Anderson, the psych doctor who's been here forever. As fate would have it, though, he's put in his notice and will be moving on to warmer climes." His head swiveled. "Hey, I gotta go talk to one of my yums—I mean, one of my social workers. Hold tight here. I'll just be a second."

He jogged over to a woman who was heading out of one of the minimum buildings. I stood, looked around, and tried hard not to appear out of place. A man walked over to me. I gave him a pleasant hello.

"You're Dr. Black, right? The new psychiatrist?"

I informed him he was correct and shook his hand.

"Well, hey, welcome aboard. The name's Jim Lundberg. I work over on one of the minimums. Glad to have some new blood. Some of these people can be difficult to deal with. They're psychotic and bloodthirsty. And that's just the staff!" He waited patiently for my reaction. I obliged with a large grin. "Speaking of the staff," he continued, "I wanted to share with you something that will help you make sense of things while you're here. Let me ask you something first. Have you accepted the Lord Jesus Christ as your savior?"

It felt as if Jim could have kept me there until the Rapture or the Apocalypse, whichever came first. Fortunately, Paul came back and rescued me.

"I see you've met our new psychiatrist. I'm going to take him from you. Thanks for keeping him company." Paul didn't wait for a response; he spirited me away from there.

"Thanks. For a second there, I thought he was going to baptize me."

"Yeah, he can be a pain in the ass, but at least he's lazy." He chuckled.

"Paul, you were saying that the other psychiatrist is leaving." I worked to keep the shakiness from my voice.

"Yeah. Sorry to tell you like this, but it's better for you to know. He's agreed to a transition period of six weeks, until you get your feet wet."

I don't mind telling you this caused me a fair amount of distress. I had little experience doing prison psychiatry and had counted on some mentorship as backup. Sensing this, Paul steadied me with a reassuring hand on my shoulder. "We'll talk about all that later. We're running a little behind, so let's get to the unit. Don't be nervous. You'll do just fine."

The unit entrance was the last hurdle. The officer saw Paul and pressed a button. The heavy metallic door opened slowly. The dazzling light behind us deepened the blackness that grew out of the opening door. It felt like a mouth opening wide to swallow me whole.

CHAPTER 3

If only there were some way of bottling the smell of that place. Without the olfactory contribution, a major facet of the unit's charm was lost. A combination of the open bathroom, the thousand-year-old structure, and the collective body odor from two dozen patients locked in a humid and stagnant room created an intoxicating potpourri. Add to the stench the wet stickiness that seemed to permeate the very walls, and you get a whole sense of what hit me when the door opened.

The unit itself was comprised of two long hallways. They were divided by the officers' trap and the dayroom, where the inmates congregated for most of the day. It had tables that looked as if they'd sprung from the ground, and everything was built around them. Putty gray and of an undeterminable material, they couldn't be moved in any way. It was the kind of furniture you might see at an ancient bus station forced to accommodate thousands of transients of questionable hygiene. In this case, the furniture had to tolerate transients with a penchant for wanton destruction. There was nothing the inmates could do to harm that furniture, so the pieces got used as God (or the DOC) intended. In one upper corner was a television hanging in a contraption made to withstand a nuclear blast. Seeing through its protective screen was a secondary objective.

One hallway was lined with rooms to house the inmates. The other had several interview rooms and the office that accommodated the treatment team. The hallway was slick with the remnants of mopping and what could only be described as floor sweat. It was a misty July morning, and there was no air conditioning in this place.

We walked to the treatment team office. It was maybe fifteen by twelve in dimensions. It held a random collection of desks likely salvaged from Cuba shortly before Castro came to power. Ostensibly made of wood, they differed from the inmates' furniture only in their movability. Opposite the door was a wall of windows covered in metal grating. To the left was a dry-erase board, and to the right was a bulletin board. The desks didn't seem to have an identifiable order.

"Here's our new doctor. And right on time."

"Cut him some slack, Rose. His first day and all." Paul turned to me. "This is Rose, our unit secretary. She is good for sarcasm and little else." He winked at her.

"I was unavoidably detained by a colleague in the yard," I whispered to Rose.

"Who?"

"Dr. Lundberg."

"Did he try to save your soul?" she asked.

"Yeah. I couldn't shake him." I smiled.

Paul sat at a corner desk and put his feet up. "Good morning, everyone. This is Dr. Black."

"Jojo," I interjected.

Paul continued, "Well, I'm sure he will introduce himself to you all after rounds. Now that he's here, we can get started. Roll 'em." He folded his hands behind his head.

As there were no chairs left to sit on, I plopped myself on the nearest desk, and rounds commenced. I quickly learned that "roll 'em" was Paul's way of saying to start rounds. This was a vastly different experience from my days in internal medicine. During that time, the medical team had walked from room to room and discussed the patients in the hallway before we invaded their personal space with an assortment of doctors, medical students, and various other hangers-on. Here at the state hospital, as in other psychiatric facilities, the doctors discussed the patients in their absence. I could only imagine what it might be like if we told our patients what we really thought about them.

Aside from Paul and Rose, several other people were in the room. The team consisted of social workers, psychiatrists, forensic evaluators (those assigned to assist the courts in determining the appropriate placement for the patients), and rehabilitation specialists.

The patients were run down alphabetically. The treatment team members assigned to their care discussed the course of their hospitalization. As I had not seen any of the patients discussed, I got lost in my thoughts. I barely took notice that there was a scramble to get to work. Paul approached me through the throng. Tall and thin, he covered the room in three quick steps. "Jojo, dig those spinning lights. You named after the Boz Scaggs song?"

"No, and not after Jo Jo Dancer either. My dad was a big Celtics fan."

He laughed out loud. "You're Jojo Black. I just got it."

I sighed. "Yeah, I know. The point guard for the Celts in the seventies. My father thought it was a nice tribute to his favorite sports team, and as a side benefit, he thought it would be hilarious that I would be Jojo Black, the white man, as opposed to Jo Jo White, the black man. It was my father's first and only foray into humor."

"It could be worse. He could have named you Hondo. OK, back to work issues. Since this is your first day, I thought we would start you with just three patients. Why don't you pick any three you want?" He pointed to the dry-erase board that had individualized magnetic strips with the names of all the patients. "That board tells you all you need to know: which patient is new, what his status is, and which doctor he belongs to," Paul said.

"Don't you know you can't end a sentence with a preposition?"

We both turned our heads.

Paul responded with a smirk. "You're right, Jack. The board tells you who they belong to, asshole." Paul swiveled his head between Jack and me. "Dr. Black, Dr. Anderson. Dr. Anderson, Dr. Black. Jojo knows he's taking the reins from you. Any tutelage you can offer him will be greatly appreciated. Anyways, I'll let you two get acquainted."

"For Christ's sake, Paul, it's 'anyway.' Not 'anyways,' goddammit," Jack shot back angrily. He then gestured to me. "Come and sit over here, and we'll talk."

I pulled up a chair opposite him. Paul sat down at his desk and worked on his computer.

"Jojo, I'm going to lay it all out for you. The whole of the work can be boiled down to trying to find the needle in the haystack—the truly sick man mixed in the criminal stew. The inmates from the other prisons will try their level best to convince you they are mentally ill and need respite. Why would a hardened criminal want to be considered crazy? I'm glad you asked."

I hadn't. That didn't seem to bother Jack. He went along with his recitation as if he were getting a flat fee, so doing it in less time meant more bang for his buck.

"See, for a lot of the max guys—inmates in supermax prisons with twenty-three-hour lockdown—time at the state hospital is like a vacation. General population here has freedoms they could never dream of seeing at the supermax. Evaluations can last twenty to forty days. That's an eternity compared to the endless time in the isolation of their locked-down lives."

"If they're obviously faking, how come they aren't sent right back?"

"Don't interrupt. Save your questions for the end. Where was I?" Jack said.

"You were educating me on the needle-in-the-haystack theory," I offered.

"Right. Needle in the haystack. So you have your max guys, right? They are one part of the equation. On the other side, you have the sick men who just got arrested off the street. The truly mentally ill. They're trying to accomplish the opposite. They really are fucking nuts, but they will move heaven and earth to convince you they aren't. It's the job of the forensic evaluators to determine which patients get sent back, but they rely on us to a large extent because we assess the inmates on an ongoing basis.

"Your mandate, my young friend, is clear. Treat the group that can be treated, and identify the group that's seeking a free ride. Then send those people back posthaste."

He made it sound so simple. At that time, everything he was saying was really over my head. I mean, it was my first day, and nothing in residency could have prepared me for this kind of work.

Once I got my feet under me, I saw that opinions of each group of inmates varied heavily according to who was doing the evaluating—whether for clinical or forensic purposes. Some were convinced that none of the prisoners were mentally ill, and all had to be returned to whence they originated. On the other side were those who believed that if you looked keenly enough, you could uncover mental illness in just about every inmate. Then there were all those in between. Their opinions waxed and waned, sometimes with the weather or what was going on in their personal lives. That will become important later, as you will see.

Jack stood. "One thing you'll learn to appreciate. We are the last line of defense for the truly mentally ill."

Paul smiled. "Not a bad summation. What you're going to find, Jojo, is that this unit will be unlike anything you'll ever see in your long and illustrious career moving forward. At any one time, we can have hardened murderers looking for a break from supermax mixed in with psychotic patients whose only crimes are their crippling delusions and disorganized thoughts. Twenty-plus men in the primes of their physical lives in a room that's maybe two hundred square feet with no air conditioning during the hot summer. They mingle, with only daytime television to divert their attention. I ask you, gentlemen, how many commercials for personal-injury attorneys and home-medical equipment could any of us take without losing our shit?"

"Paul makes a salient point, as usual. Good luck, young man. I'll be around to address any concerns you might have." Jack picked up a chart and left the room.

"Why don't you grab those three patients and get started?" Paul said and went back to his paperwork.

I looked at the board, took three names, and placed them under my magnetic-strip name. I chose two at random; the third caught my eye. His name was Thomas Jefferson. How could I pass up the opportunity to treat the author of the Declaration of Independence and a former president? I decided to save him for last. I grabbed the chart for the first of my patients and headed out of the treatment office to the officers' trap. Some of the clinicians introduced themselves as I walked. Because I was in over my head, I recalled very few of those introductions. I did see a couple of young women that my genitalic meters registered as noteworthy.

I approached the officers' trap. It was a small area enclosed by fencing and not unlike a ticket window at a stadium. There were cameras arrayed near the ceiling and a small bathroom off to one side. The officer's name was Souza.

"Is it possible for me to see Mr. Smith?" I asked in my most plaintive voice.

He pretended not to hear me. Not an easy feat, given I was standing not two feet from him and speaking through grated fence. I repeated my request.

In a slow drawl, he responded without looking at me, "You got a body alarm?"

"No. Sorry. How do I get one?"

"You got a chit?"

When I had entered the administration building, the guard at the front had given me three coin-like pieces of cheap metal that had my last name engraved on them.

"Oh, yeah. Sorry. I didn't know how it worked." I took out one of my chits and handed it over.

"Figures. Are you sure you can work here? Nobody's going to hold your hand, you know?"

The other officers' interest seemed to be aroused by the smell of ignorance and fear I emitted. On each unit, several officers were assigned with a sergeant to oversee the group. Units with more acuity, such as this one, had a sergeant and three officers. With his rising voice, the CO in the trap attracted the other COs hanging around. I had an image of fishermen dumping rich chum into shark-infested waters. They had a good laugh among themselves at my expense, and that included the sergeant. He was a massive guy with a handlebar moustache. He looked to be in his early fifties. If I were casting for a movie about classic Irish cops, he would be first on my list. His name was O'Leary.

"Sorry. Again," I tried, and I handed over my chit.

Souza reluctantly exchanged it with what looked like a garage-door opener with a clip attachment that I fastened to my belt. If I got into trouble, I was supposed to press the button. Then the cavalry would come rushing. Or so I hoped.

I chuckled at its archaic look. "Not so high-tech, huh?"

"You sure you want to be a wiseass? That button could save your life."

My hopes for rescue dimmed. Feigning contrition, I said, "Sorry. You're right."

Another officer, Johnson, approached me. "Who do you want to see?" he asked. He had kind eyes and a smile that suggested he wasn't interested in busting my balls. A welcome reprieve.

"Tyler Smith."

He walked into the dayroom, where most of the patients were loitering about, and called out the name. A well-built black guy in his midthirties came out and followed me. He wore a pissed-off look on his face. I noted from his chart that he came from one of the maximum-security prisons. I walked with him to the interview room, and we sat down. I introduced myself and gave him the necessary warning about confidentiality. This was an overture we were obligated to make by law so the patient didn't misconstrue the nature of the relationship. Normally, in a doctor-patient relationship, the patient could rely on a level of confidentiality. However, at Wampanoag, what we documented could and likely would be used in court. It was akin to the Miranda warning. We had to let patients know there was no such thing as off the record.

He shuffled in his chair, looked bored, and cocked his head to one side.

"So what brings you here?"

"What do you mean?" he asked irritably.

"Well, why did they transfer you here?"

"They been ignoring my needs since I got here. I keep telling them I need pain meds for my back, and they keep giving me the same Tylenol shit." He glared at me.

"Well, I'm sorry they haven't properly addressed your pain issue." I was already in damage-control mode. "Does your pain affect your mood?"

"What the fuck you think?" He started moving in his chair in an agitated way.

"I can imagine it makes life quite difficult. I notice you have talked about suicide. Is that still an issue?"

At this point, he became more aggressive in his stance and said, "Fuck this. I ain't going through all this bullshit. Are you gonna give me my Oxy or not?"

"Well, I don't prescribe narcotics, but I would be happy to send you to the infirmary—"

"They just gonna jerk me around like before. You a doctor, right?"

"Yes, but I'm not an internist. I'm a psychiatrist. I'm here to talk about your depression and thoughts of suicide."

"Oh, fuck this shit. You're gonna jerk me around like the rest of these guys." He got up abruptly, kicked his chair to the ground, and stalked out of the interview room.

I was left stunned and somewhat shaken at how quickly he'd escalated. It was an early lesson in correctional psychiatry. I walked out of the room and saw Mr. Smith down the hall. He was angrily cursing near the dayroom. One of the officers came over to me. "What are you going to do about this?"

I wasn't sure what he meant. I walked over to where Mr. Smith paced liked a caged panther, the menace in his eyes unmistakable. The COs congregated around him forming an impromptu circle and got Mr. Smith seated in a hallway chair. I asked if he was going to be able to calm down. He looked at me and said, "You know, you stand there with your fucking tie, and you tell me what I can't have. I ought to bust yo' fuckin' head open."

A cold sweat erupted all over my body; I was paralyzed and didn't respond. Nothing in my residency had prepared me for such a bald threat. Even my fabled wiseass retorts failed me. O'Leary steadied me with a meaty hand on my shoulder. "Do you want us to lug him or not?" He registered my blank stare and rephrased his question. "Doc, does he need the Shoe?"

I told him I believed it was the best option. The CO approached Smith who sprang out of his chair and advanced toward me. Instantly the officers intervened, quickly turned him around and placed cuffs on him. I was shaking inside as they escorted him off the unit, cursing all the way. Smith, not the officers. An overhead siren sounded short blasts and an announcement followed. "Emergency on the admissions unit. Emergency on the admissions unit."

Through the open door, I saw several officers running across the yard toward our unit. When they arrived, O'Leary told them their help wasn't necessary. In a bit of a daze, I walked toward the exit. I followed the path of Mr. Smith as he made his way to the Shoe across the yard. O'Leary held my arm gently and said, "You can't go out there."

"Why not?"

He spoke softly. "When there is an emergency, they freeze the yard. Means nobody but officers can be out there. That way, they can get to the emergency quickly. It's another way to control movement and keep the inmates in line." He paused and made sure to look me square in the eye. "Doc, you gotta be more on top of these situations. We'll help you, but if you see a guy getting pissed off, you gotta tell us so we can lug him before it gets out of control. OK?"

"Yes. Thanks." I walked back to the treatment office, hoping that my trembling wasn't visible.

Paul was at his desk when I walked in. He looked up at me and asked what had happened. I described the encounter and asked him about the "lug" phrase.

"Ah, the luggage package. It means they are going to call an emergency, cuff the poor bastard, and haul him off to the Shoe. Lug, pull, tote, whatever. It means he's done. Over. Going to the Shoe. The HSU. High-security unit."

It helped talking to Paul. His mannerisms calmed me quickly. I asked him, "Why do they call it the Shoe?"

"It's easier than 'huh-soo.'" He smiled.

"They want me to eventually be a part of a rotation of docs who round there in the afternoon to give the regular doc a break," I said.

Patients in the Shoe had to be assessed every three hours because they were in seclusion and could be in restraints. Later, I had days I was on call and had to round on those patients as well as take any calls for emergencies that came up.

Paul consoled me. "Don't worry about what just happened. Shake it off. Shit happens in this place. You just have to move on. Write it up, and see the next patient."

I sat down and wrote out both my interview and some paperwork that had to be completed with the lugging. Paul looked up and said, "And you have to call over to the Shoe and let them know what happened."

I called over there; someone picked up after a couple of rings. "Shoe."

"Hey, I'm Jojo Black, the new psychiatrist on the admissions unit—"

He cut me off. "First day, and already you're stirring shit up?"

I didn't know how to respond. A second went by, and he started laughing. "It's Mark, and I'm just trying to crank you. Don't take me seriously. Tell me who and what happened."

Mark was in charge of the Shoe much in the way Paul ran the admissions unit.

I described what had happened. After my brief summary, he said, "He sounds like a pain in the ass. If he gives me shit, don't worry. I'll dart him up."

I knew he meant tranquilizer shots given into the meaty part of the ass against the inmate's will while he was in restraints. I hung up the phone and resolved to follow Paul's advice to move on to the next patient.

I looked at the second name on the board and went to the rack. I leafed through his chart and noted he was serving a life sentence for the first-degree murder of his wife. He'd been transferred here because of suicidal threats.

I gathered him from the dayroom and walked him to the interview room. He was white and middle-aged. He had at least two days of growth on his face and a hangdog look to him. We sat down, and I gave him the confidentiality warning. He nodded, and we proceeded. I went through the psychiatric interview. He gave me small bits of his history interspersed with large doses of complaining. He bitched about the unfair treatment at the prison and then became silent and teary.

"What's causing you to become emotional?"

He looked away and said, "I thought about my wife." I stayed silent. He continued. "She was such a difficult woman. Always telling me I was no good. Always berating me. Then she left. That I could take, but when she tried to prevent me from seeing my kids, that was when it went too far."

"Do you feel badly about how things turned out?"

"Well, I don't want to be in prison, if that's what you mean. But really it was her fault. She shouldn't have done what she did."

The interview continued in that vein. The inmate detailed how difficult his wife was and how she had left him little choice but to run her over with his car. Repeatedly. Whenever he appeared to be moving toward some remorse, his face would harden, and he would state emphatically, "She brought it on herself."

I returned to the treatment team room after that interview feeling worse than before. Now I was shaken and thoroughly disgusted. Aside from the fact this man was deluding himself into believing that his wife was responsible for his actions (a stunning level of denial that, in his case, probably protected him from severe despair), he was not at all suffering from depression. He was upset and angry but not really suicidal. Just manipulating the system. Not someone in need of hospitalization or deserving of extra care. I shared some of this with Paul when I returned. He was sympathetic.

"In my fifteen years, I've seen many guys come through who killed their wives. They usually find a way to blame the wives. There is often little you can do for them. Give 'em a little buff and shine and send 'em back to their prisons." He shook his head and chuckled. "The shit you see here."

Even after such a short time, I could see Paul cut to the heart of things quickly. He and I were going to get along well.

Back on the horse. Last chart for the morning was Thomas Jefferson. The name had to portend better things, I thought, and asked for the patient. The CO yelled the name into the TV room and an older black gentleman ambled up. The officer patted him down and sent him on his way with me to the interview room where we sat.

"Mr. Jefferson, my name is Dr. Black. I am going to be your psychiatrist here. It's important that I inform you that what you say is not going to be confidential and can be used in court. Do you understand that?"

He looked at me skeptically and didn't respond.

"Do you understand the warning that things here are not confidential?"

He regarded me with contempt. "What do you mean you're black?" he finally said.

"No, Mr. Jefferson. My name is—"

"You think I'm an idiot? I can plainly see you're white. I'm black. You got a lot of motherfuckin' nerve telling me you're black. I've been around. You homosexuals here always trying to sex me up. I ain't talking to you. I got nothing to say." With that, he folded his arms across his chest and looked out the window.

"Well, Mr. Jefferson, I certainly didn't intend to offend you. I apologize. Perhaps we can start again."

"I ain't talkin' to you. I taught those bitches a lesson. They the ones should be picked up by the popo."

I failed in my attempts to learn who the "bitches" were, but I did learn "popo" meant the police. Probing further would only make matters worse so I stopped the interview and walked our third president back to the dayroom. I returned to the treatment team office fairly exhausted with what could only be construed as failed patient encounters. Paul looked up to see me come in. "Finished so soon?" he asked.

I sat heavily in a chair. "Well, I wasn't really successful. He became irate and—"

All of a sudden, an alarm sounded down the hall. Everyone froze. I stood in a panic. The sound of pounding footsteps grew louder. Several out-of-breath officers ran into our office and looked around. They all focused on me, and I had no idea why. Then they looked down at my body alarm, which I had completely forgotten I was wearing.

The sergeant shook his massive head and smiled. He announced to anyone in earshot in his booming voice, "False alarm. The newbie set off his body alarm. Go back to work."

I could feel every ounce of blood pooling in my face and ears. "I…uh…didn't…uh. Maybe it just went off." I offered the lame excuse with little conviction.

Paul smiled and shook his head. "It happens to all of us."

The last officer to leave was Johnson, the guy with the kind eyes who had helped me. He turned back to me and said, "Doc, the first time is a freebie. The second time you set off the body alarm by accident, you've got to pay us."

He left with a smile.

CHAPTER 4

The rest of that first day was uneventful. After the morning I had, it seemed unlikely I could screw up worse. By the time I left, holy shit, I was grateful to be done. A shift change had occurred at three, so the same corrections officers were not around as I walked out. My exit lacked the notoriety of my entrance. I was treated with benign neglect. That was a welcome respite from the morning's reception. Getting to my car was a joyous experience. I couldn't wait to get home.

I pulled out of the parking lot and called home. My father answered on the first ring. Old habit. He was a surgeon who covered a lot of hospitals. "Dr. Black."

"Hi, Dad."

Silence. "Jojo. How are you?" It was less of a question and more of a perfunctory statement.

"I'm OK. How are things at home? How's Donny?"

Silence. I had long ago learned not to repeat "hello" into the phone. My father was comfortable being silent. However, he forgot that, without the benefit of visualization, one couldn't be sure if he was dead or just ignoring your question.

"Dad. How's Donny?"

"Everyone's OK. Are you in the car?"

"Yes."

"I've asked you not to call when you're driving."

"I have a hands-free device. Both my hands are on the wheel."

"Nevertheless, Jojo. I'll tell your mother you say hello."

"And Donny!"

Too late. He had already hung up. Believe it or not, that qualified as a lengthy conversation with him. My relationship with my father was complicated. Lots of therapy had helped me come to terms with the father I had as opposed to the father I wanted or needed. Onward and forward.

At that time, I was living in Cambridge. For those not familiar with Boston, it's right across the Charles River and west of the city, and it's its own municipality. Being the home of Harvard and MIT lent the city of Cambridge an arrogance that had been intolerable when I first moved there. After a short while, I fell into the rhythm of my environs and developed a contempt for humanity outside the confines of the Cambridge city limits. All other people were idiots.

My home was a modest one-room apartment. "Modest" being the operative word. I had only recently completed training, where salaries were quite low. That might have accounted for my lack of a better apartment. On the other hand, I found myself on too many occasions driving out to the Indian casinos in Connecticut. Maybe that played a role as well.

I placed another call. This one was to Nigel Thomas. Despite having two first names, Nigel had been my closest friend since we met in the early stages of training. He had graduated from a Caribbean medical school. Having been born into what could only be described as a privileged life in England, he did his level best to screw up his intelligence and birthright with reckless behavior. Despite his best efforts, though, he had still been able to complete medical school and his residency and make a career for himself. While I'd gone to work in the public sector, he'd established a nice private practice and lived quite well in the swanky Back Bay neighborhood of Boston. He answered with a resounding, "Where the fuck are you?"

ᴧ

"C'mon, eleven. C'mon, eleven. Gimme, gimme, gimme." I hovered over a craps table.

I was loving life. All the difficulties of my first day melted away with each throw of the dice.

"You got 'em, Indiana. You got 'em." That was from a hat wearing guy with a southern accent.

Somehow he must have believed I hailed from Indiana or that I was Dr. Jones. Regardless, he cheered me on. So did everybody at the table who reaped the rewards of my good fortune. As I converted another winning throw, I lamented that I couldn't make a living shooting dice. Aside from the social implications (I couldn't see my mother proclaiming with pride that her son was a professional gambler with as much vigor as she announced my status as a doctor), I had to admit that my monetary comings usually did not match my goings.

Out of the corner of my eye, I watched Nigel stroll up to the table with a contented air about him. He generally played either blackjack or went into the poker room. Nigel didn't like dice games. To him, they represented too much chance. Numerous attempts to do statistical comparisons of craps and blackjack fell on deaf ears. Nigel sidled up and gave me a nod. "What's the count?"

"I'm three grand up and hot. Get in on this action," I replied.

"I've only got five hundred on me. Can you spot me some?"

I absently shoved some chips of varying worth into his hands. We didn't have the most positive influence on each other. Alone, we stood on the brink of fair and decent judgment. Together, we formed a dyad of stunning irresponsibility and recklessness.

He started placing bets as I tossed the dice. Time flew. We got caught up in the action and left the table two hours later. That was the charm of gambling when you were winning. Time couldn't move any slower when you were losing, though. I counted my chips as we headed for the cashier. By this time, it was close to two in the morning.

Nigel asked, "How much you got?"

"About six grand."

"I'm up four." He smiled.

"How much of that is mine?" I chided.

"You'll get yours. Don't worry. How about we cash in and get a big-ass breakfast?"

Our pockets loaded with money, we strutted to our favorite restaurant. A middle-aged waitress who might have once been a showgirl approached our table chewing gum. She only lacked a pencil in her beehive hairdo to complete the cliché.

"What'll it be for you gents at this fine hour?"

"You should know, honey, we are the last of the high rollers. And, darlin', there isn't another waitress in all the world who could provide sustenance better than you. Why, only a poet should describe your beauty and grace. We require your finest coffee to begin, and then I will take the pancake special."

Nobody could bullshit like Nigel. With his accent and easy nature, he got away with a lot.

I handed over my menu. "I'll just have toast and a glass of OJ." I had a light appetite—especially late at night.

The waitress walked to the kitchen.

Nigel said, "You give me three more breakfasts here, and I bet I could work my charms on that broad. I'd be banging her on the counter." This was not an uncommon proclamation from Nigel.

"Right on the counter?"

"Yeah, while the grill chef spanks it and cooks the sausage," he replied.

"You have no goddamned shame."

"What's with the toast shit? You're not eating? I hate to eat alone," Nigel said.

"I'm not that hungry."

"Where's our goddamned waitress with our coffee?" Nigel had the attention span of a coke fiend. That was, however, the only vice he didn't have.

After looking around for a sufficient amount of time, Nigel decided to refocus on me. "So what was the first day like? Any prisoner try to slip it into your cornhole?"

"No. Just rough first day, but I'll be OK."

"I don't know why you insist on working there. You should come work with me. Make your own hours. Bill privately. I'm doing pretty well."

I regarded him with a cocked head. "Then why are you always thirty cents shy of a quarter?"

He smiled. "Ah, grasshopper. It is always best to live above your means. It makes you work harder."

"But you don't work hard. You do your best to avoid anything that's too difficult."

"'Tis true, my lad. 'Tis true." Nigel did his best Irish brogue. It wasn't bad. He did have a penchant for accents.

We finished breakfast and parted ways. I didn't relish having to go to work on such little sleep, but I planned on loading up on legal stimulants at Dunkin' Donuts. In New England, Dunkin' Donuts are like stop signs. There's one on every corner.

CHAPTER 5

That first month at WSH went by quickly. Jack didn't come through with either promise he'd made. He stayed three weeks instead of six, and he was never around to answer any of my questions. With more experience, though, I honed my bullshit detector and got better at my job. This aided both my efficiency and confidence.

Each patient was assigned to a psychiatrist who handled the medications and a case manager who took care of placement and gave some counseling. Three case managers were assigned to our unit—two women and a man. The man's name was Herb. I don't think I ever got his last name. Average height. Average build. No distinguishing marks of any kind. He kept his own routine, and it involved the patients and other staff members as little as possible. Paul described him as the kind of guy who could flit in and out of life without making too much of an impact. He was the kind of guy who might disappear for months until someone noticed he hadn't been around, and cops would check his apartment and find his bloated, rotting carcass. He exemplified innocuousness.

Lina was one of the women. About Herb's age, she had a permanent look of harassment. Whether that represented an attempt to appear busy (a la George Costanza), I didn't know. The second woman, Margot, interested me from the jump. An attitude like a New York cabby but without the charm. She wore loose, unflattering clothing, but it appeared she had the goods in the body department. I found the possibility of what was beneath the clothes more exciting. I was always more of a Victoria's Secret than *Hustler* kind of guy. Regardless, I resolved to be as flirtatious as possible. It only mildly disturbed me that I found her dismissive attitude attractive. What a cliché. Treat 'em well, and they think you're a pushover; treat 'em like shit, and they keep coming back for more. Maybe I read too much into it. Occupational hazard.

I found the job increasingly interesting, and I looked forward to rounds each day. Coworkers would straggle in each morning, and when we reached a critical mass, Paul would assume his position. With his chair tilted back and his long legs on the desk, he would say, "Roll 'em." Sometimes a toothpick dangled from his mouth and really completed the overall effect.

A few of the inmates were what we called "Greyhound guys." These were the genuinely afflicted souls with mania. They were driven by impulses out of their control to get on a bus and ride to who the hell knew where. Most of the time, they got away with it. However, if they landed in Massachusetts, with its progressive nature, more often than not, they ended up getting picked up and brought to WSH. This one guy I saw stuck out. He came in crazier than hell. He looked wild-eyed and smelled like a sock that had been worn for a thousand years and then dipped in shit. When I got him in the interview room, he began by telling me he was Jesus. (This wasn't my first Jesus, prompting me to ponder the possibility that God could truly exist anywhere because he seemed to show up an awful lot at WSH.)

He started by absolving me. "I want you to know that I forgive you for holding me here against my will."

This was an unusual way for a patient to open up, but it was not terribly unpleasant.

"Well, I appreciate that. What brought you here?"

The Greyhound guys always had sparse information with them because no one had an inkling where they were from and what their histories were like. They were total mysteries.

"I am a shepherd of God. I am also his lamb. You can't understand real pain until you've walked in my shoes."

It turned out that Jesus (whose real name was James Norman) had a point about walking in his shoes. He had, in fact, walked from Oklahoma. Literally.

It seemed he had started several months prior and had made it halfway across the country. I ended up learning a lot from Mr. Norman. Given the stringency of managed care, hospital stays in the real world were generally real brief—maybe three to four days. You rarely witnessed manic patients get all the way better. They were quickly stabilized and then sent out. At WSH, evaluations were for twenty to forty days and could be extended. Therefore, I had the opportunity to see patients go from walking-fifteen-hundred-miles crazy to complete lucidity in a few weeks. I ended up really liking Mr. Norman. He had a good sense of humor and cleared almost completely of his mania and delusions. He'd led an interesting life. Only recently had his illness become so out of control. His charges were light, and it wasn't uncommon for judges to toss the charges in lieu of treatment in cases such as this. We sent Mr. Norman back to Oklahoma on a Greyhound—for real this time.

Since I'm on the subject of Jesus, it's worth mentioning another Jesus I saw. He was also quite pleasant. He was in his early thirties, and he had wild blond hair and a beard. If you had seen him, you'd have said, "Hey, at least he's dressing the part."

He also immediately absolved me. Maybe adopting the persona of Jesus led these guys to aspire to a superhuman generosity of spirit. This guy had been picked up on the highway lugging a bedroom dresser around. He was charged with loitering. He went before the judge and said his name was ET. When asked again, he changed his answer to Jesus. Astutely, the judge sent him to WSH. He appended each response to a question posed with, "God bless you." I wasn't sure if he was referring to himself as the father, the son, or what. He never clarified, and I never asked.

On the other hand, you had the inmates who weren't in the least crazy. They just thought they could outsmart the doctor with their bullshit stories. One guy was a young white kid with blond hair. He put on a bad act. I mean, it was ridiculous.

"I'm seeing things, and they scare me." His eyes darted around the room.

"What kind of things do you see?"

He leaned in closer as if unloading a terrible secret that he wanted to entrust to me. "I see a black cat walking around. And sometimes there's a greenish leprechaun guy, and he tells me to do things."

I gave him an uh-huh and started writing my note. I usually didn't write much when I saw patients. It could be construed as disrespectful to sit in the room and write while a patient talked. It was also a prudent policy when dealing with a paranoid psychotic who might become convinced you were writing negative things about him. On this guy, though, I wasn't wasting my time; I was going to multitask. I mean, visual hallucinations can occur but usually within the context of other symptoms. This guy was setting off my bullshit meter full force. Normally, if I was with a scary individual, I would never let on that I thought he was full of shit. It was a somewhat ironic aspect to the work. Those who pretended to be crazy usually weren't, and those who were crazy as shithouse rats didn't think there was anything wrong with them.

With those I thought were faking, usually I pretended I was believing their every word. It was like some bizarre poker game between the inmate and me. They might up the ante, but my words never betrayed my hand. They eventually understood that I didn't buy what they were selling. I wouldn't order the medications they were looking for, and I wouldn't recommend they stay longer than the bare minimum. Once the hard-core prisoner realized I had called his bluff, he would usually accuse me of being a liar—even though I had promised nothing. What a world! Every word out of his mouth could be a lie, but if I didn't give what he wanted, I was the liar. I never took it personally, though. I understood his behavior for what it was—an attempt to get respite from his shitty prison life. For him, why not go for it? What did he have to lose? All he had was time.

Thompson, though, played the game poorly. Shameful. Really an insult to those who put in real effort to fake it. His attempts to feign mental illness only lasted as long as he was in the interview room. Otherwise, on the unit and in the gym, he could be clearly seen laughing it up with other patients and causing mild trouble. Each time I saw him in the interview room, though, he treated me to the same cock-and-bull story about black cats and leprechauns, and I obliged him with bored looks. I would have just discharged him back to the prison without a thought, but for some reason, I felt compelled to confront him. He wasn't intimidating enough for me to worry about him going off, and I thought maybe I could do him some good.

We sat opposite each other during the last interview before he got sent back to the prison. I fixed him with a resolute look that I hoped carried equal parts forthrightness and compassion. "You know, Mr. Thompson, I have to say something. Your symptoms are quite unusual. In fact, I would go so far as to say you're full of shit."

He gave me a blank stare for a few seconds. I held his gaze without animus; I really wasn't trying to embarrass him. I sensed something in this kid; maybe he could do something with his life if he matured. After a few more seconds, he broke out in a broad grin. In that smile, he declared himself a hustler—not a psychopath. He was a good-looking guy who believed he could skate through every situation with a thousand-watt grin.

"Ah, Doc, you got me. I was just pulling your chain. I don't want to go back to prison. It sucks there. Locked away for so many hours, I'm bored out of my mind."

"Well, why didn't you just say that?" I asked. "At least then we could have talked about something real."

"I don't know. I thought maybe I could stay longer if I made up that shit. It's boring as hell in that cell with nothing to do and nobody to talk to."

"How much time do you have left?"

"About eight months if I continue working."

In prison, jobs and schooling could garner people good time and shave days per month off their sentences.

I leaned back in my chair and said, "Listen, Mr. Thompson. You seem like a reasonably smart guy. Spend the next eight months planning what you are going to do when you get out. Make it so you never end up in a shithole like this again."

He grinned again. "Don't worry about me, Doc. I got plans."

We finished and left the interview room. He turned toward the dayroom, and I went in the opposite direction.

"Hey, Doc!" He turned to me. "I had you fooled for a little while, didn't I?"

"Wise up. Stay out of prison," I said, and I resumed my walk down the hallway.

He continued his march to the dayroom while yelling and whooping it up. "I had you, boy. I had you. I could've kept it going, but I got bored. I had you."

Perhaps he wasn't going to do well after all.

Chapter 6

It was also at this time that I first met Cecil Goldberg, a notorious inmate. He had a reputation at WSH. He was like the character of Norm on *Cheers*. Everyone knew his name. However, unlike Norm, nobody was delighted to see him. He was as disruptive a force as we would see at WSH. He had a penchant for inserting things that were not meant to be inserted into places on his body that were not insert friendly. Some of those places included orifices, and I mean every conceivable hole. He was reputed to be wicked smart and could manipulate even the most hardened of clinicians. Doctors were encouraged to alternate taking care of him because he was so frequently admitted, and he was so toxic. For one person to see him consistently would be cruel and unusual. Strangely, he turned out to be a godsend for me. You'll see that later on, though.

On this first meeting, I was assigned to be his psychiatrist. Margot was going to work assiduously on getting him the hell back to his prison tout de suite. That was the best anyone could hope for with Cecil. I took the opportunity to discuss the case with her. I was making any excuse I could find to talk to her.

Margot worked at one of the desks in the treatment team office. She wore one of her big sweaters and androgynous pants. She was trying hard not to be attractive. I initially understood it within the context of WSH; I didn't imagine it flattering to be hit on by the likes of the prison partisans. Then it dawned on me. Maybe I had it backward. She always dressed down, and it happened to be convenient in avoiding prisoners' leers. I sat down opposite her.

"Margot, we should probably be on the same page for Cecil. He has the propensity to pit us against each other."

She looked up slowly with an expression that screamed, "No shit." Instead, she said, "Thanks for the update. I know Cecil quite well. I would just advise you not get into a discussion about Valium with him. He likes his Valium."

"Got it. Order him some Valium. I'll get on it right away." I stood.

She looked up from what she was writing and said, "You're not listening. I told you not to give him any Valium."

"Right," I replied. "Get him some Valium right away. Jeez. I don't need to be told twice." To heighten the effect of my shtick, I made as if to go to his chart.

She got disgusted and went back to what she was doing. As you can see, I didn't have much of a rap. My oppositional humor was the adult equivalent of pulling a girl's hair in kindergarten. Besides Andy Kaufman, who is dead, few people appreciate that kind of pain-in-the-ass humor. However, given my neurotic defenses at the time, it was the best I could muster.

Back to Cecil. I retrieved him and brought him to the interview room. We sat, and I looked him over. He didn't look like much. Cecil wore glasses that looked as if they had once been made of plastic but were now a patchwork of lenses and Scotch tape. He could have been thirty or fifty. His gray hair clashed with a youthful look. He was disheveled but pleasant and cooperative.

"I've never met you before. You must be new."

"Yes, Mr. Goldberg. I'm Dr. Black. I'll be taking care of you while you are here this time."

"What are your credentials, please?"

The expectant look on Cecil's face was priceless. You would have thought he was interviewing me for a job. His legs were crossed, and his hands were folded neatly in his lap.

I actually laughed. "Why don't you tell me what happened to get you here?"

"I don't think it's funny. You're going to be prescribing me very powerful psychotropic drugs that can have long-lasting effects on my brain—not to mention my body. I think it appropriate to know just who is going to be responsible for my care."

He continued his unsettling glare, but I had to admit he was right. I just wasn't used to being called to the carpet, as it were, in prison.

"You're right, Mr. Goldberg. My mistake." I proceeded to share my various degrees and training programs with Cecil.

He loosened up and smiled. "There. That wasn't so bad. So what brought me here is I began feeling suicidal again."

He prattled on. There was something odd about his mannerisms; he did these extensive gesticulations with his hands and spoke in a too-loud, monotone voice. It was hypnotic. All his voiced reasons to be suicidal melded together in my brain. (As it turned out, he was trying to avoid paying a large debt to an even larger inmate on a big college football game.) His litany sounded well-rehearsed.

"And I need to be on Valium. Ten M-G." He actually enunciated the letters. "At least four times a day. On that there can be no debate or discussion."

"Mr. Goldberg, you have been here on numerous occasions. You know we can't provide patients with Valium."

We were not able to prescribe controlled substances. It was a relief really. It was known throughout the prison system that those kinds of pills were verboten. That alleviated us from having to deal with the pain in the ass of prescribing anything "fun" that the inmates could fight over or trade.

He proceeded as if I hadn't spoken or said no to his request. "And I need to have a room close to the officers' trap. They put me too far down the hall. If I am away from the officers…" He put his hands up in a shrugging gesture. "Well, who can say what I'm capable of doing?"

I stood. "OK, Mr. Goldberg, I think I have enough information."

He stood as well. "Who can say? Who knows what I might be inclined to do?"

"Message received, Cecil. Loud and clear."

We walked out of the room and went our separate ways. I noticed an officer was standing by the door. He gave me a knowing look and escorted Cecil back to the common room. Cecil was still saying in a singsong voice, "Who's to say? Who's to say?"

I entered the treatment office. Paul looked up. "So how's old Cecil?"

"Well, he threatened to stir up shit if he didn't get his way. Other than that, I can't see that this guy suffers from a mental illness. He doesn't look crazy to me."

Paul stretched his legs and put his arms over his head. "Cecil is a question for the ages. There are those who would swear on a stack of bibles that Cecil is one of the craziest fuckers ever to walk these hallways. Others believe he is half a genius who has been pulling the wool over psychiatrists' eyes for the past ten years."

"Holy shit. What about psych testing?" I asked.

Paper-and-pencil psychometric tests could assist in separating out the bullshitters from the legitimate crowd.

"Oh, he's been tested. More than you can imagine. Still inconclusive. You know those tests still need to be interpreted, and the interpretations have varied."

I sat and wrote my note. A couple of minutes later, Paul spoke again. "You know what the most fucked-up part of it is?" I looked up at Paul. "He's not from around here. He comes from California and is still wanted there for some fuckin' thing. He came to Massachusetts and got picked up on a minor beef. While sitting in jail, he assaulted another inmate. Each time he has gotten close to being released, he gets into another altercation that adds more time to his sentence. He was initially supposed to be locked up for nine months. He has been in the Mass Department of Corrections for ten years. Ten fucking years! The guy can't get out of his own way long enough to be released. At this rate, he's likely to die in our prison system. Of course, if he ever does finish his bid here, he'll face extradition to California to face those charges, so I don't imagine he has much incentive to behave."

"For someone whose diagnosis is in question, he sure is on a hell of a lot of meds," I said.

"Yeah. Most of those are to control his behavior. That hasn't worked, by the way. The best we can do is keep him from doing something nasty to himself and get him back to prison in one piece."

"I'll do my best." I put my head down to complete my note.

CHAPTER 7

When the powers that be felt I was ready, they put me on the rotation to see patients in the highest security unit. Paul put his hand on my shoulder the morning I was to start there and smiled. "If you can keep your head about you while those in the Shoe are going fucking crazy, you'll be a man, my son."

Armed with that salutation, I made my way to the Shoe. It was housed in the infirmary building. Interestingly, contrary to its name, the infirmary often sheltered inmates who were not sick but would be in danger if they were put in the general population: cross-dressers, flamboyant homosexuals, the famous, and the notorious, to name a few. That contrasted with the folks in the Shoe who would be a danger to everyone else if they were released into the general population.

The Shoe entrance had a camera mounted above it. I pushed the door buzzer, looked into the camera, pulled the handle, and waited for the officers inside to let me in. With the loud buzz, I went into the sally port and waited for the first door to close so I could pull on the second door. The entrance sat on one end of a long corridor. On both sides of the corridor were individual cells that had sliding metal doors. The doors were solid—not barred like in the movies. There was a thick window three-quarters of the way up the door and a food chute at groin level. Ten rooms were on either side.

The first thing I noticed was the smell. Hard to believe, but this smell topped even that of the admissions unit. It was as if all the world's supply of stale air was being piped into the unit. After the smell, I took notice of the chatter. Because the doors were thick, inmates placed their faces near the cracks to communicate. The officers' trap and the treatment team office were located on the other side of the long hallway. This forced the staff to walk by each cell in order to reach pay dirt. I felt I was walking in the jail equivalent of the stadium wave. After each cell, new voices could be heard, and new heads could be viewed in the small windows as they talked about the new arrival.

"Hey, who the fuck are you?" This came from one cell.

"Shut the fuck up. People trying to sleep." This came from another.

"I'll fuck you up, you bitch." This was likely from the first, but it became harder to tell as I walked farther away.

"I knew you was a faggot. I'll beat your ass."

"I'll fuck you like I fucked your sister."

I didn't linger long enough to find out if the two inmates were brothers-in-law but made my way to the office. Inside, I found the head of the Shoe, Mark. I hadn't had much to do with him since he'd busted my balls on that first day. Turned out to be a really nice guy. Around my age, he had been at WSH for a while. He looked up from what he was doing and offered a smile. "Hey, Jojo. Welcome to the Shoe."

We went over what my responsibilities would be. The inmates had to be assessed every three hours. That was a state requirement. This meant frequent rounds. Three times a day those rounds included the nurse, who doled out medications taken by mouth. Intramuscular injections could be given at any time and often were needed with the more psychotic or agitated of the bunch. I was expected to go to each cell and speak with the inmate. Some were in four-point restraints—leather straps around their wrists and ankles. Though you might think that would suffice, sometimes additional "points" were needed around the chest and head. These were usually reserved for the vicious assholes, the majority of whom weren't really crazy. For the truly repulsive, there was a spit shield. That was for when they chose to use their last line of defense. I collaborated with the nurses and COs to decide who might come out of restraints and who might be deemed appropriate for release from the confines of the Shoe to be inflicted on the general population.

I stepped out of the treatment office and walked over to the officers' trap. Bigger than the unit traps, this one contained the full complement of COs who were assigned to the Shoe. I noticed that the more the intense the unit, the better quality the officer. Probably had something to do with the need for people who could think quickly and wisely on their feet.

"Look who it is. They got you in here now, huh?"

"Officer Johnson. Have to say it's nice to see a friendly face," I said. "I thought you were mostly on the admissions unit."

"Overtime, man. There's nothing like it. More money and less time at home. Win-win."

"I'm ready to start whenever you are."

"All right, young man. Let's go." Johnson and another officer stood. They escorted me, along with the nurse pushing her med cart. The second officer placed a metal rod into the wall about six inches from the end of each sliding door, preventing it from being opened more than about half a foot. Johnson stood by me. I came to appreciate their precautions.

The inmates in seclusion spent the vast majority of time sleeping. They often refused to talk to the doctor, which greatly expedited the process. Some, though, were quite talkative. I approached the cell of a guy in his fifties, and immediately it became clear he was a carded member of the crazy club in good standing. He was not looking for a vacation at WSH. His hair stood on end, and he paced the small cell with an intensity that suggested he had a lot on his mind—most of it psychotic. Coupled with that, he strode naked as the day he was born. The officer opened the door. The inmate continued his recitation to the general world.

"How are you doing this morning?" I asked.

He stopped pacing and looked at me as if I had asked to hump his mother. "I haven't gotten a goddamned hour of sleep since I been here. You got motherfuckin' state troopers making love next door, and it's keeping me up."

"Sir, I'm sorry about that," I replied in my most serious of tones. "How has that impacted your desire to wear clothing?"

"These Jamaican muff divers ain't givin' me shit to wear but those gray pajamas, and they make me itch. Besides, I know they got bugs in those things."

"You think they aren't clean?" As soon as it left my mouth, I realized it wasn't the brightest of retorts.

"What the fuck? Not insects, you fucking idiot. Recording devices. Where they find yo' sorry ass?"

I walked away, and he hurled more insults at me. I determined he was not yet ready to leave the Shoe. His nudity would probably not go over well with the hoi polloi. *Perhaps by the time he's ready to go to a regular unit,* I thought, *I will be ready to stop asking stupid questions.* I continued on and encountered a nice mix of the real patients, the bullshit artists, and the dangerous cons.

At one of the cells, Johnson opened the door, and I peaked in. Nothing. Confused I poked my head into the small, gray room. An inmate jumped from behind the door and made to pounce on my inserted head.

Johnson grabbed my belt and pulled me back hard. No harm done, but my heart threatened to pound out of my chest.

The inmate laughed uproariously—clearly one of the mischief-makers rather than legitimate crazies. The other officer chuckled too. Johnson didn't laugh. He pulled me to the middle of the hallway and placed a hand on the back of my neck.

"Breathe. Breathe. You're OK." I slowed my respirations; my perspirations didn't cooperate. I smelled the fear on myself.

Now Johnson offered a grin. "Listen to me, Dr. Black. You just got a great lesson on dealing with cons. Never, ever, put your neck out like that. You did it because you've never had something bad happen to you. And I don't want it to happen. So say a silent thanks to that who just gave you a schooling, and you came out no worse for the wear. Right?" He looked me in the eyes.

"Yes. But that lesson might not have been innocuous had you not pulled me back. Thank you."

"Don't mention it, Doc. That's what we're here for. Now you ready to finish up so we can get back to lounging in the trap?"

He allowed me a couple more minutes, and then we made our rounds again. We arrived at the last cell—the one closest to the officers' trap. Reserved for the worst of the worst. When I got there, after what I'd seen, I expected the offspring of Hitler and the Tasmanian Devil. What I got was a regular-looking guy sitting quietly on his bed. He was already staring up at the door's window and anticipating my coming around. The officer opened the door partway, and the inmate spoke in soft, measured tones. "Good afternoon, Doctor."

I looked down at my list. Lester Manson. "How are you doing, Mr. Manson?"

"I'm good. How about you?"

I ignored that. "What led you to be here?"

"No idea, Doc. I am but a pawn in the corrections department's vast machinations. I goes where they tells me."

The officer holding the door handle shook his head. I smiled, and he slid the door shut. I walked back to the treatment office accompanied by the officers.

"That guy is bad news."

"How so?" I asked.

"He is the leader of a white-supremacist gang. A real rabble-rouser."

"Rabble-rouser? I haven't heard that particular phrase in a while."

He smiled. "I feel it important to bring back the oldies for you young'uns."

I thanked him for helping me with rounds and continued to the treatment office. I took a seat opposite Mark. He was busy writing in a chart.

"Tell me about this Manson character."

He looked up. "He's a lifer."

"Meaning?"

"He's got several life sentences, so he's got nothing to lose. For most of these guys, the prospect of having time added to their sentences can keep them in check. Others are so criminal by nature that they can't control themselves—regardless of the consequences. Then there are those like Manson, who are dangerous and have nothing to lose."

"Thanks for that. Say...Manson. That his real name?"

"No. He changed his name. It was Earl Lufkin."

"You being straight?"

"No shit. His name was Earl Lufkin. Can't blame him for changing it to Manson."

"Why Lester?"

Mark shrugged. "Hell if I know."

"Anyway, the only person who looked ready to leave the Shoe was Manson."

"No way. He's on the Shoe plan. Stays here, chills for a few days, and then returns to twenty-three-hour lockdown at Walpole." That was the supermax prison in Massachusetts.

I stood. "I'm going to write my notes. By the way, you are now a Jamaican muff diver."

"What the hell is a Jamaican muff diver?"

"I have no goddamned clue. But the nude guy over there said it, and I made a promise to myself I would repeat it."

He smiled. "Have a good one."

I took my leave.

I got back to the admissions unit office and found Paul sitting in his chair with his legs propped up on the desk as usual. I went and sat down heavily. He took note.

"So what'd ya think of the Shoe?"

"That's a fucked up place."

"That it is. Lots of hard cases there."

We sat in silence for a few minutes, each doing his own work. I put down my pen. "How do you do it, Paul?"

He stopped and looked up over his feet. "What is it I'm doing?"

"How long have you been here?"

"I've been in this prison for damn near sixteen years. I get paroled in eight." Paul grinned broadly.

"So how do you do it? How do you deal with the craziness that goes on here and not get crazy yourself?"

Paul swung his legs down to the ground and stood. "Look at me. You see this body?" He gestured to his tall, skinny frame. Seemed in good shape. "I run almost every day. I go home, and I spend quality time with the wife and kid. In other words, I leave this shit right here at work—where it belongs.

You'd be wise to do the same. Put too much of yourself out there, and you'll burn out in a hurry. I've seen it too many times to count."

"Exercise, huh?"

"Yes. There's a staff gym on the grounds here just outside the state hospital. And it's free for us."

"Is it nice?"

"What the fuck do you want? Fancy machines and coeds in those thong workout outfits? This is a fucking prison. It's good enough for you."

"All right. All right. I'll check it out."

Paul got back to his work.

"Paul?"

"Yeah?" he said without looking up.

"Thanks."

"No problem. You'll be OK. Go work out."

CHAPTER 8

The next day, I brought workout clothes. Inmates were confined to their cells several times a day for count. The lunch one chewed up a good hour and a half. Because I couldn't see patients, it proved a perfect opportunity to catch up on paperwork, screw around, or work out.

I walked out of the state hospital and scanned the different buildings, finding the one with the staff gym at the far end of our parking lot. It looked like a big garage on the outside. Cutting through the cars to get to the building, I stumbled upon Margot leaning against a car, smoking a cigarette. If candor is my ultimate goal, I must admit a fetish for women smokers. Sure, the oral fixation (and all its connotations) is the low-hanging fruit, but, whatever the reason, it turned me on to her even more.

"Hey, Margot. I never envisioned you as a smoker. Makes you seem like the bad girl."

She offered a wry grin. "You don't really know how to talk to women, do you?"

"I'll admit my approaches can tend toward the infantile, but 1 grow on people."

Margot pointed at my bag with her cigarette. "Going to the gym, huh?"

"Paul's advice."

"I would go too, but it interferes with my smoking schedule." She dropped the cigarette on the ground and mashed it with a sneakered toe. "Have a good workout. See ya after."

It wasn't the warmest of sendoffs, but it felt like a small opening. I felt a lift in my step and promised myself a good effort in the gym.

I swiped the card reader on the outside with my ID and opened the door. The interior looked better than I'd expected. I took a cursory tour. On the left was a locker room with a couple of showers; there was no way in hell I was going to use those. I didn't care if I ended up smelling like a horse's ass after a marathon shit. I wasn't going to shower anywhere near a prison. It was a vow I'd made to myself at the get-go.

The main room was divided between some cardio equipment and a decent amount of equipment for weight training in the back. A lone guy worked out. He looked as if he spent a lot of time there. Big as fucking hell. Cutoff shirt, cargo shorts, and no shoes. He eyed me as if I was going to steal his wallet or fuck his sister. He seemed prepared for both. I averted my eyes in an attempt to suggest submission and retreated to the locker room to change.

There have been times in my life where I resolved to work out consistently only to have it peter out shortly after I began. This routine at the prison staff gym, though, had real promise. I could see myself doing this every day. What I didn't realize at the time—what I couldn't know—was that the gym would prove a real haven for me. The jacked-up, steroid-looking guy who was as unfriendly as a junkyard dog when I first came in? He would become an invaluable source of information and support to me. Who could figure?

CHAPTER 9

I met Nigel in a bar in Harvard Square. We had a place we liked to frequent called the Crimson. Nigel said he went there to pit his cocksman wits against smart pussy. He believed that anyone who showed up in a bar near Harvard was in fact a Harvard student. This made his potential conquests all the more prestigious. Like I said, Nigel had a way with words. Not being blessed with the ability to pick up woman like Nigel did, I enjoyed the bar because it was within walking distance of my home. Aside from the pain in the ass that is parking anywhere within five hundred miles of Boston, I am averse to driving drunk. Lest you think of me as saintly, I should disclose that I drove home inebriated on one occasion and was so scared I was going to be pulled over that I shit myself. It could have been fear, or it might have been the copious amounts of alcohol. Who knows? But the shit was very real indeed.

After I entered the joint and my eyes adjusted to the light, I spotted Nigel. He was sitting at the bar and chatting up the bartender, a lovely woman in her midthirties named Kathleen. The other nice thing about going to the same place repeatedly was getting to know the bartenders who offered up complimentary shots if we were likewise tipping graciously. Kathy and I had begun a flirting exchange when I'd first come there as a med student. I didn't believe I really had a chance with her, so it felt quite harmless to me.

I sidled up to the bar and said, "Gin sour, Kathy, if you please."

She nodded her head. "Oh, a Tanqueray night, is it?"

I gave a playful nudge to Nigel, who I hadn't seen for a couple of weeks. Kathy set to work on my drink.

"Where've you been?" I inquired and took a seat on the barstool.

He smiled and replied, cockney-style, "I've been 'itting the casinos, I 'ave."

"How bad is the damage?"

This was a serious question for Nigel. Though he had money, it was a constant struggle getting his funds from his mother. She guarded the family treasure as if it was...treasure.

"I'll be OK," he replied while taking a sip of his single malt.

"That bad, huh? What was it? Poker? Twenty-one?"

He shrugged. "Who cares? It's only money. What's happening with you?"

I knew better than to push. Eventually—with time and enough Glenlivet—he'd end up spilling the beans anyway. I turned to more pressing matters. "Have I told you about this one social worker where I work?"

He shook his head.

"Well, there is this one woman I'm interested in. I just don't know if it's wise."

He nodded gravely. "Dipping your pen in the company ink. Risky business."

"Yeah, something like that. But how am I supposed to find a good woman? In here?"

Nigel swiveled his stool to face me. "Jojo, what the fuck do you need a good woman for? What's the matter with you? Have you learned nothing from me? All you need is a solid lay. A good woman is for down the road. We are living the bachelor's dream. Why fix what's not broken?"

Nigel could always be counted on to give his perspective.

"While I appreciate your vote of confidence, Nige, I don't really have the bachelor's dream life like you. You're able to say all the right things to a woman at night and then have the callousness in the morning to break away from a long-term commitment. I'm not built like that. If I am going to sleep with a woman, I have to be able to look her in the face in the morning and feel the same way I did the night before."

He inspected me with a cocked head. "Are you sure you're not gay?"

I bristled—not at the intended insult but that I knew he was yanking my chain and not taking me seriously. "C'mon, Nigel. I mean it. I like this woman. I find her interesting." At that, Nigel raised his eyebrows. "She is seductive without even trying. It drives me wild."

Nigel took a thoughtful sip of his scotch. "I can see you're smitten. OK. You need to remember you are a Harvard-trained psychiatrist, my son. Have some confidence. Ask her out, but do it casually." He grabbed my arm and looked me in the eye. "Don't come on too strong. You hear me, Jojo? Casual at first. Like you're at the Texas Hold'em table and you've got a killer hand, but you want to sweeten the pot a little. You go betting all in, and you're going to scare away the fish. You have to be patient to grow the pot."

Kathleen had been casually listening in on the conversation while washing and rinsing glasses. She spoke when Nigel was done. "You're a great catch, Jojo. Any woman would be lucky to have you."

It was probably the booze that caused me to flush, but I could feel the heat coming off my face in waves after she said that.

⅄

Armed with the confidence that only a beautiful bartender can give you, I resolved to be more direct in my up-to-then ham-handed attempts to woo Margot. Whenever we had interactions, I focused on being open and pleasant with her. No bullshit. No neurotic defenses. It seemed to have the desired effect. She became less hostile and opened up. I learned all manner of things about her. For instance, one day I finished notes in the treatment team room while Paul and Margot conferred on something. Focused on my task, I missed the initial part of their conversation. I entered their conversation about horses midstream. Margot described the types she rode and jumped.

"Well, I have a Belgian Warmblood. His name is Sparky, and I've ridden him since I was in college. Before that, I had a Hanoverian. Fritz. I loved him."

"How does one get into riding horses?" I asked.

She turned toward me. "My mother rode, and she got me interested at a young age."

"You do the steeplechase?" I asked. I was eager to show interest in anything she did. I struggled mightily to keep the horse dick and shit jokes rattling around in my head from coming out of my mouth.

"Well, I do jumping. Not the steeplechase."

"What's the difference?"

"Steeplechase is a race where rider and horse navigate obstacles. Jumping is more about your ability to work with the horse in collaboration. You have to develop a good relationship with the horse. In my opinion, it's a lot harder work."

"That sounds, uh, fascinating."

Margot deflated. "You're making fun of me."

"No, no, no. I'm not." I stood up and waved my hands like a madman. The great irony of being ironic is that when you're serious, nobody believes it. "I really mean it. You're very passionate about horses. I like that."

She softened.

"This is truly fascinating, but I have work to do," Paul said with a smile, and he walked out of the room.

Now it was just the two of us, I seized the opportunity. I walked over to her desk. "Hey, how about telling me more about this after work?" Margot's face instantly registered genuine apprehension, so I hastily added, "No pressure. Just a friendly get-together."

"I don't know. Not a great idea to mix business with pleasure. You know what I mean."

"One harmless dinner. If it doesn't go well, I promise to back off," I pleaded. I'm not proud, but I felt sure that if I could get one audition with her, I'd get the part.

"It could get weird in here. You know, at work."

"You mean weirder, right?" I smiled broadly. "C'mon. One dinner. I'm harmless."

"One dinner, and you'll back off if I give the say-so?" I nodded. "You're gonna bet on your ability to win me over, aren't you? You that sure of yourself?"

"Hey, nothing ventured, nothing gained. Or is it that every journey of a thousand miles begins with a single step? Or is it some other bumper sticker I can quote?"

"Wiseass." She laughed. "Where should we go?"

"I've got just the place."

Chapter 10

Back then, I took all my first dates to the same piano bar in Cambridge's Inman Square. My thought was that even if the date turned into shit, I would at least enjoy the experience. The food was mediocre, but the ambience was killer. They kept the lights dimmed just the way I liked it. Not groping-in-the-dark dark but soft and subdued. A guy in a tuxedo, John, played lounge music on a baby grand. During the day, he worked at a biotech firm in town. If you asked him, though, he'd say he worked there to pay the bills. His real vocation was musician. The placed oozed cheesiness in an unapologetic way. I dug that.

She refused to let me pick her up, so we met there. The hostess seated us, and we ordered drinks and looked at the menus. There was small talk until a waitress took our orders. Then I turned to my upbringing and focused on Margot. My mother always admonished me to ask a lot of questions about others. "People don't grow tired of talking about themselves," she said repeatedly. Training in psychiatry had honed that skill. Margot, it turned out, had an interesting story. Grew up in a wealthy suburb of Boston. Her parents were both professionals who enjoyed a steamy, albeit brief, love affair that was doused by the daily grind of marriage. They argued incessantly until their divorce when Margot was eleven. Then they argued through Margot.

An only child, Margot was the recipient of the classic excessive attention from each parent. This was both as a way of winning her allegiance in the battle royal that was their parting and a method of getting back at each other.

To hear Margot speak about them, I could see their behavior had forced her to be the adult to her parents. She didn't sound bitter. More annoyed that the antics hadn't really stopped, even in her twenties. She proved an eager conversationalist and threw in anecdotes and self-deprecating humor. Then she turned the tables on me.

"But what about you? You've asked about me the whole night."

I took a sip of wine. The pianist played some Dave Grusin. "Well," I said. "I grew up on Long Island. I'm the youngest of five boys, so I spent a lot of time trying to get attention."

She smiled. "That much anyone can see, based on your daily antics at work."

I was inwardly stung. She looked as if she meant it in an endearing way, but I've never been able to shake that internal core of insecurity. I forced myself to smile back. "That's just my way of making connections with people. Not often elegant or sophisticated, but at least I got you here."

"That you did. So tell me more."

"There isn't that much to tell. My father's a surgeon. He always told us we were free to choose whatever careers we wanted—from within the field of surgery. Three of my brothers went into surgery. When it came time for me, I chose psychiatry. Probably just to stick it to the old man, on a subconscious level."

"What about the fifth brother?"

I paused. I was not really prepared to divulge this much. "The brother who is closest to me in age is also probably the most brilliant of us all. He finished high school at sixteen and college by nineteen. He suffered a nervous breakdown while working on a combined MD and PhD program. He hasn't been able to get back into medicine since."

"That's really sad. Where is he now?"

"He lives on Long Island with my parents."

"Are you guys close?"

"He changed a lot after the breakdown. Hard to communicate with. I try my best to stay in touch, but you know. It's hard for him, having his brothers be successful, but he's stuck where he is."

"He shares that with you?"

"Not really," I said. "Probably just my own survival guilt."

We sat quietly. In the background were the comforting sounds of hushed conversations and adoring couples clinking wineglasses. John launched into some spirited Burt Bacharach.

"So what does he do?" Margot asked.

"He's not able to do much. You know, he's on disability. Does a lot of drawing. Spends a lot of time on the computer. He goes out very infrequently. It's had a big impact on my parents."

"What's his name?"

"Donald. We call him Donny."

She leaned back in her chair. "You know, I don't get you."

"How is that?"

"I'm seeing a very different side of you tonight. No bullshit. And you're a nice guy. Why do you act like a fool?"

I was speechless.

Margot reached over and touched my hand. It was such a warm and tender gesture. In that moment, there was nary a lascivious thought in my head. It was truly a respite from the near total domination of lewd images that constantly populated my mind. She leaned in and said in a low voice, "You put on this wiseass facade, but I see you, Jojo Black. You say you went in to psychiatry to piss off your old man. I say you went in to save your brother."

I smiled broadly—despite the sting of Margot's comments. Her comments went straight to my core. It was a genuine smile. The kind that blossoms of its own accord when you're revealed in a safe setting. "Perhaps," I said. "But enough about me. What do you think about me?"

We both laughed.

CHAPTER 11

The next morning at work, we exchanged sly glances. I couldn't be sure, but I thought Paul took notice of this new development with Margot. He didn't say anything. Just had a knowing look on his face. He looked as if he was going to say something, but an intervening incident diverted our attention.

We got through rounds, and Paul assigned patients. I got a couple of run-of-the-mill guys. The third, a black kid named Higgins, wasn't so usual. At six foot six and three hundred pounds, his size alone set him apart. Those dimensions scared the hell out of COs. How did you take down such a big guy? Spending a minute with Higgins, however, exposed his mental deficiency, if not retardation. To top it off, he was exceedingly gentle. Arrested for a bullshit charge of trespassing. I'm sure his massiveness had worked against him.

I should remind you of the kind of men this young kid now kept company with. Hardened criminals with no real mental illness beyond lacking the basic capacity to empathize with fellow humans. Bullies when they were kids, they grew into cruel men who delighted in tormenting someone weaker. In this case, mentally weaker.

I met with Higgins. It was like dealing with a large kid. Immense. He blocked out the sun, but he possessed the mental age of a nine-year-old. I escorted him back to the TV room and turned in my body alarm. I talked breezily to the trap CO when a big ruckus emanated from the dayroom. Two guys, no more than 130 pounds apiece, were antagonizing Higgins. It was easy to see this was going to turn out badly. I went to the COs office to find the sergeant. The unmistakable sounds of a brawl carried down the hall. I ran and saw the two little guys whaling on Higgins. Two little guys going after such a big guy was an oddity. A couple of COs watched with lighthearted banter. They did little to break up the fight. I quickly alerted the sergeant. He prodded the COs to cuff the two antagonizing parties and break up the rabble that surrounded the threesome. As the handcuffed pair was being lugged to the Shoe, they still hurled taunts at their quarry, who was now bleeding profusely from his nose. I pulled Higgins from the dayroom and spoke calmly to him. He sobbed gently.

"Hey, Sergeant, can we get young Higgins here to the infirmary to get looked at?"

O'Leary was a hard-ass, to be sure, but a good-hearted man. "Right you are, Doc. Come over here, Higgins. We'll get you over to the infirmary. Get that nose looked at." He got on the radio to call over there.

Nothing I'd seen in my lifetime to that point matched the pathos of that scene. I returned to the treatment team office. I must have looked every bit as depressed as I felt at that moment. Paul noticed.

"What was the hubbub?"

"They beat up Higgins."

This got Paul's attention. "You mean the big retard?"

There is nothing like a New Englander throwing out the word "retodd."

"Yeah. I can't fucking believe it. It was two scrawny kids taunting the shit out of him."

Paul sighed and said, "Fucking Serengeti."

"What?"

He sat back in his chair, put his feet on the desk, and laced his fingers behind his head. I smiled and settled in for a good one.

"You see, the admissions unit here at Wampanoag State isn't unlike the harsh savannas of Africa. Like the Serengeti. You got your predators and your prey. A guy like Higgins, big as he is, is just a sitting duck for these hardened max guys. They smell him a thousand miles away. They are the lions to Higgins's lumbering elephant. And he's a wounded elephant at that. They aren't content to kill him. No. They want to injure and then play with him."

I nodded at this well-laid-out analogy. I replied, "The thing that really pissed me off was the COs. They didn't seem to be in a rush to break it up."

Paul contemplated this briefly. "Yeah, I don't know exactly how they fit in with the Serengeti theme. Gamekeepers, I suppose. Some of them are little better than the inmates they look after. Hey, this place can make a cynic out of anyone."

Interestingly, I would not have described Paul as a cynical guy. He would use all manner of dark and sardonic language, but his actions always belied an idealism that smoldered beneath his gruff exterior. Paul was my boss, and I respected him because he made it easy to work for him. There was more to it than just that, though. I related to his demeanor. On the surface, he appeared laid-back, and he was flexible on many issues. However, he maintained a very distinct level of intensity with all patients, staff members, and CO dealings. In turn, everyone respected the hell out of him. I admired that.

"Paul, you a religious man?"

"I'm a lapsed Catholic, but like a baserunner, I keep a toe on second just in case the Lord wants to pick me off. My ace in the hole is extreme unction."

"Extreme what?"

"Unction. It's repenting on your deathbed and getting last rites just before you kick off. That's the key, Jojo. That's the key."

"We are a strange bunch to be working here," I said.

"You gotta love the chaos in a place like this. Learn to roll with it and even feed off it at times."

Paul put his feet on the ground and straightened the items on his desk. He looked up at me. "Hey, why don't you come out to lunch with us?"

"Who's us?"

"Me and some of the other social workers. We go to lunch in town. Come along. You'll like it. Blow off some steam."

It meant missing a workout, but I didn't have much energy anyway. "Sure," I said. "Sounds great."

The restaurant was a German-themed place—the kind of family-owned restaurant that was quickly becoming extinct thanks to the TGI Fridays of the world. The place had a nice decor—lots of dark wood, pictures of

Bavaria, and the like. The carpeting looked as if it had been installed circa 1967, but it was clean. Big wooden chairs and tables and the kind of giant steak knives I loved. If a fight ever broke out, I would be more confident grabbing one of those bad boys than the typical butter knives on restaurant tables.

There were supposed to be five of us, but two didn't show. That left Paul, Margot, and me. Paul smiled knowingly at me when I sat down opposite Margot and him. He put his arm around her.

"Known this one from when she was a wee lass." Margot blushed but looked pleased. "She interned with me. It was my subtle powers of persuasion that kept her working at the old state hospital."

"And we're all better for that persistence." I picked up the menu. "What's good in this joint?"

"Wiener schnitzel. Or schnitzengruben. Or any of your bratwurst and sauerkrauts." Paul turned to Margot. "So what do you think of young Dr. Black here? A keeper, no?"

She turned to me. "I'm always so confused when someone ends a question with 'no.' Do I say no to say yes? Or do I say yes to confirm the no? Which, in fact, is the initial way of saying yes."

I laughed. "A good question. What do you say, Paul?"

Paul beamed. "I say I've got my young guns here. The new talent to take over when old farts like me do the fade into retirement. I've got my Florida condo already picked out. The white shoes are next."

A heavyset woman approached our table and stood expectantly. "What'll you have?"

"How come you're not wearing lederhosen?" I attempted to feign innocence.

"Lederhosen are for men. Traditional German stein-carrying women sport dirndls, but I can't see you being able to handle me in one of those. Can you?"

That clammed me up quickly. We placed our orders and were silent.

Paul rescued me. "How long do we get to keep you, huh?"

"What do you mean?"

He leaned forward on his elbows. "C'mon. You know what I mean. You're a highly trained—and highly skilled, I might add—psychiatrist. You could make it in private practice and rake in the big bucks."

"You sound like a friend of mine," I said. I was a little defensive. "I like it at the state hospital. The work is challenging. When I was in residency, I found the jail rotation the most interesting. It was like fishing for marlins in the deep blue sea."

Margot touched my arm. "Come again, Ahab?"

"Nice," Paul said.

"Hear me out. The prison is the one place where the mentally ill can't fall past. They can avoid treatment but not the law. They get picked up by the cops and thrown into the pot with the hardened criminals. I enjoy fishing through a sea of cons who are looking to score sedatives for the one guy who is truly sick and needs my help."

"Well said, matey," Margot said.

I looked at Paul. He smiled at me and nodded his head. "I know what you mean."

"So why did you go into this work?" I asked him.

"Me? Shit, my mother told me I would never amount to anything. To prove her wrong, I surround myself with the lowest scum of the earth. Now I look good in comparison."

We all laughed.

Our waitress came with our food, and we dug in. Cutlery on the Corningware punctuated the silence. After the initial hunger abated, Paul spoke to Margot and me. "Listen, you two."

"OK, Paul. So serious," Margot said.

"This is important. If I believe what I'm seeing with you two, I'm here to tell you to be very careful. Any outward indication of a relationship between employees is problematic on a couple of fronts. First off, the corrections folks frown on fraternizing within the ranks. Now that doesn't mean it doesn't happen. Of course it does, but you gotta make sure you're not obvious. More important—and more dangerous, if you ask me—is if the inmates get wind of it. They will try to exploit it if they can. So a friendly warning."

"I appreciate that, Daddy. You want me to be home by ten?"

"I'm serious, Margot. I've seen a lot of bad things happen in this joint, and I wouldn't want that to happen to you."

"Thanks. I really do appreciate it. No bullshit," I said. "But just so you know, there's nothing going on between us."

"Hey, I'm just looking out for you two. I'm not kidding about you guys being the future. I think highly of both of you."

One look at Margot's face, and I confirmed she was just as heartened by those words as I was.

CHAPTER 12

The rhythm of life. You get into a routine. It can be a grind, but the grind is part of life. There's comfort in developing mastery. I liked going into the interview room and knowing I could handle whatever came my way. I worked out every day and went out at night with Nigel. Lots of gambling. Some wins. More losses. My only frustration came from Margot. She was playing coy again. I worked on my psychiatric and gambling crafts. Overall, life was good.

But…humans crave change. It's in our nature. We love the departure from the usual. Embrace the delta, a psychology professor used to say, and you will successfully navigate the bumps in life. We humans are curious, even if it is to our detriment. So it was for me, and it was so insidious I didn't see it coming.

On the day that my life changed radically, I arrived at WSH the same time I did every morning and got to the unit for rounds. I looked at the board to see who the new people were and saw the name Lester Manson. I knew I had seen it before, but I couldn't place it. We rolled through rounds and got to his name. Paul spoke. "This guy is hard-core Walpole. He's a white-supremacist gang leader and should be back in supermax in no time."

I then recalled seeing and hearing about him in the Shoe. "Isn't he supposed to stay in the Shoe? Not come out?"

Paul looked at me. "Normally, yeah. But they got so backed up there. They needed to unload some of theirs. He's usually well behaved, so they put him here with an expedited review to get him sent back."

"I rounded on him in the Shoe. He was, in fact, pleasant and calm."

Paul pointed at me. "Why don't you take him, then, since you know him? Be extra careful. He's a dangerous one. Try to keep him 'pleasant and calm' until we can get him the fuck out of here."

Everyone laughed. When rounds adjourned, I approached Margot. She was hunched over a chart.

"Are you going to pick up Manson?"

Smiling, she said, "I'll work on him with you, if you like."

I smiled in return. "That would make my day." I lowered my voice. "When can I see you again?"

She stood. "Jojo, I like you. I just don't know if it's a good idea for us to get involved."

"What if we go out, and it doesn't work, and someone gets hurt, and we have to see each other every day, and it's awkward, and one of us brings an AK-47 to work and blows a lot of people away before offing ourselves but not before cursing the other person? Something like that?" I asked with a straight face.

She chuckled, and I loved that she got it; I didn't have to verbalize that I wasn't serious. "You have a hell of a way of putting it. But yes."

I sensed her resistance was low. "Margot, life is short. It's not as if I'm meeting a ton of people I want to date. When I am interested in someone, it means something to me. I can't just throw it away."

Smiling wryly, she responded, "Was that your best shot? The 'what if there's a nuclear war, and life is short' routine?"

"It was pretty convincing, no?"

"Hey, you two. You going to see patients or fart around in the corner?"

Margot picked up a chart and walked out the door, leaving just Paul and me in the room. "Thanks, Paul. Good timing."

"Jojo, don't you remember our discussion? Don't dip your pen in the company ink."

"Holy shit, Paul! My friend used the same expression."

"Wise friend. Get busy."

"I'm going. I'm going."

I grabbed Manson's chart and walked down to the officers' trap. I handed over a chit and collected the body alarm as Johnson approached.

"Who you want?"

"Manson."

"I'll bring him down to the interview room."

"Thanks, man." I made my way to the room and began filling out my initial assessment. It included name, age, and that kind of basic data. Manson walked in, escorted by Johnson.

"I'll be right outside the door, Doc."

"Thanks, Officer Johnson."

Manson sat opposite me. "We meet again, Dr. Black."

I was not wearing my ID tag, so I was surprised he remembered me. I told him that.

"I rarely forget a name. Especially someone who's competent. You have to keep track of those types of people. There aren't that many in this world." He said.

As a psychiatrist, I was automatically suspicious of someone giving me a compliment. Patients were always looking to divide staff by talking up one and bad-mouthing another.

"Nice of you to notice."

"Well, I've seen a lot of shitty psychiatrists in my time. You must have trained at a good place."

"Harvard."

"It shows," Lester said.

We sat in silence for a moment.

"So what brought you here?" I asked.

"I told them I was suicidal. I needed a break from the monotony of twenty-three-hour lockdown. Weeks can go by without them letting me outside. Even though that's against the law."

"That's not right."

"Tell me about it."

"So you're not really suicidal?"

Manson paused. "I'm certainly not delighting in my current situation. This is no way to treat a human being."

"That doesn't really answer my question."

"Maybe it's the question that's off target. You're supposed to be looking out for those folks who have been swallowed up by a corrupt justice system that criminalizes mental illness. They get thrown in the slammer when all they really needed was some Thorazine. You're not asking the right questions."

"Are you saying you're psychotic and in need of Thorazine?"

"I'm in need of help that only someone in your position can provide. These primitive COs see things only in black and white. If you're here, you're a criminal, and you deserve nothing more than time in isolation. You, though, you can see the grays. Psychiatry is all about the grays. You are mandated to cut through the haze, zero in on problems, and remedy them. That's what you do."

"I appreciate the endorsement. But you still haven't answered my question."

"What is it you want to know? That the situation I'm in has brought me to my knees?" Here Manson looked genuinely perturbed. "That I have to make claims of suicidality just to have some light shone on the injustices someone in my situation has to endure? That isolation for weeks at a time has an impact—even on someone as educated and resourceful as me?"

I was speechless and entertained. A smile must have been on my face because he gave a hint of a grin.

"That's quite a talent you have there," I complimented him.

"Talent?"

"For bullshit. I mean, that was well done. You avoided my question, and in the process, you gave me a lecture suitable for a college kid who just discovered injustice in this world. Then you took it to another level by opening up just enough to draw some possible compassion from me. Well done."

"I'm glad you approve."

"Well then. What is it you'd like? An antidepressant?"

"Hell no. Do I look depressed?" Manson was genuinely offended. "No. No pills for me. I would like to speak with the social worker, though, and see if I can get help with reassignment to a different prison."

"OK, Mr. Manson. Everyone sees a social worker." We sat in silence. "Well, that's all the questions I have. So if there's nothing else, I'll get you back to the dayroom."

We stood. As we were walking out the door, Manson stopped. "No ring, I notice. You single?"

"Have a good day, Mr. Manson." Turning to Officer Johnson, I said, "He's all yours, Officer."

Manson smiled and walked away.

That afternoon, I changed in the locker room as the big guy got dressed in his uniform. We'd had a predictable relationship up to that point. He shot me occasional looks suggesting comfort with violence toward me, and I did my best to seem unobtrusive. I finished tying my shoes when his phone's ringtone allowed Willie Nelson to tell us how great it was to be on the road again.

"Hey, Mom." He turned his back to me. "No. No. That's not happening. No. They are not plotting against you. No one is looking to transfer you to Guantanamo Bay. Yes. I'm sure of it. Mom—Mom." I could hear her yelling into the phone. "Mom. Calm down. I'm coming over." He hung up and began buttoning his shirt. He turned to me, looking both embarrassed and pissed.

I quickly apologized. "I'm sorry, man. I wasn't trying to eavesdrop."

"Nah. I know that," he said.

I found the silence uncomfortable. I finished getting into my gym clothes, and he got into his CO blues. I stood to leave.

"Hey, Doc. You're a psychiatrist, right?"

I was a little taken aback; I didn't think he knew anything about me. "Right."

"Well, do you mind if I ask for a little advice?"

I sat. "No problem."

"Well, you heard—I mean, you can see there is something wrong."

"Why don't you tell me what's been going on?"

"My mother's been acting crazy. And I mean crazy. Paranoid. Batty. Out of her freakin' mind."

"Who's her psychiatrist?"

"She don't got one."

"How long has this been going on?" I asked.

He looked at the ceiling. "I don't know. Maybe two months."

"Any prior history of mental health problems?" He shook his head. "How old is she?"

"Sixty-six."

"Any memory issues, such as being forgetful? You know, like Alzheimer's?" He shook his head.

"That's interesting. People generally don't get crazy like that when they're older unless they're getting demented. Anything else going on? Other changes in her?"

"Well, she's lost a lot of weight. And her face has the look of someone who drinks all the time, but she doesn't touch the stuff. I've asked her to get checked out, but she ain't in her right mind, you know?" he said.

That was worrisome. "Let me ask you something. Does she or did she smoke?"

"Like a chimney."

I took a deep breath. "Listen. Take your mother to the ER and tell them what's been going on. Tell them they need to do a chest X-ray or CAT scan."

"A chest X-ray or CAT scan?"

"Yeah. Best would be a CAT scan of the chest."

"Should I be worried?"

"Let's not jump to conclusions. Right now you need someone to see and assess her. Force her if you have to."

He stood and grabbed his bag. "Thanks, Doc. I appreciate it."

He left the locker room, and I went and did my workout.

Chapter 13

As gamblers, Nigel and I couldn't have been more different. I placed small bets most of the time. I didn't have the energy or smarts to count cards, but I believed I could sense when the table might get hot. Runs of low cards meant some face cards were coming. With well-placed bets, I could grind out a nice stack of chips. Not a people-standing-behind-me-oohing-and-aahing stack of chips, but respectable. Nigel lacked patience. He could grind it out for a little bit, but he grew restless. If he had a winning hand that had a small bet, he would smack the table and curse. He would convert to big bets and take bigger risks. I was quiet as a church mouse at the table. Nigel never stopped bantering with the dealers, the other players, and the deities that controlled the cards.

"C'mon. Give me something good. Make it happen, mate. Make it happen. You can do it. You can bring joy right here, in this little section of the world. Make it happen."

There was a lot of gesticulating. When we'd first met, Nigel had told me he was an Englishman with an Italian's penchant for expressing himself with his hands.

When he lost big, he would engage in the classic degenerate gambler habit of chasing his bad bets with stupid bets. Occasionally, he might do well. On most nights, though, he ended up bust early and would annoy the shit out of me until we left.

Tonight, we were both doing OK. We had to move tables a couple of times because Nigel wouldn't gamble when there was an Asian woman dealing cards. Don't ask. We had a nice flow on this particular table.

"How's the practice going?" I asked him.

"Boomin'. Word got out that I'm loose with Adderall. I have a steady stream of students from BU getting treatment for their long-undiagnosed ADHD."

"You're a piece of shit. You know that?"

"Jojo, I can see six patients in an hour. Six! I have afternoons where I'm close to twenty-five. And they're easy as shit. All they want are the scripts. No small talk. No 'do you have any thoughts of killing yourself?' Do you know how refreshing that is? Wait until I can grab some of that Cambridge business across the river. Harvard. MIT. Then I'll be rolling."

I absently doubled down. "You're just a licensed drug dealer."

"Not true. Most of these kids legitimately have ADHD. They grow up with Nintendo, PlayStation, microwaves, and texting. They can't focus for more than the time it takes to write something stupid on Twitter. I'm doing them a service. Hell, I'm doing the entire world a service. I mean, we've got athletes with performance-enhancing drugs, and all they're doing is hitting bloody balls or throwing balls into iron hoops. These are smart people. The kind of people we should be enhancing. If anything, I'm a humanitarian looking out for the betterment of humankind. Dealer bust!"

We both collected our chips. I tossed a ten-dollar chip to the dealer. "That's for you."

He nodded thanks, tapped it on the felt table, and put it next to my next hand. A nice compliment to me; he was playing my hand with me.

Nigel continued. "I don't see anything wrong. It's as much an affliction as schizophrenia or depression. And the treatment is more effective. The patients are happy and satisfied. How often does that happen in your work with felons and half-wits?"

"Of course they're satisfied. You're keeping them plied with speed. Shit, I would be happy too with enough Adderall in my system."

I showed a jack and a three. The dealer had a king and a four. I stayed pat. Dealer got a queen. All players rejoiced. Dealer smiled at me and put his two checks in a chip collector for the dealers.

"Why are we talking about college students? Tell me what's happening with your love interest at work. Has she blown you in the yard yet?"

"Lovely, Nigel. She's playing coy again. Saying she doesn't think it wise for us to date, given that we work together."

"So she's got more self-control than you. Good for her. Anyway, fuck her. What do you need that kind of headache for? She sounds like an intelligent, willful woman. Otherwise known as a pain in the ass."

"I like her, though. And it's not as if I have other prospects."

"That's because you walk around with your eyes closed. Not seeing the myriad opportunities at your disposal."

"It's you who sees women as disposable."

He stopped. "Very fucking clever. Well, if this girl means that much to you, don't be overzealous."

"Meaning?"

Nigel turned to me and placed a hand on my arm. "Don't be you. In other words, play it loose. Nothing reels a woman in like not paying her any mind. Be coy yourself. Play hard to get."

"That's not my style."

Nigel turned back to the table. "Can you believe this, folks? You all don't realize it, but before you is a real-life hermaphrodite. Looks like a man, right? But there's a giant vagina in those Farah slacks."

The other players, all men, smiled. The dealer held up his cards. "Should I deal or what?"

I elbowed Nigel. "Prick."

The table got cold after that, so we called it a night. As we drove back, I had to admit that maybe Nigel had a point. A needy man was a big turnoff to a woman. I had to play it looser and be patient. It was funny to get that kind of advice from Nigel. With his patience, he made junkies look positively Zen.

I soon put Nigel's advice to work. I wasn't a prick, but I wasn't overly friendly with Margot either. With everyone else, who knows? Maybe I was a prick, but I didn't pay as much attention. It was hard to tell if my strategy was working because Margot treated me as she had before. Christ. Having to play these kinds of games made my skin crawl. I'd rather things be simpler and out in the open.

Toward the end of the week, Paul pulled me over to the side after rounds. "What's happening with Margot?"

My skin went cold. "Nothing. We're just friends."

He looked at me funny. "What the fuck are you talking about?"

"What are you talking about?"

"She's acting strange. She doesn't seem herself."

"I hadn't noticed."

Paul scratched his armpits absently. "What's the story with Manson?"

"Nothing. Just here for a little R and R."

He looked intensely at me. "That's not a guy to fuck around with. You understand?"

"Yeah. I know what you're saying, and I'm on board."

"Good. 'Cause a guy like that can get into the head of even the most experienced clinician."

"How come he's still here?" It had already been almost four weeks. Twenty days was usually enough to turn around the troublemakers. "I thought they were expediting his return to Walpole."

"I don't know. That's what bothers me. I'll look into that. But you're not making any medication changes or any treatment plan changes, right?"

"Right."

Paul patted me on the shoulder and smiled. As he started to walk away, he spoke over his shoulder. "You should have seen your face when I asked about Margot. What a guilty look. Ha!"

"Thanks for not busting my balls."

He laughed his way out of the office. Had it been anyone else, I probably would have been pissed off. Paul was sharp, though. No point in trying to snow him. Besides, I hadn't done anything to feel guilty about. Yet, I silently hoped.

The morning kind of dragged until Margot made it infinitely more interesting. She approached me and asked if we could speak after work. From that moment on, the time couldn't pass quickly enough. At the end of the day, I leaned on my car and waited for her to come out. She walked out, and I straightened up as she approached.

"Hey, Jojo."

I kept a straight face, but inside I was grinning from ear to ear. "Hello, Margot."

"Why have you been giving me the cold shoulder?"

Keep calm, I told myself. "I'm not sure what you mean."

"Give me a break. You've been acting like a jerk, and I want to know why."

"I hadn't realized I was acting differently toward you. But then again, why should that matter? You were the one who set the terms for our interactions."

She paused. "Well, I've been thinking about that a lot. I turned it over in my mind and have come to the conclusion that I would like to see you again." She hastily added, "If you're willing."

I kept my poker face. "I am willing. Did you have a time in mind?"

"I don't know exactly. I'm kind of busy in school."

"That's an interesting response. You just told me you did want to see me."

"Oh, I'm sorry. I don't mean, 'I'm busy. Fuck off.' I mean, 'I'm busy, but I had a good time with you, and I decided that just because we work together doesn't mean we can't have something special.' I mean, I spend most of my time working. It's only natural I would meet someone where I spend a lot of my time."

"I can get behind that reasoning."

"Can you?"

"I think you're a great girl, and I would really like to get to know you better. I'm not good at sleeping around. So when I meet someone I like—"

"I know. You've made that pitch before. So let's find a time to go out. Soon."

"Great. How about this weekend?"

"Can't, but we'll talk more tomorrow and come up with a good time. I'm in a bit of a rush." She stood, gave me an awkward hug, and walked quickly over to her car. A Prius.

Well, nobody's perfect, I thought.

I waited until she pulled out and then unlocked my door and climbed in. I slipped my manual into reverse just as another car pulled right behind me.

This caused me to stop short and stall. I turned as the big CO from the gym exited a blue corrections car and walked over to mine. I lowered my window. "Everything OK?"

"Yeah, yeah, Doc. I just wanted to...you know...I just needed to tell you that I took my mother to the ER."

"Oh, right. How did it go?"

"Well, they did the CAT scan of her chest like you suggested. And they, uh, found something in her lungs. They think it's lung cancer, and they said that kind of cancer can produce things in the blood that can make someone crazy. They said she wasn't really crazy and that when they treat the cancer, she'll get better. They also said they thought they caught it early enough to give her a good chance to get better. So...I'm saying thanks. I really owe you one."

He had his hand out to me. I smiled and shook it. "Don't even think about it. I'm just glad I could help."

"OK," he said and turned away. I was about to start my car when he stopped short and returned to my window. "By the way, I'm Steve Gomes."

"Jojo Black."

I was about to start my car when he stopped short again and returned to my window. "By the way, I would be very careful about who you talk to and how you interact with people in the parking lot."

"What do you mean?"

"You see those buildings?" He pointed toward the minimum-security units in the state hospital on the other side of the fence. "You know those are the mins, right? Well, guys look out those windows, and they check to see who drives what and who talks to who and all that shit. And they report it everywhere. You've got to be mindful of everything you do around here."

"You're shitting me."

"Serious as a heart attack. You gotta be careful."

"I appreciate that, Officer Gomes."

"All right, Doc. You drive safe now."

"Thanks."

This time I waited until he was in his car and clear out of sight before I started my car. I gave some brief thought to what he had told me. Then the realization came over me that my plan had worked with Margot, and I drove home with a smile.

Chapter 14

"C'mon. You got it. You got it. Give, give, give."

I put up the last rep on a bench press of 185. Not a ton of weight, mind you, but I had made a lot of progress and was proud of myself.

"Good job, Doc."

"Thanks, Steve."

Since our meeting in the parking lot, Officer Gomes started offering spots when I lifted heavy weights. He never asked for a return favor, and he lifted a hell of a lot more than I did. Steve opened up a lot. He introduced me to classic country music, regaled me with great prison-guard stories, and taught me the history of corrections in Massachusetts.

Steve, an eighteen-year vet of the DOC, worked second shift and lifted every day before his tour. After twenty-five years, a CO can retire with a good portion of his or her final salary. Steve had come here right out of high school. He was only thirty-seven and close to being able to choose another career with a generous safety net. Not bad.

He drove the perimeter every day. That meant patrolling the areas around the state hospital, the boot camp (for alcoholics), and the treatment center for sex criminals. Not a rigorous job, it was usually assigned to someone the corrections department wanted out of the way. I didn't ask him about that. He walked to the preacher curl bench and did biceps training with nearly the weight I had just benched.

"Hey, Doc, I hear you're tappin' that hot social worker from the admissions unit. The one I seen you with in the parking lot."

That got my attention. Margot and I had yet to go on another date. Seemed someone put the rumor before the cart, if you'll pardon the mixed metaphor. "Who's saying that?"

"Word gets around," Steve said.

"Well, it's not true. We just work together."

"C'mon, Doc. You can tell me. There's a locker room etiquette here. Omertà of the lifters, you might say. Open up."

I walked over to the dip bar. "I would tell you—if it were true. But it isn't."

"So you just work together, huh? She's a piece of ass, though."

"I would agree with that assessment."

"'I would agree with that assessment.' You're funny as shit," Steve said.

I did a set of dips. He continued to curl.

"Steve."

Grunt. "Yeah?"

"Who's talking about me?"

Grunt. "Are you kidding me? There is nothing in this place that's private. It's like a high school with steel bars. And many in the prison population are bigger meatheads and gossips than you find in the cattiest high school. That goes for the inmates and the staff too."

"I didn't know that."

He grunted and kept curling; his biceps looked as if they were going to explode from his skin.

"You better get it into your head. People see everything, and they tell everything. It ain't like a priest's confession or a psychiatrist's office." He nodded his head to me in deference. "Things are not kept in confidence here. So if you're thinking of confiding something you don't want everyone to know, don't. Just don't."

He finished and flexed in front of the mirror. He didn't kiss his biceps.

"Steve?"

"Yeah?"

"Not to put too fine a point on it, but then how can I confide in you?"

He turned to me. "Fucking omertà of the locker room. I told you. I won't say shit to no one. You might be a highfalutin doctor, but you're all right. I will always have your back. You can bank on it."

"All right. I'll start with a question I've wanted to ask a CO."

"Shoot."

"Inside, there are no weapons. No batons. No guns. What happens if all hell breaks loose? What advantage do the COs have over the inmates?"

He pulled a fifty-pound weight, sat down on a bench, and started doing triceps extensions above his head. "The real key to controlling a population is to control movements. You know that everything is timed and regulated. We limit their actions as a group. Routine and more routine. The guys who have been in for a long time come to rely on that routine. Something about the human psyche. You'd probably know more about that than me. So you restrict their movements, and they are less likely to act out. It takes some time for the new ones to get used to it. But they get the message."

"OK, that makes sense. But what about if a whole group acts out?"

"A riot, you mean?"

"I guess."

He switched arms and continued the triceps extensions. His breathing barely changed. "The thinking about weapons is that you don't want them to fall in the wrong hands. And besides, let's say you've got a gun. And let's further say your gun can hold sixteen rounds. What will you do with the seventeenth guy? Huh? You get it?"

"I get it. But I'm still wondering why there aren't more attempts to overwhelm the COs with numbers."

"Because that has to be coordinated. Here at the state hospital, the ones who stay for a long time are cuckoo. You've seen them. They couldn't coordinate to tie their own shoes in sync—much less attack and overwhelm the staff. The troublemakers, the ones who are looking for some time off from the max places, we send them back quickly."

"So this is more of an issue at the other prisons."

"It can be," he said. "And you know there have been riots, right? Some here in Massachusetts. But at the state hospital, it isn't likely for the reasons I gave you. Controlling movement is a big part of that."

"I get it. Thanks, Steve."

"You got it, Doc. Any time." He put the weight back and walked to the preacher curl bench.

"Steve?"

"Yeah?"

"Omertà?"

"Absolutely."

"I got a date with the social worker tonight."

"Hot damn. I'm happy for you. Let me know if you get some."

Margot agreed to meet me at a trendy diner near her apartment in Braintree. She eschewed being picked up again, so I drove there alone. The place wasn't much. Somehow, crappy was the new chic. She was already there when I arrived, so I bypassed the bored hostess and sat down opposite Margot.

"I thought this might be a fun place," she said.

I sat and took the menu she handed over. "It seems like the kind of hip place that is a breeding ground for *E. coli* and the next great writer."

She chuckled. "You always have a line, don't you?"

The waitress came over, and we ordered. For me it was a filet. She got a salad with grilled chicken. I would have paid for the lobster. We sat regarding one another in silence.

"I've been thinking, Margot. Why does a woman like you want to work in a place like the state hospital?"

"That sounds like a variation of 'What's a girl like you doing in a place like this?' You think it's too rough for me? I'm not up to the challenge?"

I held up my hands in surrender. "I'm not questioning your ability, just your rationale. I mean, it's such an ugly place filled with depraved and deprived men. It's hard for me to see beautiful women and keep my mouth shut. Inside prison, you're all the inmates have to look at, and you're nice to look at. I can't imagine the kind of comments you have to put up with."

She smiled. "That was a most awkward but nice compliment." She dipped her fingers into her glass and put some ice in her mouth. "I like it there because my work is consequential. In most hospitals, as a social worker, I'm looking for placement for the patients. Boring. At Wampanoag, I'm involved in therapy. I get to be a part of the treatment team, and I love that."

"You hold your own. That's for sure. Ever been scared?"

"Hell yes. What about you?"

"What? Scared?" I asked. She nodded. "Nah. I'm a tough guy when there are tougher guys just a button push away."

She laughed. Our waiter brought us warm rolls.

"Why did you choose to work at the state hospital? You going to repeat all that shit you said to Paul when we had lunch together?" Margot asked.

"It's true, though. My best mate, Nigel, is in private practice, and he's always busting my chops to give up the state job and come work with him. I don't get the same satisfaction working with the upper crust. I prefer the bottom of the barrel."

"Mate? What are you, British?"

"Nigel's British. I guess it rubbed off."

Margot buttered a roll and cut it in half. She took a bite and handed me the other half. I took it without saying anything. Kind of sexy, I thought. Intimate. Like sharing a cigarette.

"I'm glad you're with us and not him," she said. "You know what you're doing. It makes my job easier."

"We're here to please," I said. "The royal 'we,' that is."

Our entrees were served. There was a moment of quiet as we dug in.

I broke the silence. "I'll admit that I have a thing for crime and criminals. The environment interests me. And if I'm really being honest, maybe the idealism of working with the dregs allows me to feel better about myself. Like Paul, I place a lot of stock in being able to look down my nose on other people."

Margot laughed. "Are you being serious or not?"

"Sadly, it's the truth. I like knowing I'm treating people who are needy. "

"Look out, Jojo. You said that without a joke."

"True enough."

A good meal. The conversation didn't wane, but it didn't feel like a chore. I sensed Margot was feeling the same way. We walked out of the restaurant together.

"Where's your car?" I asked.

"I walked. I only live about ten minutes from here."

"Let me give you a lift home."

"It's OK. I don't mind walking."

"What kind of gentleman would I be if I let you wander the streets of Braintree on your own?"

"All right. But I'm not inviting you up." Margot wagged her finger, and we walked over to my car.

"You don't have to worry about me. I wouldn't dream of accompanying you upstairs. We hardly know each other."

When we pulled up to her five-story apartment building, she turned toward me.

"Well, I really had a great time."

"I did too."

We kissed. It started out as a nice, soft kiss, but it quickly became more intense and passionate. Our hands started groping; she pulled back, short of breath.

"I think we should stop."

"Right."

I leaned in, and we kissed a little more. She pulled away and opened her door. "If I don't go upstairs now, I probably will act rashly. And I really don't want to rush things. You know?"

"I do. And I do. Want to rush things, that is."

"C'mon. You understand, right? You're not going to sulk?"

"I'm hurt you would say that. I'm not the pouty type. Besides, I have patience and an extensive porn collection at home." I reached out and palmed her cheek. "No, really, this feels like the start of something really good. I can wait."

She touched my hand. "I'll see you tomorrow."

"Have a good night."

I watched as she walked to the front door of her building. She looked back and waved after unlocking the door and entering. I drove away. I was sexually frustrated, but in a good way, you know? Or is that not believable?

The next day, Margot and I exchanged pleasantries, lots of grins, and an occasional accidental but purposeful touch. It didn't go unnoticed by Paul. I went about seeing my patients. It barely registered that Margot spent a fair amount of time in an interview room with Lester Manson.

I had a spirited lift in the staff gym at lunch. Steve and I argued about country versus rock 'n' roll. We were doing squats. Steve was a hell of a good sport about it. We had to take off four forty-five-pound plates each time it went from his turn to mine. He never complained. He did castigate me, though, for my opinions about music.

"Doc, you tell me. You got the Highway Men. That's Willie, Kris Kristofferson, Waylon, and the Man in Black, Johnny Cash. Name me one band that had that kind of firepower."

"How about the Beatles, the Stones, Led Zeppelin, The Who. The list goes on and on."

"Yeah, but those were bands. I mean, these were successes on their own that got together. Nothing like that in rock."

"How about the Traveling Wilburys, huh? You've got Roy Orbison, George Harrison, Tom Petty, and Jeff Lynne."

Steve finished his set of 405 pounds and placed the bar back on the rack. Really, the idea of me spotting on that much weight was pretty much a joke. If one of his legs gave way, he was truly fucked. Again, he never complained.

He nodded his head. "OK, the Traveling Wilburys. That's a good one. Though, Roy and Tom Petty had a kind of country thing going. And you missed Dylan."

We moved on to donkey raises for the calves. He liked to lecture me on the calves. He said most body builders usually neglected them and that Schwarzenegger had to model in the water until he blasted out his calves. I changed the subject.

"Steve, what do you know about Lester Manson?"

"Bad man. Head of the White Dawn."

"Never heard of them."

He finished his set and sat down on a bench. "Imagine a group of skinheads who didn't just want to fuck up minorities and shit. Yeah, they hate blacks and Jews like the other white-supremacist groups. But they also are a gang that is looking to make money and get turf. It's like two groups rolled up in one. That's the best way to put it."

"What kind of shit are they into?"

"You name it. They sell drugs, peddle stolen shit, hijack, and extort."

"On the inside?" I asked.

"No. Manson's inside right now. But he can run the operation just as easily on the inside. He has a right-hand man on the outside."

"How does he know that guy won't try to take over?"

Steve smiled. "Manson is a sharp fucker. The guy on the outside is his son, so he knows he can trust him. He runs the operation while Lester is locked up. In some ways, Lester is safer in the joint than his son is on the outside."

"How does the antiblack thing go over in a prison with black inmates? I mean, I've seen him fraternizing with all races, and I didn't see any tension."

"Inside the joint, no one really cares who you hate. It's about who you can control," Steve said.

"How do you know so much about these things?"

"Shit. It's my job to know. You work long enough in corrections, you have to pay attention to all the politics. To not do that is to risk getting yourself fucked up or killed."

We lifted in silence for a few minutes.

"Jojo, why are you asking about Manson?"

"He's on my unit. I haven't seen anything worrisome from him, but he has my boss spooked, and I've never seen him spooked about anyone."

"Paul's spooked?"

I smiled. "Yeah. You know him?"

"Everyone knows Paul. He's a smart fuckin' guy. If he's worried, you should be too. He's right to warn you about a guy like Manson. You know what they say. By the time you know you're in quicksand, you're already fucked. Well, it's the same with Manson. You don't even see him coming. When you realize something is wrong, he's already got his hooks in you. I'm surprised they let him out of the Shoe."

"Thanks for the info and the heads-up."

"You bet, Doc. Now let's do some delts."

Chapter 15

I experienced a bounce at work. I hadn't yet made another date with Margot, but it didn't seem to matter. It was a foregone conclusion that we would be dating regularly. *Today's the day I'm going to make it happen,* I decided. When rounds finished, I walked up to her. "How you doing this fine mornin'?"

"Not now, Jojo. I'm really busy."

At first I thought she was joking, but the look on her face said otherwise. Icy. As if the date hadn't happened.

"Holy shit. What's going on?"

"Look, I'm sorry. I can't talk right now. I've got a lot on my plate. Let's talk later."

"OK."

She walked out of the treatment office. Paul walked over. "From the look of you two, I would say you had a fight recently."

I lowered my voice. "No. Actually we had a good date. Went great. This is coming out of the blue for me."

"She's been prickly to everyone. Not just you. Just so you know."

The next day, Margot continued her standoffish attitude toward me. I tried not to take it personally, but I failed. I thought it best not to pester her; I decided to do my best impression of an adult, and I gave her space.

That night, I hobbled over to Harvard Square to meet Nigel at the Crimson. My legs still killed me from the squats I had done two days previously. I promised myself no more squats from that day forward, and I planned to consecrate that vow with alcohol. Nigel sat at the bar and talked with Kathleen.

"Lady, gentleman." I tipped my imaginary hat to both. Kathleen gave me a nice smile and placed a napkin in front of me. "A Caucasian please."

As Kathleen turned to mix my white Russian, I reached for the pretzel bowl. It pained me to admit to Nigel that his advice regarding Margot had proved right.

"So, Nige, I had a date with Margot earlier this week."

"Oh. So my advice worked, did it?"

"I will admit your advice helped. Along with Kathleen's little boost of my confidence, I might add." I gave a nod to Kathleen, but she appeared busy making drinks.

"I notice you held onto that little piece of news for a few days. Is it painful to admit that old Nigeldomus knows his shit? Well, tell me how it went. Spare no details."

"It was fun. I took her to dinner."

"Where?"

"Some shithole in Braintree of her choosing, but that doesn't matter. The great company and conversation. Those matter."

"Did you get a BJ at the end of the evening?" Nigel asked with a leer.

"You're a demented fuck. You know that? We kissed, but that's all."

"You going to see her again?"

"Well, that's where it gets sticky."

"I thought you said you got no action."

"You can't help yourself, can you? You have to throw in sexual innuendo whenever possible."

"You'd be bereft if I didn't. By the way, do you even know what 'innuendo' means?"

"Of course. Insinuation. Intimation," I said.

"No. It's an Italian suppository."

"What is that joke? Like a thousand years old? Do you mind if I continue with my story?" I feigned exasperation. "Anyway, things went really well. Then the next day, she was cold as ice to me. Has me real confused."

"That makes sense. She's probably just playing a little hard to get. Wants to see how much you dig her. That's all. Play it cool. Don't be overzealous. It will turn out well."

Kathleen came over and said, "You know, Jojo, wouldn't it be great to just go out with a woman and have there be no games? Just straight talk and no bullshit."

"Amen," I said.

"You have to stop dating these educated, stuck-up types. Go out with a down-to-earth blue-collar gal. Like a bartender."

I looked at Kathleen. "Someone like you?"

"Sure. Why not?"

"That's nice of you, Kathleen. If I could get with someone as hot as you, I would have it made."

"Who says you can't? You just gotta have confidence."

I sat up straighter. "Thanks, Kathleen. You're always good to me."

She smiled and made her way down to a couple of frat guys who were arguing about who could drink the most shots of Jäger before puking.

"She's a hell of a woman," I said to Nigel.

"Mate, she fancies you."

"No way. Hot piece like that?"

"You always sell yourself short. She's into you, and she's telling you so."

I was about to refute his theory when my phone rang. The number was blocked.

"Hold that thought, Nigel. Hello?"

I heard a woman's voice, but I couldn't make out who it was over the din of the bar.

"Hold on," I yelled into the phone. "I can't hear you." I walked to the bathroom area. "Are you still there?"

"Jojo, it's me. Margot." She sounded tense.

"Oh. Hey, Margot. What's going on?"

"Can you come over?"

I looked at my watch. It was almost eleven. "Are you OK?"

"I just need to see you. Can you come over?"

"I'm a little indisposed at the moment."

"Are you with another woman?" she asked.

"No, nothing like that. It's just that I've had a couple of drinks."

"I really need to see you."

"Fuck it. I'll cab over."

I hung up the phone and walked back to the bar. "That was Margot on the phone. She says she needs to see me right now," I said to Nigel.

"Whoo!"

"Take care of my check for me, will ya?"

He was still hooting it up when I left the bar.

I rolled up in the yellow cab about twenty minutes later. Cost a bloody fortune, but I had a feeling it might be worth it. At least I hoped it would be.

Margot must have been standing right by the door because she buzzed me up right away. She opened the door wearing sweats. Don't get me wrong. I love a woman in sweats. Especially if they're not baggy. And these weren't. But my besotted mind was envisioning some sort of negligee—though I'm not exactly sure what constitutes a negligee versus a nightie versus lingerie. Regardless, I'd imagined her standing with one arm extended over her head, leaning on the doorframe. No such luck.

"Thanks for coming over."

"Sure."

She had a small place. One bedroom. Step-in kitchen. Cozy. Lots of plants. We sat on the sofa and faced each other.

"You sounded upset on the phone."

"Yeah. I'm sorry about that. It really wasn't such a big deal, but I didn't want to be alone. You know what I mean?"

I actually swallowed hard. "I think so."

Margot moved a little closer to me on the sofa. "You're quiet tonight. No quick jokes."

"I'm a little thrown off. That's all."

"Why?"

"Why? First you're receptive to my advances, and then you tell me it can never happen. Then you agree again. Then you're cold as ice to me. I don't know whether I'm coming or going."

She moved closer. "I hope you're coming. And, yes, you know what I mean."

I laughed and moved in. Soft kisses. We began some timid hand searching followed by less-than-timid groping. She pulled back. "Let's go into the bedroom."

I nodded and followed her. As she walked, I began pulling her sweatpants off. She giggled and jumped on the bed. What followed confirmed my suspicions about what was beneath the baggy clothes: a veritable treasure. Athletic legs and ass. Breasts were bigger than I had thought and were very sensitive to all manner of touch. We had really good chemistry. We crescendoed and climaxed together.

Afterward, I was on my back with my eyes closed and my hands laced behind my neck. Margot's head was on my chest. The room had little light save the blue neon coming from an alarm clock near the bed. It made for a killer ambience in the afterglow.

"Jojo."

"Hmm?"

"That was nice. Yeah?"

"Yeah." I was in twilight, halfway to sleep.

"This Manson guy. He's pretty scary, huh?" she continued.

"He is. Needs to get back to prison."

"I'm having some difficulties with him."

That got my attention. "What do you mean?"

She lifted her head up. "I kind of did him a favor."

My eyes were wide open now. I turned and propped myself up on an elbow. My look of consternation caused her to lower her eyes. I regretted it, but I didn't have full control over my faculties—what with the booze and sex and all.

"What kind of favor?"

"I did something really stupid." Margot started to cry.

I stroked her hair. "OK. Just tell me what's going on."

"I'm in really bad trouble. He...he..." She cried hard now.

"It's OK. We'll figure it out. Just tell me."

Margot got a tissue from her nightstand and collected herself. "I approached him like I did the rest. I knew he was a dangerous guy, but they all are to an extent, right? I wanted to make sure I wasn't neglecting what might be a real problem for him. Anyway, he was really grateful for my efforts.

"Two days ago, he told me this story about his daughter and how he knew of a possible attempt to kill her. You know, to get back at him. And he had to warn her somehow. When I offered to call the police, he said he didn't know where she stayed. He only had her number in his cell phone. He said that was all he had because he wanted to shield her from all his criminal activity. He was so convincing. He asked me just to let him have his cell phone for a minute so he could get the number. Well, I was wary, but I thought, 'What can he do with his cell?'"

"Where was his cell phone anyway?"

Inmates didn't bring any personal items to the hospital. They didn't really have any personal items.

"He said his son would bring it to me."

I sighed. "So you agreed to be the go-between and brought him the phone."

"Yesterday. I brought it into the interview room and gave it to him—with the intention of taking it right back. That was the agreement. But just as I handed it over, an emergency sounded on the unit, and it forced him to go back to the dayroom. I couldn't get it back. Then he refused to see me."

"Uh-oh." My addled brain was putting the pieces together.

"This morning he asked to see me, and I thought he was going to give it back. Instead, he coldly told me that I owed him one. 'Funny,' I said. 'I thought it was the other way around.' He explained to me that if I didn't do what he wanted, he was going to report me as the one who gave him the cell phone. Obviously I would be fired."

"Jesus. Have you told anyone else?"

"No. I thought about telling Paul, but I'm just so ashamed. You know, I've been there for three years. I didn't just fall off a turnip truck. I don't know how I got suckered by such a cheap ploy."

"He's a very skilled psychopath. So what does he want you to do?"

Margot didn't say anything. The very air seemed to grow thick.

"Margot, what does he want?"
She looked at me. "He wants to speak with you."
I didn't stay the night.

CHAPTER 16

The next morning, my senses were heightened by orders of magnitude. I walked into the prison aware of every step I took. The doors slamming behind me caused me to jump. By the time I got to the unit, I was a wreck.

Rounds went so slowly I thought someone had fucked with the clock—or with time itself. The moment Margot told me Manson wanted to speak with me, my mind went into overdrive. I needed to know how this was going to play out right away. I bounced up when rounds ended like I'd sat on a spring. I went to the officers' trap. Johnson sat reading the paper.

"Hey, Jojo. How they hanging?"

Before I could answer, he looked into my face.

"Shit, boy, you look like you just seen a ghost."

"Rough night," I said. "Could you get Manson for me, please?"

"Sure, man. You go sit down in the interview room, and I'll bring him to you."

"Thanks."

Manson wore a blank look on his face when Johnson brought him into the interview room. I expected some smugness.

"Dr. Black, you want me to stay in here with you?" Johnson asked.

"No, thanks. I appreciate it, but I'll be OK."

"I'll just be down the hall," he said and closed the door after himself.

Manson folded his hands and placed them on the table. "Young Dr. Black. How are you this morning?"

91

"Cut the shit. What do you want?"

"Wow. Hot damn. I mean, I knew she would get to you, but I thought it would take a bit more time." Manson was delighted.

"You're a goddamned genius. Small wonder you're in prison and not heading up a NASA think tank."

"Temper, temper, Dr. Black. If this is to be a negotiation for the future of young Margot, we need to be civilized."

"What do you want?"

"Nothing from her. It's you who have what I need."

"How so?"

"Well, as you might know, I run an organization. The rules and regulations of this prison are so confining it makes it difficult to hold proper meetings. I've asked for GoToMeeting, but you know the cheap bastards in the prison system." He smiled at his own joke. "Anyway, I need to have some people here for an important powwow. They know how to get here, but it isn't always easy for them to stay long enough for us to get down to the real work. That's where you come in. I want you to recommend that they be held here for extra observation time."

"You know I'm not an evaluator. I don't make those decisions."

"Come now, Dr. Black. I know how it works here. If you make the recommendation, they will follow it."

Fucker was right. "It's not that easy."

"It is, Dr. Black," he said more insistently. The smile vanished from his face. "And you will do it, or I will make it very unpleasant for your girlfriend."

"She's not my girlfriend."

He leaned in close. "You've already lost, man, don't you realize it? Just by showing up and talking with me today you've confirmed what I already know. Get up to speed. I don't have time to educate you."

The room grew very cold for me as the weight of my dilemma began to sink in. "How many guys are we talking about?"

"I don't know just yet. I'll let you know how many and which ones."

"You know, there have to be reasons for them to stay longer. It will look suspicious if I'm keeping guys who are perfectly healthy—apart from their criminal tendencies."

"You'll have to be creative."

"Once I've done this, what assurances do I have that you won't keep asking for more things?" I said. It came out like a plea, and I hated that I couldn't control the whiny quality of my voice.

"None." My face must have registered the full realization of what I was into because he smiled. "Now you're up to speed. Good boy." He stood. "We done here?"

Without waiting on my reply, he walked out of the room and whistled his way back to the dayroom. I sat for a few minutes to collect myself. It dawned on me that Manson had planned this for some time.

⚔

It didn't take long for Manson to put his plan into place. After lunch, I returned to the treatment team room. Paul immediately called me over to his desk. "There's a new one asking for you specifically. Normally we don't accommodate these kinds of requests, but you've already seen him before. Makes sense for you to follow-up with him."

I didn't recognize the name on the chart. When I got him from the dayroom and sat down with him, though, his face brought the memory flooding back. It was Thompson, the kid who'd reported seeing leprechauns and other associated falsehoods; the one I'd called out on his bullshit. He wore the same all-knowing grin on his face.

"How the hell are you, Doc?"

My temper flared. "What kind of shit are you pulling now?"

"Just the God's honest truth. I need to stay here for the next few weeks and was hoping you might make that happen." I stood up. I was ready to put a wrap on this reunion. He quickly added, "Oh, and Lester says hello."

I don't know if it's physically possible, but my blood simultaneously boiled and went cold. "You've got to be shitting me."

On my walk back to the treatment team office, I came up with a reason to justify keeping Thompson. I felt like shit. Seeing Paul behind his desk intensified the guilt. At that moment, I badly wanted to open up to him. Spill the beans right then and there. End it. Because I already knew that was my only real option in this blackmail scheme. I knew that when digging yourself a hole, the first rule was to drop the shovel. I couldn't, though. Whether because of shame, bullheadedness, or stupidity, I can't say. But I chose to ride it out and see if I could manage it, like thousands of knuckleheads who came before me and attempted likewise.

That night, I met Nigel at the Crimson. He sat hunched over the bar, shooting the shit with Kathleen.

"Hi, Kathy. Can I get a beer?"

She shot me a cold look. Without a word, she pulled a pint of Guinness from the tap. She didn't really give it time to settle. She set it in front of me and walked away. No banter. And the beer was mostly foam. Shit.

"I pissed her off, huh?"

"I told you, mate. She fancies you."

"I've got bigger problems."

"So you said on the phone. Talk to Nigel. The doctor is in."

I told Nigel everything that had happened up to that point.

"Jojo," he eventually said. "I'm surprised at you."

He got my attention by using my name. A rarity for him. He turned, faced me, and looked in my eyes. This was even rarer. "You've been manipulated up and down on this one, mate."

"No shit."

"You walked right into the trap this Manson character set for you. He knew you would help Margot, and you obliged. Like a fucking actor in a shitty play."

"Manson played both of us."

"No. He got to Margot through his usual devious means. But she's the one who dragged you into this."

"What are you saying?"

He sighed and downed his shot. Looking over, he caught Kathleen's attention, and she poured us each another.

"Look, I know you have this thing for Margot. But if I have the timing right, she only called you over after Manson had laid the trap for her. Then she got you into the sack knowing you'd be easier to manipulate once you'd ejaculated."

My hackles were up. "No. What are you...no." I shut up. It occurred to me he might be right.

The warm robe of naïveté came off. Realization crashed over me in waves. How stupid could I be? How fucking gullible had I been? Here I prided myself on my ability to read people and to know how to gamble both in the casino and in my work. When push came to shove, though, I folded like a house of cards. Nigel must have read the epiphany on me because he softened his stance. He actually put a hand on my shoulder.

"Don't be so hard on yourself, mate. I'd cut off my left arm if a chick asked me nicely after she finished sucking my cock."

I took a long drink of my beer and breathed deeply. My thoughts swirled without landing anywhere. I turned back to Nigel. "What am I going to do? I mean, what can I do?"

"I take it you've decided against going straight to the authorities."

I nodded my head. "I already spoke with the evaluator about the guy I saw today, and I recommended he be kept in the hospital for extended observation." My anger rose. "Why should I lose my job over this? I'm a victim here; I was just trying to help a woman. It's not as if I'm bringing in drugs or profiting by this in any way. Just trying to save her ass. No, I'm not going down for this." I huffed for a moment and then calmed myself with a gulp of my beer. "Besides, I can handle it. I'm going to double down and power my way through."

"You do realize that all screwballs do the same thing before they are eventually caught. Then people wonder why they didn't nip it in the bud right away and come forward. When digging a hole—" Nigel said.

"I know, the first rule is to stop digging. But the only reason you're thinking that is because the ones who double down and then get caught are the screwballs. You don't ever hear about the ones who successfully manage these kinds of situations. That's going to be me." I downed my shot. "I'm not taking the fall for this. Where would I even go from here? Who's to say they wouldn't take action against my license to practice medicine? I could be drummed out of the profession."

Nigel beamed. "I'm proud of you. You're walking into the coliseum, into certain death, with your head held high in defiance. If that's your decision, you'll have to buy yourself time until you can figure a way out of this. You know, though, it's going to get worse. Manson will push and push and eventually ask you to do something you are absolutely unwilling to do, and then he'll crush your bollocks into dust."

I nodded my head. I'd already arrived at that same conclusion.

Chapter 17

I walked into the unit and saw an inmate look at me and then nudge a big, bald, white guy in the ribs. He came to the door of the dayroom and called out. "Hey, Doc. Doc. Can you see me today?"

I had no idea who he was. I scanned the dayroom and saw Manson smile and nod. That made the walk to the office dreadful. The board had five new names. Paul sat at his desk and twirled a pen.

"Who's the new skinhead guy?" I asked.

Without looking up, Paul said, "Big guy? Maybe six three? Two fifty?"

"Yeah."

"Think his name is John Whitney."

"I'll take him."

"No problem. We'll do rounds, and then we'll divvy up the rest."

I sat down hard in a chair in the corner. Margot was on the other side of the room, and she was avoiding any eye contact with me. I was already on edge; that nudged me over the cliff.

"We going to start any time soon?"

Paul looked at me, puzzled. "OK," he said slowly. "Roll 'em."

Margot started reading off the names. "Jimmy Smith. He just got out of the Shoe. From Walpole. Says he's suicidal."

I snorted. Margot didn't dignify me with a response. She went to the next name. "John Souza. He comes from the treatment center. He's been pretty demanding. Angry at the way he's been treated over there. Asking for all sorts of accommodations."

"Just like those goddamned pederasts to be so fucking entitled. Then when you confront them for what they did, they make up all sorts of shitty reasons why they are not responsible but victims themselves." I made my voice whiny. "The priest made me what I am. The boys wanted it. If NAMBLA ran the country, you people would be the odd ones."

Paul put his feet down. A sign he wasn't happy. "OK, Jojo, enough of the commentary. Go on, Margot."

She read the next one. "Manuel Gomez. Sounds as if he wants out of Los Reyes, and his compatriots aren't too happy. He's mostly here to avoid getting beaten up."

"Ain't that a fucking shame? Just when I thought I was out, they pull me back in." My Al Pacino impression was passable, and I thought it warranted some grace for that smartass interruption.

Paul thought otherwise and let me know with an exasperated look. I held up my hands in surrender. "OK. That was the last one."

Margot went through the rest of the names, and they were assigned teams. Everyone stood to go about his or her morning routine. Paul asked me to step outside the office. He waited until others were out of earshot and then said, "What the fuck?"

"Sorry, Paul."

"Something you need to tell me?"

"No," I replied after a pause not lost on him.

"If you're stressed out, then you gotta let me know so I can help. If you keep it to yourself, there's not much I can do."

Boy, did I want to open up in that moment. More than anything. I chickened out, though. My mind offered instant justifications, and I jumped on them. *What have you done thus far that's so wrong? You've recommended some guys get lengthier times in the hospital. So what?* I knew they didn't need to be there, but anyone would be hard-pressed to find evidence of wrongdoing on my part. I documented well. So some scumbags would spend more time possibly getting help. There were bigger issues in this world.

Still and all, I avoided looking into Paul's eyes. I had a ton of respect for him, and it killed me to be dishonest. I had to offer him something, though. "I've been under some stress outside of work."

"Margot?" he asked.

An opening. "Yeah. You were right. I shouldn't have mixed business with pleasure. It was a mistake."

"Anything I can help with?"

"No. But I appreciate the offer. We'll work it out. I'm sorry I brought some of that with me to work."

"Look, I understand how that can get you upset. But, you know, you gotta keep it professional. All right?"

"Yeah. Thanks, Paul."

I went back into the office and got Whitney's chart. Then I got the man himself. He gave me a spiel similar to Thompson's. Whitney made a feeble attempt to describe mental illness and then smiled broadly when he dropped Manson's name.

I walked the big man back to the dayroom and asked to see Manson. He took his sweet time coming down the hall. He was schmoozing everyone in his path, inmates and COs alike. He was a politician working a rope line. We sat down. The smugness was on full display.

"What the fuck is going on? Just how many guys are you trying to bring here?"

"I don't know yet. Right now I'm just working my core guys."

"That little shit Thompson is one of your core guys?"

He didn't seem bothered. "Nah. That was just a side favor for someone else."

"Well, all these guys, it's too much. It's gonna draw attention."

"That's for you to manage."

My frustration and panic were boiling over. "At the very least, you gotta educate these morons on how to act the part. If they say they're crazy, then they have to be consistent on the unit at all times. If they're seen yukking it up in the dayroom and looking normal, everyone's going to know they're full of shit."

"How's that my problem?"

"You want this to work, right? So tell your guys. No bullshit voices or seeing the devil or dead people."

"OK, Doc. That's a fair point. What should I tell them to do?"

"I don't know." I thought for a minute, and an answer came. "Have them pretend they are catatonic. You know, say little. Walk around with blank expressions. Look dumb. That shouldn't be too hard for them. The evaluators will suspect they're full of shit, but they won't be able to prove it."

"If they're acting catatonic, how am I supposed to talk to them?"

"You can figure out times to converse where there won't be that much attention."

Manson contemplated this. "That's not bad."

I felt I had wrested a modest amount of control back. Manson seemed to sense this and said with some irritation, "Don't get cocky, Doc. Just do your part, and nothing too bad will happen."

"What are you threatening me for? You need me in this. If this falls apart, what are you going to do then?"

He leaned in menacingly. "I'll find another shithead just like you and lean on him. Don't you worry about me. Just worry about you and that pretty little girlfriend of yours."

CHAPTER 18

In the gym that afternoon, I vented my frustrations on the weights. Steve noticed.

"You got a lot of energy today. Either you're on speed or you're pissed about something."

"I'm in a bit of a jam."

"Want to talk about it?"

"I can't just yet, Steve. I'm sorry."

"No sorry needed. You know I'm here if you do want to talk."

We each worked out on our own for a few minutes, but we reconnected at the dip bar. One of us would do a set for the triceps, and then the other would try to do five more. This went on until we couldn't do any more dips. I jumped up onto the dip bar.

"You remember asking me about Manson?" he asked.

I grunted my affirmation.

"I'm hearing a lot of things coming out of the state hospital."

I stopped at fifteen reps. "What kind of things?"

"I hear the power players from the White Dawn are convening at the state hospital for an important meeting. You know anything about that?"

I shook my head. "Nah. I'm not into the gangland stuff."

Steve looked at me hard. It was as if he was trying to see through me. It was unsettling. I was finding I wasn't as good a liar as I hoped to be. My World Series of Poker aspirations came unglued.

"All right, Doc. You want to talk to me, you let me know. I haven't forgotten what you did for my mother. Just remember that. If you need something, you come here first. I might look like a meathead, but I've got a lot of connections."

I smiled for what felt the first time in a long time. "Thanks, Steve. I appreciate that. Just so you know, though, you don't owe me anything. What I did was for the sake of your mother. Not to be used as some sort of chit to exchange in the future."

Steve smiled back. "You don't get it, Doc. It's precisely that attitude that makes me want to help you."

He got on the dip bar and did twenty-five. Fucker.

⋏

I recommended two more guys for longer-term evaluations. It wasn't that unusual for me to urge for more time for an assessment. There were some legitimate inmates with mental health issues. Because I didn't want to fall into the trap of sending back guys who really needed to stay just to make my numbers work, I was keeping more people in the hospital. I mean, nobody really counted up how many guys I kept or sent back, but I worried my change in habit would get noticed. It did, but not like I thought.

Paul pulled me aside near the end of the day on Friday. He waited while people cleared out of the treatment office and then sat on the edge of his desk. "Everything all right?"

"Sure. Why?"

"Because, Jojo, I've worked in this joint a long time. I'm seeing an uptick in admissions from the max security prisons, and I'm hearing scuttlebutt concerning gang activity. Then I see you're looking stressed, and you're dealing with Lester Manson. Give me a little credit, will ya?"

"Nothing like that, Paul." I set my face to the most earnest look I could muster.

"Nothing, huh?"

His expression reminded me of my parents' faces when I was caught red-handed as a kid and was trying to lie my way out of it. The look was equal parts anger, incredulity, and shame at my idiotic attempt to pass off an obvious lie as truth. I'm sure the guilt registered on my face, but mercifully, Paul relented. He put a hand on my shoulder. "You've got the weekend coming up. Take the time to figure things out. By Monday, hopefully you'll have sorted things out. OK?"

"Thanks, Paul. You have a good weekend."

I committed myself to confronting Margot. I finished my paperwork and hurried out of the office. As fast as I could, I made my way through the many locked doors to the parking lot outside. I found her car still in the lot and waited by it. She finally came out, and I could see as she approached she wasn't excited to see me.

"We have to talk."

"Jojo, I have lots on my mind. Could we do this another time?"

"Another time? Are you freaking kidding me? Do you know what you got me into?"

"Do I know? Of course I know!" Her voice rose shrilly.

Others in the parking lot took notice. I recalled the sage insight Steve had told me about the prison system and its parallels to high school. It got me under control in a hurry.

"Calm down. Nobody needs to know what we're talking about. Let's take it down a notch."

"Calm down? You're the one who started the yelling."

I took a deep breath. "You're right. Let's calm down together." I leaned against her car. "Can we sit in your car?"

She nodded and unlocked the doors. I got in the passenger side and exhaled loudly. "I'm in a world of shit. He's asked me to do things that are job-threatening, not to mention possibly illegal."

"I'm in the same boat." Margot was defensive.

"Yeah, but—"

"But what?"

"Well, I wouldn't be in this if you hadn't sicced him on me."

"What the hell are you talking about?"

"You were upset. I comforted you. One thing led to another," I said.

"Fuck you. I was in trouble. I wasn't looking for pity."

"It feels to me as if you manipulated me all along."

Margot recoiled. "You think I slept with you to manipulate you? That's what you think?"

"Look at it from my standpoint. You sprang this on me just after I came. Not exactly when a man is thinking his best."

"I would disagree. Before you assholes ejaculate, all you can think about is tits and ass. Some of the best conversations I've had with men are when they aren't thinking about sex because they just got some."

"So you admit you fucked me just to take advantage of my kindness."

"Is this what you call kindness? Disrupting me during rounds?" Margot asked.

I mumbled an apology to the dashboard, but it was perfunctory. Inside I seethed. I turned back to her. "Like I said before, I'm in a real jam here. So if I'm not behaving the best, you could cut me some slack."

"If you would stop thinking about yourself for a second, maybe we could help each other."

"Oh no, sister. No thanks. You've helped me enough already."

"Then why did you want to speak with me?"

"I guess to clear the air. To tell you I feel used."

Margot got more agitated. She angrily took a cigarette and lighter from her purse and lit up. She didn't open the window until she had exhaled the first plume in my direction. "Then you're dumb. Sleeping with you happened for several reasons—none of which had to do with manipulating you. I thought you were attractive, smart, and funny. Those are nice things to look for in a partner. But I can see you're also self-centered, cynical, and callous. So this is obviously not going to work out. Why don't you get the hell out of the car so I can go home?"

"I'm self-centered? And you're what? Mother fucking Teresa? You flirted with me, avoided me, flirted again, played the damsel in distress, and then indebted me to a psychopath. That about right?"

She inhaled the shit out of that cigarette. "I didn't force you to help me, OK? I just passed a message. If you're too chicken shit to handle that, I'm sorry."

I looked away and spoke softly. "I wouldn't be in this shit if it weren't for you. I would still be living a quiet life, earning a paycheck, and handing it over to the casinos."

"You know what? Fuck you. Get out of my car, and you will be shot of me for good. I can see I made a mistake with you."

I opened the door. As I stepped out, she said, "And you were wrong about one thing. I didn't put him on to you, as you said. It was you he wanted all along."

I slammed the door, and Margot pulled out.

CHAPTER 19

I got home and dumped my keys on the foyer table. I like to give important-sounding names to areas in my apartment. So what? I have a foyer, living room, sitting room, office, and rumpus room. That they are never any two of those things at the same time makes me no never mind. I even have a greenhouse, if you count the dying plant perched on the windowsill. Which I do.

My cell phone rang. Nigel.

"Are we meeting at the Crimson?"

"I don't know, Nige. I had a hell of a day."

"Aw, c'mon. Don't be a prat. You'll come out and drown your sorrows. I'll pretend to be listening. I'm getting really good at that—especially when I have a wealthy Beacon Hill housewife pissing and moaning how she's been driven to distraction."

I laughed. He was always good for that. "That's enticing. Give me some downtime. Let's meet at ten so I can decompress beforehand."

"Ten it is."

I went to my freezer and pulled out my SKYY. I don't know if it's a good vodka, but I love the cobalt-blue bottle. I poured a generous helping of Russian courage and reached for the Kahlúa. A white Russian. It was like adult chocolate milk—and I had liked it even before the Dude made it popular. However, he had cemented it as my go-to drink when I felt shitty. And man, was the shit flowing.

I sat down heavily on my loveseat, which doubled as a barrier of sorts to cut off the living from the sleeping area. I halfheartedly flipped through the channels and finally settled on SportsCenter. It proved hard to focus on what they said. Sports were diminished at that moment. I let my mind wander.

Paul had given me an opening. I figured he must know something was going on. The smart thing would be to go in on Monday morning and let him know the dilemma first thing. Take my lumps. If they fired me, I could always find other work. There were always headhunters sending me e-mails and texts about "great opportunities" in Horsehump, Nebraska. *No. I shouldn't even wait until Monday. I should call him now.* Did I have his home number? Why would I think I had his home number? I was sure I could get it, though. How hard could it be? He lived somewhere on the South Shore. Or was it near the Cape? *You know, I've been in this state for six fucking years, and the closest I've come to the Cape is eating a lobster roll in the summer.*

I took a big swig of the drink. If nothing else, I was saving on buying booze at the Crimson. Those fuckin' bastards and their seven-dollar mixed drinks. Put so much goddamned ice in there. You were really getting very little alcohol.

What the fuck are you complaining about? Kathleen hooks you up with so much free booze. On average, you've probably paid a dime for each drink. Kathleen. I groaned. I hadn't seen that one coming. If Nigel was right, I had to fix things with her. Tonight I was going to grow some balls and see what I could do to repair that friendship. My thoughts drifted as the alcohol set to numbing my feelings.

I woke up to a different SportsCenter show and dark windows. I looked down and hissed. I had fallen asleep with the drink in my hand. My adult chocolate milk now adorned the cheap rug in Rorschach splotches. The clock read just past two. Holy shit. I was more tired than I had thought. My cell phone had several missed calls; That would be Nigel. The stress of this past week had taken everything out of me. I'll sort it out tomorrow, I thought, and I got into my bed—clothes and all. What serendipity that my boudoir was so close to my parlor.

After thirteen hours of sleep, I felt better. I hadn't slept that long since my teenage years and I awoke with resolve. Today I would get my shit together. It started with cleaning my apartment. I gave every surface a passable scrub. The toilet and the tub were especially needy. What can I say? It had been a long time since a woman was up there. After I cleaned, I had a sensibly light lunch and got my gear ready to go to the gym. I belonged to a local club that over-charged me, which I made up for by not showing up. My use of the prison staff gym had allowed me to feel better about neglecting the expensive one. Funny about Paul asking me whether I needed to work out with coeds in thongs. This gym had plenty of those, and I avoided it and them. Today my focus was entirely on the workout. The lifting I had done with Steve had paid off. I enjoyed a great session. I topped off the weights with a three-mile run. It took me a little longer than usual; I blamed that on Margot's secondhand smoke.

On my way home, I called Nigel.

"What the fuck happened to you last night?"

"I fell asleep after we spoke."

"Jesus. Are you OK? Got some of that narcolepsy that's going around? Can I assume you're all right now?"

"Yes. Wanted to see if you would take a rain check and go to the Crimson tonight."

"Technically, the rain check would have been given out last night. And no. Tonight I want to hit the casinos. You in?"

I didn't have the money—not that Nigel would take that as an excuse. He would spot me whatever I wanted or needed. I really wanted to see Kathleen and clear the air, though. Shit, you would think I'd had enough air-clearing after Margot, but I sensed things would go better with Kathleen. I didn't have the courage—or the energy, for that matter—to tell Nigel about the conversation I'd had with Margot. I couldn't bear his lecture.

"No. Now, can I take that rain check?"

"You can't 'take' the rain check. You can 'ask' for one. Jesus."

"Goddamn you and your king's English shit."

"Queen's English. There is no king."

"I would very much like to ask for a rain check on the casino, gov'na." My cockney accent was shit.

"All right, buddy. You be good."

"You too. Don't lose your shirt there."

"Ta-ta."

I showered and shaved. A hint of cologne. Dressed decently but not too formally. I walked down to the Crimson at Harvard Square.

"Hey, Tommy."

"What's happening, Doc?"

"Not much. Have to bounce any underage drinkers thinking they can outsmart Tommy Gun?"

"Not tonight. Dammit. But the night's still young."

I walked past the larger-than-life bouncer and into the bar. I immediately spotted Kathleen working behind the bar. As usual, she sported jeans and a tight top. Magenta this time. She wore the shit out of a tube top. I took my seat on an empty stool and looked at Kathleen. Incredulity washed over me. There was no way this gorgeous woman had feelings for me. *Just look at her,* I thought. *She's fucking beautiful.* That was why it was so easy for me to flirt with her. I didn't think I had a snowball's chance in hell. Nigel had to be wrong. Tonight I would find out.

Kathleen did her best to ignore me. She tended to two men sporting out-of-date ponytails and earrings. They flirted with her unabashedly—and clumsily. Fed up with that, she finally came over to me.

"What will it be?" She placed a napkin in front of me and avoided eye contact.

"For my drink, I would like a beer. But I also want to know why you're so pissed at me."

She pulled a glass and began pouring the Guinness. Tonight, she was the consummate bartender. She poured a little, let it sit, poured some more, and let that sit. Really built up the head and made those bubbles dance. The blacks and tans. No beer was more enticing than good old Guinness.

"You know, Jojo, you might just be the most thickheaded bastard I've ever seen."

"That's a bit harsh."

Kathleen finished pouring the beer, knifed off the head, and pushed it to me.

"No. I don't think it's harsh. I spend my days fending off the juvenile advances of every undergrad and grad student. Meantime, I'm sending you hard-core signals, and you're oblivious to them."

I was speechless. The thought that Kathleen was interested in me was fun to toss around with Nigel, but having her say it to me point-blank was something else. My heady rush came to an abrupt end when I remembered something.

"Don't you have a boyfriend? You're always talking about him. Big guy. Personal trainer."

"Yeah, we've been together for three years. He's OK. But he bores me. You don't bore me."

"How do you know that? We barely know each other. We only ever see each other here. It's all fun and games. I'm a bigger pain in the ass than I let on."

She leaned over the bar and rested her chin on her hands. She was so close to me I almost fell backward off the stool. "I'm thirty-six, Jojo. I've been around. Met and talked with thousands of people. Hell, it's what I do for a living. I know when someone's a keeper."

Someone down the bar yelled for Kathleen.

"I'll be right there. Hold your water."

"Hold your water? Did you really just say that? That expression has to be a hundred years old," I said.

She broke out into a smile. "You're clever and fast. And you make me laugh. Those are qualities to value." She walked down the bar.

I called after her. "But you don't know me. I can be a real prick."

Some wiseass wearing an MIT hat a few barstools down chimed in. "Yeah, man. You are a real prick. Hogging the hot bartender like that. You should listen to him, hottie." Running his hands over his torso, he said, "Take a look at me. I'm a catch."

"Go fuck yourself, MIT, and mind your own goddamned business." I half stood on the stool and glared at him.

He quieted down. That was what I loved about this college place. A pussy like me could bluff his way into the tough-guy role.

Kathleen stayed busy filling orders. She looked upset that she couldn't come back and talk to me. I got antsy. I walked over to where she stood. Her back was to me, and she was ringing up a customer.

"Can we talk someplace more private?"

She gave the customer change. "I can take a break in a few minutes. I'll signal you, and we can take a smoke break outside."

I waited at the bar and finished my beer. It occurred to me that I had been so preoccupied with Kathleen that I had completely forgotten the world of shit I was in at work. I figured a quick gulp of the beer and another shot would take care of the returning dread and keep it at bay. I leaned over the bar. "Kathy, can we do a shot?"

Between mixing drinks for the bustling Saturday night crowd, she poured us each a Goldschläger, and she downed it with me. In no time, my mind refocused on this lovely bartender who (for reasons unknown) found me irresistible. She signaled her partner for a break and nodded at me to follow. We walked out the front door to the parking lot in back. She lit up a cigarette.

"Secondhand smoke is a killer."

She blew a plume in my direction. By now I was used to it. "How much collective smoke is built up in those casinos you and Nigel frequent? Huh? And is that what you wanted so badly to get me alone to tell me?"

Good point. "No. Look, Kathleen, I wanted to tell you that I never meant to lead you on. To be honest, I didn't think you'd ever go for a guy like me."

"I fucking hate it when people say 'to be honest.' What the fuck does that mean? That everything you said before was a goddamned lie?"

"OK, OK. I just meant that I thought it was harmless flirting because you're out of my league." The Goldschläger had hit me like a ton of bricks. Made me a little unsteady on my feet and lent the night a surreal feeling.

"That shows what you know about women. Jack shit."

"No argument there. When it comes to affairs of the heart and me, you're absolutely right."

We paused to take some breaths. Mine were deep inhalations of the Cambridge night air. Hers involved nicotine and a thousand different chemical carcinogens.

"And I don't know why you're so upset. You've got a good thing going with Bruno the Wonder Trainer."

"Don't you get snarky with me. His name is Jeff. And he's a decent guy. You'd like him."

"No, I wouldn't. I would hate him on principle."

She smiled. "I don't know why I see past your sarcastic, self-deprecating facade. But I do." Kathleen leaned in close and caused my head to go fuzzier.

I stammered. "I'm sorry, honey, if my stupid comments hurt you. It's not in my nature to repeatedly and purposefully try to hurt someone."

"How could you know that I felt such a connection to you? I loved you almost from the beginning." Her whisper drove me crazy. I offered no retort. She rescued me by saying softly, "It's 'honey' now, huh?"

Before I could say anything stupid, she leaned in and gave me a kiss. It sent my head reeling and my nether regions exploding. In fact, I was afraid she might lean in close enough to gauge how wild it made me. I kissed her back, and it got more passionate in a hurry. My mind raced with all the implications of our union. But I didn't have as much time as I might have hoped, though, because we were interrupted.

"What the hell?"

We pulled apart, and a big guy came stalking up to us and gave me a shove. I'm not insubstantial, but this guy must have been six four. He also must have weighed 220 pounds, and his push nearly put me on my back.

"Jeff. Holy shit." Kathleen stepped between us.

Jeff. Oh. Oh fuck! I threw up my hands. "Man, this is certainly not the kind of thing I wanted."

"Shut up, asshole. Kathy, baby, what the fuck is going on?"

"Jeff, calm down—"

"I'm sorry, man. It's not right to be kissing another man's girl. I know—"

"Shut the fuck up, asshole, before I put my foot through your chest!"

"Jeff! Calm down. It's not his fault. I kissed him. Not the other way around."

"No, Kathleen, don't do that. I can take responsibility for myself."

The punch landed squarely on my upper jaw, the zygoma. Had it hit my mandible, or lower jaw, it would have shattered it to pieces. Still, I didn't just feel the force of his fist hitting my face. I heard it—both outside and inside my head. It was the first time I had received such a blow to the face. When people talk about getting your bell rung, I can confirm that it felt as if my head vibrated to the frequency of his fist. It's possible that I blacked out, but I'm not sure. My senses came back to me while I inhaled concrete and listened to Kathleen yell at her boyfriend. I pushed myself to a sitting position just as another country was heard from.

"Hey, tough guy. Back the fuck away from the doctor."

I opened one eye (on the other side of my head) and saw two guys standing with their hands on their hips. They were opposite the gargantuan personal trainer. One of the guys was of medium build. He wore a blazer and had a crew cut. The other was tall and lanky, and I could see a tattoo on his right arm that read, "Thug 4 Life."

Jeff moved his neck back and forth like a prizefighter. "Who the fuck do you think you are? You want a piece of me? Come the fuck on."

"I ain't going to fight you, pecker breath," the smaller of the two said. "I'm just going to blow your fucking head off and file a report." He peeled back his blazer to reveal a gun and a badge.

Jeff turned white and started to back away.

"That's right, tough guy. Take the woman, and get the fuck out of here."

Kathleen shot me a look of fear. I didn't have the energy to speak. I just sat on the concrete and looked, I'm sure, like I felt. Jeff and Kathleen walked away.

"Keep going. Stop looking back, tough guy. Just keep walking." When they turned the corner, he looked down at me. "You can get up now."

"Thanks for your help, Officer. I'm not looking to press charges." I got to my feet, feeling grateful to be rescued from the Jeff situation, blissfully unaware I was living out the idiom from out of the frying pan into the fire.

"I ain't no street cop, fucko. I'm state police. That means I don't walk a beat looking for drunken brawls to break up. No, my interest in you has nothing to do with that meathead or the girl."

My throbbing head made it damn near impossible to focus. "So why are you here?"

"I'm here to tell you to stop helping out that scumbag Manson."

"I don't know what you're talking about," I mumbled.

"Yeah, you do. I know all about what you're doing. I've spent the last five years working on keeping that piece of shit behind bars and incapacitated. I'd like to continue that work unfucked by a chickenshit doctor who fools around with big ape looking assholes' girlfriends. So if I find out you're still helping Manson out and I have to come back and pay you a visit...well, it won't be pleasant."

I stood up straighter and attempted to rally. "Officer, I can't speak about any patients I might or might not see at the state hospital. You must know that. So I will repeat. I don't know what you're talking about."

"I heard you the first time. You just remember that I'll be watching."

The two men walked off. I thought I'd seen the tall, skinny guy before. He had a familiar look to him, but I couldn't place it. After they turned the corner, I considered going back into the bar to find Kathleen and make sure she was OK. Then I remembered Jeff—all six four of him. I decided against it, and I walked home as fast as my addled brain allowed. Once home, I grabbed a ziplock bag, filled it with ice, and crashed on the sofa. The ice stung my face, but at least it turned it numb. After a few minutes of contemplating all these new developments, I gave up. I fell asleep sitting up on the sofa, and I woke up in the middle of the night with a puddle of water in my lap. Fuck. I had to stop doing that.

Chapter 20

Monday morning arrived, and my cheek remained swollen and many shades of purple. I couldn't face the folks at work, so I called in sick. That was one of the nice things about working in a prison. The patients weren't going anywhere, and no insurance company was breathing down your neck to discharge them. I spent the day running errands to keep busy and prevent my head from exploding from the building pressure in my life. The encounter with the statey refocused my attention on work and pushed out other considerations. Like Kathy. By day's end, after a punishing workout motivated by an intense desire to hurt myself, I resolved to nip this in the bud. I would go to Paul and enlist his help. It was the only way forward.

Lying in bed before going to sleep, I ran scenarios in my head. In my mind's eye, I waited until after rounds and pulled Paul aside. I told him everything from the start and asked him how to proceed. I put my fate in his hands. Whatever lumps had to be taken, so be it. It seemed more sensible than going down a path where a psychopathic gang leader led the way. A sense of calm came over me after I completed the scene in my head, and I fell asleep easily.

The next morning, I'm proud to say I held the same sense of purpose. Sometimes I have brilliant thoughts at the edge of sleep only to find they aren't that brilliant when exposed to the light of day. Not this time. I stood firm in my resolve. I drove to work, parked my car, and walked with my head high. I would soon be beholden to no man. In the first sally port, the officer behind the glass tapped.

"Dr. Black, you need to go to administration right away."

"OK. Thanks." My mind started racing.

The administrative offices were on the second floor of the main building of the prison hospital complex. I started up the stairs slowly, reliving all my childhood trips to the principal's office. It was never good to be called to the office. I broke into a run up the stairs and immediately regretted it. The combination of anxiety and the flight of stairs left me feeling dizzy. I had to hold onto the railing at the top to keep from falling. A secretary saw me.

"Are you OK?"

"Yeah. I'm all right."

"You sound as if you just ran a marathon."

"I'll be OK."

"Are you Dr. Black?"

"Yes."

"They're waiting for you in the medical director's office."

That didn't help the dizziness. I walked in. Sitting at a boardroom table were the medical director of the hospital, Dr. Porter; Paul; a big CO; and a woman. I didn't recognize the latter two.

"Come on in, Dr. Black. Have a seat." The medical director seemed to be MCing the meeting.

I hadn't had much contact with Dr. Porter. He held monthly staff meetings, but my attendance lagged when they conflicted with my workout routine. I nodded to Paul, who looked stricken.

Dr. Porter spoke. "Dr. Black, we have some disturbing things to discuss and hope you might shed some light on the situation."

"Sure," I croaked, and then cleared my throat.

"First of all, do you know everyone here? I know you know Paul, but next to him is Mary Policy, nursing administrator, and to her right is Captain Fogel." I nodded my head at each introduction. "We're all here to get to the bottom of this situation.

"There is a social worker on your unit, Margot, whom I'm sure you know. She's in a bit of trouble."

I snuck a glance at Paul. He gestured to my black-and-blue face with a quizzical look, but I waved it off.

"What's going on?" I said.

All my energy went to maintaining my composure. Faced with the prospect of 'fessing up, I found myself scared shitless. I wasn't going to be able to go through with it. So now I focused on keeping a blank face—putting all those hours at the poker table to some real-world use. I didn't know what they knew, but I had to assume they didn't know what cards I held. *Avoid giving any information they don't ask for,* I coached myself.

Captain Fogel picked up the narrative. "The social worker in question provided contraband to a very dangerous inmate whom you also have been working with. Lester Manson."

"OK."

"Well, Dr. Black, we need to know what your involvement has been in this incident."

I took some deep breaths and gambled. "I'm not sure what you mean."

Fogel looked at Porter. The latter said, "She mentioned your name."

"In what context?" I asked with all the nonchalance I could muster.

"She said you could provide some background to this that would help corroborate her story. Frankly, it looks really bad for her," Captain Fogel said.

"What did she bring in?"

"The specific contraband is not important." Fogel looked like a man to be reckoned with.

Paul put an arm on Fogel. "Easy. Dr. Black is a good psychiatrist. Hard worker. Don't make this out to be an inquisition. She brought in a cell phone and some other items."

"So can you shed any light on this? Is there something you know that will help Margot?" Porter looked saddened as he asked.

I looked at everyone in turn and shook my head slowly. "No. I'm sorry. I wasn't aware of anything unusual happening with Manson or any involvement he had with Margot. He's been a sarcastic pain in the ass, but he hasn't caused me any trouble."

Porter smiled and looked over at Fogel. "OK? Good. Thank you, Dr. Black. Why don't you go to the unit now."

I stood. "What's going to happen to Margot?"

The three looked at each other. Fogel answered. "You don't have to worry about that. Just be on your toes with Manson until we ship him back to maximum security."

I walked to the door. I don't know why, but I looked back. You would have thought I would have learned a lesson from Lot's wife. Paul's expression hit me like a bolt of lightning. It held a mixture of disgust and sadness.

As soon as I entered the treatment team office, the room went quiet. Then a barrage of questions all came at once.

"What did they say?"

"What's happening with Margot?"

"I heard she brought stuff to an inmate."

"I heard she was caught having sex with an inmate."

"What? You're crazy."

"Is it true, Dr. Black? Is Margot being fired?"

"Holy shit. I didn't realize it was that serious."

Just like high school. Steve couldn't have been more right. The staff members acted like a pack of teenagers delighting in the intrigue of someone else's misfortune. The news of the meeting with the uppers had obviously gone around. I didn't have time to answer. Paul entered and silenced the group. He conducted some dispirited rounds. New inmates had arrived over the weekend and requested yours truly as their psychiatrist. Paul assigned teams to the new ones, and rounds broke. He came over to me.

"What happened to your face?"

"I got mugged over the weekend."

"Holy shit. You OK?"

"You mean aside from the Gorbachev bruise on my face?"

He smiled. "Gotta keep your sense of humor. I like that. On a more serious note, we need to process that meeting. You know?"

"Yeah. I know. Let me get my bearings. It took me by surprise. I walked into the first officers' trap and was told to go to administration. It's the first I've heard of all this."

Paul was scrutinizing me like nobody's business. He pulled me to a corner and leaned in. "You're holding out on me. I know. I don't know exactly what or why. But it will make it more difficult to help you when the shit goes down."

I stayed silent, but I maintained eye contact. This was not an easy feat.

"Thanks for not insulting my intelligence by going into a big denial song and dance, Jojo." He sighed. "There's something building here, and it's got the potential to cause a major shit storm."

"You're not just talking about Margot, are you?"

He shook his head. "Everyone's on edge about gang activity. There's a lot of traffic this way. It's hard keeping the warring parties separate."

"Have there been incidents?"

"Not yet, but everyone's on pins and needles. And when COs get itchy, they make our lives more difficult. Let me tell you, I've been here when there were major emergencies. They once locked down the prison for seven hours after a riot broke out. Seven fucking hours we stayed in this room. There was no movement allowed except to go to the bathroom, and that was with a lot of begging. They don't give any deference to clinical staff. When the shit goes down, everyone is equally a security risk. Unless properly contained." We stood in silence. "OK. Enough of that, Dr. Black. Why don't we get to work." He started to walk away. "Oh, by the way, Cecil Goldberg is back. You mind picking him up? You did a good job last time."

"What did he do to get here?"

"Put something on or in his body in a place that wasn't meant for anything."

"Nothing like consistency to bring a smile to your face. No good deed goes unpunished, I guess. I'll try to do a shittier job this time so someone else can pick him up next time."

"I like your reasoning. Meantime, tee him up, grab the three-wood, and get him back to Walpole."

Rather than start my day with Cecil, I picked up the chart of a name I didn't recognize and headed for the trap. I was expecting another lousy interview. A bad actor with a smarmy grin eager to stay for the gang convention. Still, it felt preferable to another round with Cecil. As it turned out, the interview went rather differently. His name was Andrew Hart, and he wore makeup.

I asked one of the officers to get him. Cecil paced back and forth like a caged animal in the dayroom. He was eyeballing my every movement. Cecil's reputation clearly preceded him. The others offered him a wide berth in an already tight space. Manson stood at the door's opening. "You gonna see me today, Doc?"

"Yes, Mr. Manson."

A CO escorted Hart. Some of the men gave wolf whistles.

Manson grinned maniacally and said loudly, "I guess it's ladies first, huh, Doc?"

I didn't reply. I followed Hart to the interview room and gestured for him to sit down. "Mr. Hart, my name is Dr. Black."

"Please call me Anjelica."

He had a slight build with long, dark hair. A feminine quality to him. I mean, apart from the blue eye shadow and blush he wore.

I gestured to his makeup. "How did you do that?"

He smiled. "Thank you for asking. I make my own makeup from materials I find. I know it's contraband, but the COs look the other way."

"I have to assume that's a hard way to do time—with guys like this. No?" Anjelica's face fell into a droop. I continued softly, "You tried to kill yourself by cutting your wrists."

He spoke to the ground. "It's not easy being a woman trapped in a man's body. Everybody thinks I do it to get attention. Some sort of homosexual come-on to the other cons. I'm not even gay, but try explaining that to this group. I did this on the outside too. Being in prison has got nothing to do with it."

"And that's why you cut your wrists?" I asked.

"Yeah."

"What did you use?"

"I broke a lightbulb and used the shards. It wasn't hard. There are dozens of things you can find inside to use," she replied.

"Is that going to be a problem while you're here?"

"It depends on what's going on. I can't predict the future, can I?"

She was coy and flirtatious. That was probably a mixed bag for her. Helped her manipulate some, angered the shit out of others.

"You make sure to let us know if you need to be transferred to the infirmary."

Patients could be kept there in relative safety without having to be in the painful seclusion that was the Shoe. We always had to be on the lookout for inmates like Anjelica who were at particularly high risk.

"I will, Dr. Black. I appreciate it. You know, you're kinder than most of the psychiatrists I've seen here."

"That's nice of you to say. How many times have you been here?"

"More than I care to remember."

I walked her back to the dayroom and nodded to the CO to retrieve Cecil. He was already in the middle of a monologue as I walked him to the interview room. It was as if I had arrived late to our conversation.

"I haven't received my Valium since I've been here—"

"We don't have Valium here, Mr. Goldberg. You know that."

"I don't like my room. It's too far away from the officers' trap. You know I am the victim of assaults by these common criminals, and I'm not one of them, and they know this, and they victimize me, and you all don't care because we're not—"

"Have a seat, Mr. Goldberg."

"Humans to you all. We're just cons. I had status on the outside. All this here is a misunderstanding gone awry."

I contemplated that statement as he prattled on. Great thing about Cecil was I could complete all the paperwork while he talked. It mattered little to him whether he had my full attention, but I made sure to make eye contact with him periodically and nod my head strategically.

Rather than terminate the interview, I simply stood and walked to the day-room. Cecil followed me. He chattered on as if our scenery hadn't changed. He continued to talk even as I walked Manson back to the interview room.

"You better be careful with ol' Cecil there. He is a shit disturber extraordinaire. He is the proverbial fuse that could set this whole place off," Manson warned.

"Seems to me you don't really need a reason to set things off. Besides, why pick on Cecil? You feel the need to go after the mentally incompetent?"

He threw his head back and laughed. "I had you pegged for smarter than that, Doc. You think Cecil is mentally incompetent? That guy is savvier than all the rest of us combined. So you be careful."

"I'm grateful for your concern."

"Hey, I'm just looking out for you, man. You know, like you scratch my back, and I'll scratch yours." He said it seriously—not as a taunt. That surprised me.

Then I got angry at his blasé mention of our arrangement. I hadn't prepared for that kind of vulnerability in front of an inmate. It took all my effort to contain my emotion.

"Well, I don't have any additional questions for you. So if there aren't any issues you need to discuss with me, we can end this interview."

He was about to speak when we both reacted to a commotion outside the interview room. I got up and walked down the hall to find the dayroom cons pressed against the glass. They watched as Andrew/Anjelica struggled in the clutches of the COs. It didn't stop him from lunging and screaming after Cecil. "He stole my shit! He stole my shit! Do you know how long it took me to collect all that? How hard it is to keep anything of mine in these hellholes?"

Cecil modeled indifference; he spoke in a monotone voice. "I didn't take anything. I swear it. Someone's trying to set me up, and I am tired of being the fall guy. All the shit that happens in the joint isn't my fault."

The inmates did their best to fan the flames into a bigger conflagration.

"That faggot is calling you a thief. You gonna take that?

"You gonna let that transgender freak own you?"

"Cecil, what you need his tampons fo' anyway?"

Sergeant O'Leary intervened. "You assholes, shut the fuck up, or I'm going to lock this place down." That calmed the dayroom in a hurry. He turned to Johnson, who stood holding Cecil's arm. "Pat him down."

Johnson smiled. "How thorough do you want? 'Cause I don't need to be exploring Cecil's body. I just ate."

O'Leary shot him a look.

"Take Andrew to his room. Find out what's been taken. Meanwhile, lug ol' Cecil to the Shoe for a more, um, thorough inspection."

"Wait." I walked over to O'Leary and Johnson. "Why do you assume Cecil is guilty?"

"Years of experience dealing with Cecil, Doc."

"Would you give me a minute to meet with him to see what his story is?"

"I don't have time for this shit." The sergeant said.

Johnson nudged O'Leary. "C'mon, Sarge. Let the doc get Cecil's story. It'll only take a minute."

"OK, Doc. Knock yourself out. We'll even stand outside the door for you."

"Thank you, Sergeant. C'mon, Cecil. Let's talk."

He huffed a little, but Cecil looked grateful for the opportunity to get away from the rabble. We walked to the interview room, the COs trailing behind us. We sat while they stood outside the room, the door open a crack.

"So what happened, Cecil?"

He talked more to himself than me. "Always trying to blame me. Always assuming I'm guilty."

"Cecil, you're not really answering me. You're just protesting your innocence, which I heard. But there's no audience here. Just me. So tell me what really happened."

Quiet. Then the hint of a smirk. "What can I say, Dr. Black? He's got some real nice stuff. Pretty."

"Are you saying you stole those things from his room? That this whole protest has been an act?"

As a substitute for answering, Cecil squirmed in his seat and then se-creted from his body—from some unknown catacomb of his well-explored corpus—a makeup kit and a pair of tweezers.

I shuddered and motioned to the COs outside the window. I needn't have bothered. Having observed our little tête-à-tête, they practically fell over each other in laughter.

CHAPTER 21

The day dragged on forever. At lunch I went to the gym. I walled off my lies to the administration, but the mendacity and betrayal of Margot to save my own ass oozed out like pudding in a child's fist. Then I remembered that she'd trapped me, and I felt justified. Those emotions warred inside me and cultivated a shitty mood. I took it out on the locker door. I changed into my workout clothes and found Steve already working out.

"Oh, look who decided to show up," he said sarcastically.

"Sorry, Steve. Things have been a little nuts next door."

"Is that where you got that shiner?"

I touched my cheek. "No. That came courtesy of an irate boyfriend."

Steve dropped his weights abruptly and looked at me. "I didn't know you swung that way."

I laughed. "Good one. I needed that. No, I flirted with a woman. It turned into kissing, and her 'roided-up boyfriend saw, and, well, you can see the result."

He broke out into a grin. "Nice."

We settled into the day's routine. Chest, squats, and triceps.

"I'm glad you're back. I need some skinny on what's happening in your neck of the woods," Steve said, and he stepped away from the bench.

I took off a fair amount of the weight and got on the bench. "What kind of info are you looking for?" I said on the exhales.

"There's talk of an all-out gang war."

I put the bar back on the rack and sat up. "I've not seen too much out of the ordinary."

"Jojo, either you've got your head in your ass, or you're a world-class liar. There is some serious shit going down. You were asking me about Manson a little while back. He's still there. I know that. You mean to tell me you haven't seen nothing?"

Playing dumb was becoming a habit. "I don't have your experience. These guys come and go. All I'm looking for is mental illness—you know, what I can treat. I leave the security issues to the COs."

The workout induced sweating, heavy breathing, and a rapid pulse. These gave me cover for my lies; I would have failed a polygraph sure as shit.

"Well, you'd be wise to keep your eyes open and watch your ass." He picked up a barbell and curled it.

"Out of curiosity, which gangs are involved?"

"Way I hear it, it's a reflection of the turf wars on the outside. Los Reyes trying to muscle in on White Dawn territory. They strategize inside the joint as much as on the street. I hear Los Reyes are trying to intimidate Manson. Maybe bump him off. It's dangerous for him outside, but inside, he's getting a lot less safe."

"Los Reyes? White Dawn? Where do they come up with these names?"

"I don't know that I would joke about their names. Those folks take that shit awful serious. It's their identity. Some of them get branded."

"Branded? Jesus. That's dedication."

Steve put the barbell down. He went into a crouch opposite me. "Jojo, you need to get serious because this is very real. There is a distinct chance that people will be hurt. If you think you're outside that danger, you're fooling yourself. With that in mind, is there anything you want to share with me?"

"No, Steve. Again, though, I appreciate the heads-up. I guess because I grew up in the suburbs, this whole experience still has a surreal quality. Don't think that I'm stupid, though. I keep my guard up."

"Nobody thinks you're stupid. Just stubborn." He stood and offered a smile. "OK. I see you don't want to share. But remember what I told you. You get yourself in a bind, you come straight to me. OK? I still owe you one."

"That's nice of you, Steve. But like I told you, you don't owe me anything. By the way, how is your mother?"

"Still smoking."

"No."

"Yeah. Do you believe that shit? She's needing oxygen at times and is going to have to get surgery, but those things have a hold on her."

As I was changing back into my dress clothes, my pager went off. I went over to the house phone in the gym.

"Hi. This is Dr. Black. Someone paged me?"

"Jojo, it's Paul. You at the site?"

"Yeah. At the gym."

"Good. Come on back to the administration building for an emergency meeting. There's a guy here going to brief us on some gang activity. Can you be here in five minutes?"

"Sure."

"OK. See you."

I entered the conference room and found most of the staff already seated. Paul stood and talked with someone just outside the door. I sat down next to one of the social workers from the maximum unit.

"Any idea what this is about?"

He shrugged his shoulders in lieu of an answer. Paul walked in next to a man in a blazer and a crew cut. I almost shit myself when I recognized the statey who had rescued me from Jeff and then threatened my life. Paul held his hands up for quiet.

"Thanks for coming here on short notice. As many of you are aware, we are experiencing an uptick in gang activity right here at the state hospital. This reflects a growing concern throughout the corrections department. In response, the DOC has asked the state police and their specialized gang unit to get involved. Officer Wilson heads up that unit and was kind enough to come here and give us a primer on what's being done and how we can help. So, Officer Wilson." Paul stepped aside.

Wilson buttoned his blazer. "Thank you, Paul. I appreciate the introduction and the ability to have your attention today. For too long there has been a divide between my department and the DOC. The gang stuff doesn't end when we arrest them. That's when you folks take over. So I am grateful to bridge the divide and share with you what we know—and especially what we fear."

That voice brought me right back to other night and his threats. Feeling very exposed, I slowly sank down in my chair. Wilson scanned the room as he spoke, but his eyes didn't linger on me. I caught half of his spiel, but my concentration was waning. Something about Los Reyes and the White Dawn and territory. How we shouldn't fool ourselves into thinking we were safe or they were not a threat just because we worked in a prison. How we should let our supervisors or the COs know if there was something suspicious. How we shouldn't be heroes. There was some other stuff thrown in too. He asked for questions. The shrugging pinhead next to me asked a stupid-ass question, and then everyone went quiet so enough time could pass and we could adjourn. Somebody said, "Well, thanks."

We adjourned.

I didn't want to bring attention to myself by running like hell out of there. I calmed myself with the thought of what you do when you're sitting on the nut at a Texas Hold'em table and you want people to bet more money. Play it cool, baby. Play it cool. I shuffled out with the bulk of people. Once in sight of the stairs, I hauled ass back to the gym. Thankfully, Steve was still there.

"Hey, man. I thought you were done with your workout."

"I am. I have to return to work. But I need you to answer a question for me."

"Shoot."

"Well, it relates to what we were just talking about. You know, the gang shit. We just had a talk by a state trooper on that subject."

"Steve here is always ahead of the curve, man. Always. Best listen to me."

"I'm happy for you. I really am. But my question is this: Do you know this guy, Wilson, from the state police?"

"Can't say I do."

"Oh. Because I saw him once before, and he was with another guy who didn't look like a state trooper. Tall and dressed like a young hood. You know, baggy jeans down around his hips, expensive sneakers, and hat with the brim just so. He also had a tattoo on his arm. It said, 'Thug 4 Life.'"

"Thug 4 Life? You sure?"

"I was kind of wasted, but when the statey flashed his badge and gun, that sobered me up pretty quickly. So yeah. I'm sure. Why?"

"That sounds like Manson's kid. The one I told you about who's running things for Manson on the outside. The kid's name is Toby, but he makes everyone call him Flash. In school, he was a gifted sprinter. Even had his hopes pinned on the Olympics before he went into the family business. Rumor is he got the tattoo as a teenager to piss off his father. How did you happen to run into him?"

"I was in a bar when I saw him get into a fight," I lied easily. It came naturally now.

"He's one of those people you want to avoid. Bad temper and chip on his shoulder, they say. Something to prove. Not a good combination."

I mulled that over. Every time I thought things were loosening up, they seemed to be spiraling further out of control. I needed air. "I'm going to get out of here. Thanks for the info."

"Any time, Jojo."

I turned to leave. At the door, I stopped. "You know, Steve, with your fund of knowledge, how is it you're driving a perimeter gig and not more involved with internal security matters?"

"Just lucky, I guess. Who needs that kind of headache?"

He went back to lifting, and I went back to work.

CHAPTER 22

After dropping my stuff off at home, I needed a drink. I walked to the Crimson and played out some Kathleen-encounter scenarios in my head. I went so far as to mumble the conversations to myself. That got me some odd glances, even in the colorful Harvard Square where talking to oneself didn't usually warrant attention. It turned out I'd embarrassed myself needlessly. She wasn't working tonight. Tommy, the bouncer, had the skinny.

"She ain't been back since Friday night. Taking some time off."

"You heard why, Tommy?"

"Just something to do with her boyfriend."

I pondered that as I sidled up to the bar and ordered a gin sour. Drinking alone usually made me feel like an alcoholic, but tonight I relished not having to make conversation. The first drink melted away the anxiety from the day. By the third, I felt better about my life's prospects and had to micturate.

"You really need to mix up your routine, Doc."

I turned to see Manson's kid at the end of the bar. He was dressed in jeans and a T-shirt that had the gun-toting image of Tony Montana and the caption, "Say hello to my little friend." He ordered a beer and sat next to me.

"This ain't really my kind of place. Too snobby. But you, an educated man—I can see why you might like it." He drank from the bottle. "You know who I am?"

I nodded. "Where's Wilson?"

"He not here. Just little old me. I wanted you to know what's at stake. Things on the outside change minute to minute. In there, Lester runs things. Out here, I'm the man. The man. You understand?"

Truth be told, I had no idea what the fuck he was getting at. Remember, though, I was three drinks on board, so I nodded like a well-oiled bobblehead.

"My old man's been in the joint for three years. Whatever loyalty I might have felt is gone. It's a dog-eat-dog world, and loyalty, while important, has to take a back seat. See, I like being the man. Making important decisions and being respected. So I have little incentive to work toward Lester's release. Or escape."

That got my attention. "Just what are you insinuating?"

"Don't play dumb with me, Doc. I know my father plans on using you to escape prison."

That was news to me—as my bladder attested. I feared losing my urine.

"Let me make this clear. If you help my father get out of prison, I will kill you. I know where you live, and I obviously know your routines. I'm not big on empty threats. You make a statement that you're going to kill someone, you better do it, or word will get out that you don't back up your word. My word is important to me. You following me?"

I nodded. Power of speech had not yet returned.

"Good. Play it smart, and don't go against me. I represent the new generation. The future. Lester, he's the past. His time is over. Mind me, not him." He patted me on the shoulder. "Sure, you're a smart man. You know where the power is. You be good, Doc."

I watched him walk out in the bar's mirror and then signaled the bartender for a shot of anything. After the second shot of anything, I shuddered and headed off to take a piss. I staggered into the bathroom and shook more violently. I gripped the edges of the sink to hold myself steady. How the fuck had I gotten into this shit?

Two college-aged guys entered the bathroom.

"So then she says, 'How 'bout you come over and party with me and my friend?'"

"No fucking way."

"I'm telling you. How fuckin' player is that?"

"That is some sick shit."

I took a piss, splashed cold water on my face, and walked out. Twenty on the bar and out the door. Just as I turned the corner, someone called out.

"You got a busy life, Dr. Black. Mixing with gang leaders in prison and gang leader wannabes in bars."

Shit. Flash was right. I was way too fucking predictable. I turned to the origin of the voice. It belonged to a man who looked to be in his midforties. He wore a flannel shirt, jeans, cowboy boots, and a Red Sox hat. He was big, broad, and in shape.

"Can we take a walk?" he asked.

I didn't have the energy to argue. Instead, I started toward the Cambridge Common, a park near Harvard Square.

"Who are you?"

"My name is Hatchett. I'm here to talk to you about what's going on at the state hospital."

"You know I'm not at lib—"

"Liberty to discuss patient information. Yeah, yeah. I'm familiar with the laws governing protected health information and its responsible dissemination."

Here he stopped and put his arm on my shoulder. Through the haze of alcohol and fear, this small gesture impacted me. The combination of his size and flannel was calming.

"Dr. Black—Jojo, if I may. I'm here to help you. We both know you are in a world of shit. If you want to hide behind a law protecting medical information, then you can do that. But what would you accomplish? You'd remain alone in a battle that is *way* out of your league. You with me?"

I exhaled for an eternity, and we walked again. Harvard Square gives way to an open park with fields, trees, and a children's playground. On the opposite side is the university with all of its collegiate buildings. It helped me to be on my territory, so to speak. I felt more confident. "I'm with you. But I still don't know who 'you' is."

He smiled at that. "I told you. I'm Hatchett."

"C'mon. Who do you work for?"

"I work in a special division of the US Marshals Service." He showed me his badge. "My special focus is on fugitive gangland criminals. Normally I spend my time out in California, but I flew out here because of what's happening with Lester Manson."

"What's happening?"

"We'll get to that. But first, I want you to know that I'm aware of what you have already done for him. Before you interrupt and get indignant, I have been following the career of Mr. Manson for many years and know just what kind of manipulative psychopath he is. Someone like you, young and naïve. Yes, naïve. Don't take that the wrong way. You're bound to get suckered by a criminal mind of his caliber. I'm not judging you. But I do need you to get your head on straight because you'll need it for what's coming."

"Again with the 'what's coming' stuff. Why the cryptic shit? Can't anybody just speak plainly?"

Hatchett stopped. "You have a point. More importantly, you have a right to know. All of Manson's manipulations will end with him forcing you to help him escape from prison."

I stopped. "I can't process what you're telling me, OK? This is too much and doesn't make any sense. I mean, it's ridiculous for Manson to want my help. How the fuck am I going to spring him from prison? With a spoon and a lot of elbow grease?"

"We can discuss the how later."

Some hippie guys were playing Hacky Sack to our left in the park. I turned toward Hatchett. "Obviously I'm not going to let that piece of shit escape. Apart from aiding and abetting a criminal escape from prison, which I'm sure would lead to my incarceration for a long time, I have no desire to inflict this bastard on the rest of society."

He nodded his head. "I thought you might say that. Commendable. Really. But I'm here to ask you to consider helping him." Hatchett went silent.

I stood silently too. Then I burst out laughing. "You're yanking my chain, right? This is some sort of test that if I fail you'll throw me in jail." I began looking around for cameras or Hatchett's backup.

"It's not a test, Jojo. You're caught between a rock and a hard place. Needless to say, there are those of us who feel the best outcome would be Manson being out in the open. There are machinations taking place on the street that could tear this and many cities apart. The gangland warfare could be unlike anything this country has ever seen."

"Way to sell the melodrama," I said.

It helped that he was asking me to do something ridiculous. It allowed me to act righteously indignant. Not much else I had done recently warranted that. I milked it for all it was worth. "I didn't sign up for this. It's more than I'm willing to consider. And how would letting him out help avoid murder and mayhem on the streets?" I hit my forehead. "Let's not forget that somehow I would have to get him out of there—past the guards. And not get in deep shit myself."

He looked at me with a placid expression. "Jojo, take some time to consider what I've told you. It might not seem like it, but I'm here to help you."

"How? By asking me to help a murdering thug escape from prison? By putting myself in danger of, at best, going to prison myself and, at worst, being killed by the piece of shit's son? Did you know he was with a state trooper the last time they threatened me? A state fucking trooper. What chance do I have?"

For the second time of the night, Hatchett placed a hand on my shoulder to steady me.

"I can't imagine how this sounds to you. Or how difficult this has been for you. Understand that I am here to help you." He continued. "Look, get some rest. Here's my card. A lot of things are happening that you aren't aware of. There are people on your side. Guys who have a lot invested in making sure that Manson is properly dealt with."

"Look, I appreciate your help, or whatever. But you really haven't fully answered my questions."

"I'm not at liberty to divulge more information right now. But I have faith in you. You'll do the right thing." Hatchett smiled and tipped his hat. (He actually did that. I'm not making it up.) Then he walked away.

What the fuck had he meant when he said I'd do the right thing? My head was spinning so much I didn't even know what the right thing looked like. How did he have confidence I would figure it out?

It was not the best time to call home. Too vulnerable. Knowing how it would play out, I wrangled with the decision even as I pulled out my phone and dialed.

"Dr. Black."

"Hey, Dad."

Silence. "What's wrong, Jojo?"

"Nothing, Dad." My voice cracked. Why did I insist on calling him in this state and then prevaricating?

"OK. You want to speak with your mother?"

"No. Just wanted to touch base."

Silence. "If you've got something on your mind, share it. Otherwise, I'm doing the taxes."

Here goes, I thought. "I have some trouble at work."

Sound of breathing. "More specifically?"

"It's complicated."

"If you're not going to fill me in, there's little I can do to help."

"I don't think there's anything you can do. I was just looking for some moral support."

"Are you behaving morally?"

"What is that supposed to mean?"

I could actually hear exasperation coalescing on the other line and making its way through the fiber optics to reach me with crystal-clear precision.

"Jojo. Don't pretend we just met. It insults my intelligence—and all your forebearers' to boot. You've always been guided by your own sense of morality, and it was loosely based on those laws of humanity you deemed worthy of consideration. Now I have to hand it to you, you've made it far without screwing your life up too badly, but we are always on pins and needles when it comes to your antics. So with that in mind, why don't you tell me what is really happening?"

He had me there; I had to hand it to him. After inhaling deeply, I said. "I'm in over my head with a psychopathic inmate who might blackmail me into trying to bust him out of the joint." I exhaled.

Silence. "Go to the authorities right away. But if you were planning on doing that, you would have told me that. Instead, I can infer you believe you can outsmart this criminal who has nothing to lose whereas you have everything to lose. Jesus, Jojo."

"Just Jojo."

He exploded. A rarity for the ever-in-control surgeon. "Is now the time to be a wiseass with me? By now you should have outgrown the belief that you're smarter than everyone."

"I'm sorry. You have a way of making me feel small."

"Don't start in on the psychobabble. The 'I didn't live up to Daddy's standards' bullshit. This isn't about me. This is—"

"Wait a second. Let me get a word in edgeways. Why is it you explode on me and assume I am responsible for the trouble I'm in? Maybe I was manipulated. Huh? Maybe I am the victim here."

"Come off it. This isn't going to help you. You want to feel sorry for yourself, save it for your therapist's couch."

Ouch. We were both silent.

"How much trouble are you in? Could you lose your job?"

"Yes."

"Could you be charged with something right now?"

"Probably not."

"Then bite the bullet and goo to the authorities. When it comes to blackmail, that is the only way to diffuse the issue. Take away the blackmailer's power to bring you to your knees. Remove the potential energy."

"It's more complicated than the guy in prison."

"All the more reason to involve the authorities. Listen, Jojo. I know you well. Better than you think. I know you're thinking you can still manage this. That you can find a way out. Stop. Bite the bullet."

"I hear you."

"Oh, Jojo, I wonder if you do. Regardless, I'm not going to tell Mom. She would stop sleeping."

"Agreed."

"Keep me apprised."

"OK, Dad."

We hung up. This was the second person to tell me my understanding of the world and myself was not reflective of reality. Not an easy thing to hear. I comforted myself with the knowledge that neither my father nor Nigel knew all the information. It wasn't feasible to go to the authorities right now. I mean, Hatchett counted as an authority, and he wasn't telling me to cash in my chips. I still had the opportunity to double down and find a way through. If they'd had all the info, I was sure that would be their move as well. I repeated that mantra all through the rest of the evening.

Chapter 23

The next day during rounds, I got word that one of my patients had asked to see me right away. It was Whitney, the big guy. He was one of the first guys to stay under Manson's auspices for their powwow.

I wrestled with seeing the guy. I was under no obligation to see each patient every day. In fact, doing so would set a bad precedent because most of these fellows weren't mentally ill, and they would drain my energies for those with real needs. I knew myself, though. If this hung over my head, if I had to pass by the dayroom and ignore his stares, it would piss me off. I decided to see him right away and get it over with.

He sat down with a smarmy grin. "How you holdin' up, Doc?"

I ignored that. "What do you need?"

"Manson's going to need another favor from you."

"He's using you as a messenger now? Why doesn't he ask himself?"

"Don't you worry about that. He's got more important things to do."

It suddenly dawned on me. What leverage did they think they still had? Margot had gotten canned. I was feeling less concerned about my job with each passing nanosecond. Burnout from living on the edge approached rapidly. As if reading my mind, he continued. "Maybe you think because the lady got fired you're off the hook. But getting fired from here should be the least of your concerns."

"What kind of threat is that?"

"You don't think we can get to you anywhere? You can't be that fuckin' stupid."

I was too tired of this shit to be scared. "Did you ask to meet with me so you could threaten me too?"

"What do you mean by 'too'?" Whitney looked genuinely perplexed.

"Nothing."

"C'mon, Doc. Don't dick me around. I'm not a man to be trifled with."

"Mr. Whitney. Is there anything else you need from me?"

He leaned in menacingly, grabbed the edges of the table, and spoke in a low growl. "I'm two seconds away from leaping across this table and wringing your fucking neck. By the time the COs get here, you'll be dead. And it will be worth it. So enough of your shit. Tell me who else has threatened you."

Reflexively I reached for the body alarm on my side. It wasn't there. In my haste to see this guy, I hadn't gotten a goddamned garage-door opener. The one time I forgot, this happened. Figured. I rallied.

"Take it easy. I'm just referring to your boss. No need to get worked up."

He shook his head and grinned. "You take it easy. C'mon. I wasn't going to hurt you. I just needed you to focus. Get you serious. Because we need you to come up big for us. Mr. Manson needs you to have some of Los Reyes sent to the Shoe."

"What?" I wasn't expecting that.

"Some of these Reyes on the unit are getting in our way. Rather than risk a full-on gang war on your unit, Manson thought it best for you to pass along to your superiors that some patients would be better served elsewhere."

"In isolation? You gotta have a reason to send someone to the Shoe. It's not arbitrary."

"Think of it as lifesaving. 'Cause if some of them guys stay here, some shit's going to go down. And besides, they can go to the maxes, can't they?" He stood and pushed his chair out with a kick. "From what I see, you're a clever guy. Got some capacity for deceptive shit. I'm sure you'll come up with something."

Whitney walked out. As he did, my body shook to rid itself of the excess adrenaline coursing through my veins. I had grown up sheltered. Movies were not a reasonable facsimile for the toll real stress could have on a person. I was getting a crash course. A distant part of me registered that this was what I had wanted, right? A little action. Well, here it fucking was. For all my imagination, I couldn't have predicted the impact of long-dormant brain chemicals surging into areas previously untapped. The fantasies were most definitely better than this reality.

I wondered why he hadn't raised the escape issue. I didn't know what information Hatchett worked from, but maybe they'd gotten it wrong. In any event, I needed another break. I was going to crack if I didn't get away from here right now. Thankfully Paul was the only one in the office. I cleared my throat. "Can I talk to you?"

He withdrew his feet from atop his desk when he saw me. "Jesus, you look like shit."

"Yeah, I just got threatened by Whitney."

"Did you lug him? I didn't hear the emergency called."

"No, no, no. It's OK. He just wanted to scare me a little. Get me worked up."

"Looks like he succeeded."

I sat down opposite Paul. "Just when I thought I'd achieved a measure of mastery, I get spooked by someone trying to yank my chain. I'm not feeling too well. I wondered how you'd feel if I called it a day and went home. I don't think I can handle more right now."

"OK. I know that look. Best you take a break. Better than boiling over."

"Thanks." I started walking toward the door.

"You will be coming back, right?" Paul said it with a straight face.

"You're serious? You think I'd walk away without saying anything?"

"It's happened before." He got up and walked over to me. "Listen, Jojo. This isn't an easy place to work. And right now things are tenser than I can remember in a very long time. You seem to be right in the middle of it and not willing to let me in on what's going on. So yeah, I'm worried about you taking a powder."

"Taking a powder? What the fuck does that mean?"

He laughed genuinely hard. "That's what I like about you, Jojo. You're able to see the lighter side. Even now."

We laughed together. I managed to say, "I really don't know what that means."

"It means leaving and not coming back."

"I surmised that, but where does it come from?"

"What do I look like, a fucking etymologist? I read, and I repeat."

"Paul, I will not be taking a powder, but I do need a break."

"Take it, my young friend, and come back to us refreshed tomorrow."

As soon as I got to the parking lot, I called Nigel.

"Hey, buddy. How you holding up?"

"I'm fried. How do you feel about going out tonight?"

"A scalp run?" Nigel couldn't just say "Indian casino." He had to make it as offensive as possible.

"Yes, Nigel. I am referring to a trip to the casinos."

"I'll pick you up in an hour," he said.

"Right on."

CHAPTER 24

"**W**hy so quiet?"

We approached the Rhode Island border, and I hadn't said more than hello.

"I'm having a hard time getting my feelings in order."

"What are you, a fucking chick?"

"Fuck you."

"OK. OK. Talk to Dr. Thomas. He'll cure your ills."

"You going to listen or bust my balls?"

He put on a straight face and looked at me for as long as he could without taking us off the road. "I'm serious. Lay it on me. We've got another hour at least."

"I haven't told you all the things that have happened to me at the prison."

Nigel stayed silent to draw me out and to prove he could actually shut up. I continued. "You know about Manson and his threats about Margot."

"Yes."

"There's more. I seem to be in the middle of different warring factions. I can't even keep the sides straight myself."

"What are you talking about?"

"I've been threatened by Manson's son and from a rogue state trooper if I help Manson. And I've been—"

"What do you mean if you help Manson? Are you saying Manson's kid is looking to usurp his power while Daddy's in the clink?"

Nigel's perspicacity impressed me. When he wasn't being a fuckup, he was quite astute.

"Yeah, that's what it looks like. But it gets better. There's a US Marshals Service member who is all but ordering me to help Manson escape."

"Holy shit. I've got to pull over. This is too much." Nigel slowed down, got on the shoulder, stopped, and put the car in park. He turned to face me. "You're telling me that one of the good guys wants you to help Manson escape."

"So it would seem."

"US Marshals Service member. Like Tommy Lee Jones, yeah?"

"Yes."

"Those marshal blokes are the ones who capture fugitives from prison?"

"That was the gist of the movie, yes."

Nigel shook his head. "That's fucked up. Him asking you to help Manson escape. I can only imagine he thinks something more permanent can be done to Manson once he attempts an escape."

"I hadn't thought of that."

"Go on then."

"Anyway, today Manson asks me to have some rival gang members banished from the unit. Well, he didn't ask me. He sent his lieutenant to threaten and intimidate me."

"Is that why you took off early and called me about going out?"

I nodded. "I have to get out of this situation and have no idea how. I didn't sign up for this."

Nigel looked away and grunted.

"What?" I said. "You got something to say, spit it out."

"You're not going to like it, mate."

"I appreciate your touching concern, but I'm a big boy. I can take it."

"OK, here goes. You can start by acting like a man!" he said in a spot-on imitation of Brando doing Vito Corleone. "Long as I've known you, you always make it seem as if you're at the whim of cosmic forces pushing you to and fro."

"To and fro? What are you, Shakespeare now?"

"Don't interrupt. You act as if you've got no agency in anything that happens to you. As if you have no control. Just because you choose to be passive doesn't mean you haven't made a choice. To quote Rush, 'If you choose not to decide, you still have made a choice.'"

"So you're saying I brought this on myself?"

"In effect, yes. You flirt with women and then are shocked when they respond. You gamble and lose money and then bemoan that you are broke."

"Ha! Look who's fucking talking. Always spending a thousand more than you have."

"I don't complain about it, though, do I?"

Fucker was right. He never complained; he just got more cash.

Nigel continued. "My faults are myriad and grand. It's true. But we're not talking about me, are we? We're focused on you. Maybe that's why you see fit to attack me."

"Give me a break. What are you now, a psychoanalyst? You don't believe in that shit."

He put on an exaggerated aggrieved face. "More personal attacks. I must be hitting close to home."

I turned toward the window. After a few moments of silence, Nigel steered the car back on the road and sped up to his customary eighty-five. I thought hard about what he had said.

"That's not fair about the women. I assume you're talking about Kathy."

"I am."

"For me it was always a flirt, never something serious. I feel bad that it turned out like it did, but the reality is I'm more interested in someone like Margot."

Nigel thought about that and responded in a soft voice. "Maybe you need the negative feedback to feel like you're earning something." He glanced at me and then looked back at the road. "I joke about it, but a lot of people respond more to the negative than the positive. We're a fucked up race, we humans."

"It's pathetic, isn't it? I don't know what I'm going to do."

"All right. All right. Let's think this through." He rapped on the steering wheel. "OK, first option. Obviously. You do a runner."

"What do you mean? Just don't go to work again?"

"Yeah."

"Maybe I didn't tell you, but they threatened bodily harm no matter where I went. Besides, it's not an option. I don't like the idea of tucking tail and running."

"Don't rule anything out. Number two. Go in first thing tomorrow morning and call in the cavalry. For that matter, you could call the authorities right now."

I shook my head. "Which authorities? The stateys? US Marshals Service? FBI?"

"That's got to be part of the calculus. We have to think that through."

"The one thing that's bothered me all along is the feeling that I should be able to outsmart Manson. After all, he's behind bars, and I'm free. I should have options at my disposal that he doesn't. Even if he commands a legion of gangbangers."

Nigel beat on the steering wheel with greater enthusiasm. "Now you're thinking. Now you're really thinking. But how? That's the rub, isn't it?"

"Maybe there's a way I can use Hatchett."

"Which one is he?"

"The marshal."

"Right. Tommy Lee Jones. Call him Tommy Lee so I don't get confused," Nigel said.

"What does Manson really have on me? The worst that can happen is I lose my job at the prison."

"Don't forget the threats, mate."

"Oh yeah. Fuck."

"If you put yourself at the mercy of your superiors, I'm sure they'll provide you with the appropriate protection. Even if you do lose your job," Nigel said.

"I would hope. Not much to go on, though. Seems I'm more use as a pawn."

"That kind of self-pity shit isn't going to work."

"You sound like my dad," I said. We drove in silence. "Fuck it. You got any cigarettes on you?"

Nigel shot me a look. "You gonna take up smoking now?"

"I used to smoke in college when I drank in bars. Then they cut out smoking in bars. The cigs never had a hold on me, so quitting was nothing. Now I feel as if I've got nothing to lose. You got any?"

He leaned over. One hand was on the wheel, and the other groped for the glove box. He opened it and rummaged through loose CDs, parking tickets, and assorted other shit. Pulled out a battered pack of Camel Lights.

"Here you go, junior. Smoke up." This was his Judd Nelson from *The Breakfast Club*.

I laughed. "Thanks."

"No problem. I'm glad to recommence the assault on your lungs. And listen, if you do get fired, it's not the end of the world. You come into business with me. We make a mint providing stimulants and sedatives to the hoity-toity of Back Bay and Chestnut Hill. We'll be the toast of the Brahmins."

"Hoity-toity?"

"Hoity-fucking-toity. I'm expanding my vocabulary."

"I don't think I'm ready for the Brahmins. But I am feeling better, and I'm ready to tear the shit out of the casino."

"That's the spirit."

Nigel put his foot down and pushed the car to one hundred. He turned the radio up. I opened the window and let the air rush on my face and blow some of my worry away.

CHAPTER 25

Casinos had a way of picking up my spirits. I think it had something to do with the warm glow of the lights and the serenade of beeps from the slots. I felt so good in there. Lights always on. People in a good mood. So much opportunity. The part of my brain that encouraged my addiction kicked into overdrive, and I felt no pain. Its effect was no different than a drug. I scolded myself for not becoming a professional gambler. I could have taken my chances grinding it out at poker or blackjack. Why did I choose a profession like medicine with its attendant responsibilities? Who would care if I didn't come to my job at the blackjack table trying to hit the natural twenty-one? I'd never get threatened by psychopaths pushing the buttons on slot machines. Only pushy old ladies trying to horn in on a machine that's paying off.

It was no way to live, though, right? Immature. Irresponsible. Not realistic. Can't cast your fate with the fickle whim of Lady Luck. She could be a real bitch, I knew that. Right now, though, I felt reckless and pushed to the edge.

We walked around and tried to find a good blackjack table. I settled on a middle-aged, white, male dealer. Nigel kept walking. There were three others at the table. I took third base. First base, or the seat immediately to the left of the dealer, set the table. Mistakes made there reverberated to the rest of the players. Third base is the last place dealt on the table. It's not easy explaining to someone who hasn't played blackjack that there exists a rhythm to a table—expected moves for every situation. Most dealers were willing to offer tips for play.

I nodded to the other players and put my money on the table. The pit boss came over and watched the exchange. He tilted his head in my direction. I didn't know if I'd seen him before, but I nodded in return.

I pulled out the pack of Camels. One left. I looked around for the drink gal.

"Drinks are flowing like mud in this joint." This was one of my icebreakers.

One of the guys at the table chimed in, *"Scent of a Woman."* He had on a leather jacket and Kangol hat, and he had a toothpick in his mouth that he rearranged incessantly.

"That's right. Lt. Colonel Frank Slade. Hooah!"

The dealer motioned for one of the servers. A nice perk of a casino. Free drinks. Watered down, to be sure—but free. I gave the server a buck or two each drink. Vegas culture. Tip, and good things will happen to you. My only superstition. The dealer laid out the cards nice and quick. No superfluous movements. Economy of motion. Both cards up. I lit up my cigarette.

First hand dealt. A king and then an ace. Hot damn. Paid out one and a half. Like a beckon from a beautiful woman. It was a great way to hit the table running.

"Nice way to start off your evening, sir," the dealer said.

He was a real pro. I nodded in appreciation and tossed him a five-dollar chip. The table flowed nicely. When it was like that, I could sit for hours, the time just sailing by on calm waters. I leaned across to another smoker and bummed a cigarette. My chip stacks grew slowly but steadily. I made all the right moves: pulling back on my bets when my cards were bad or the dealer got hot, upping my bets, splitting my cards, or doubling down at the right time. I felt great. Except I was out of cigarettes. I was about to get up when the pit boss came over and laid a pack of cigarettes next to me just as the server brought me another drink.

"Thank you. Both of you," I said.

The pit boss must have seen me bumming a cigarette. I understood the ulterior motive of the casino. Keep 'em happy, and most importantly, keep 'em gambling. Those kinds of gestures impacted me, though. Kangol looked over. "That's some service, huh?"

"It most certainly is." I took a big gulp of the drink. Stronger than usual. Had a gritty aftertaste. "What the hell are they putting in these things?"

"Sir, you haven't placed a bet. Are you in on this hand?" The dealer waited. The cards were poised for action.

"You bet your ass I'm in on this action."

I put down a hundred. A big bet for me, but I felt it. The dealer laid out the cards. He showed a four. For me, a five and a queen. Technically, I should have stood pat. Dealer has to hit on sixteen or lower. Odds were he was going to bust, but I had a hunch that if I stood pat, I would lose.

"Hit me."

The table groaned. They were not happy with me bucking the norm. I ignored them. The dealer gave me a six. He dealt his own card. A four. He didn't bust, but I had him twenty one to nineteen. I felt invincible.

It just kept getting better. Aside from a few misses, I won on almost every bet. When the dealer got tapped out, I was up three grand. It was usually my practice to use a dealer exchange to take a break myself, but I wasn't going to be denied this evening. I started making more aggressive bets. At some point, Nigel came over and sat next to me. He saw my stack of chips and my bets.

"Holy shit, mate! How much you got there?"

I guesstimated by looking at my stacks. "I don't know. Maybe six, seven G's."

"Why are you still gambling? Walk away."

"Fuck that. I can't be beat tonight." The others at the table whooped it up at that bit of bravado. I played up to it. "That's right, baby. The action is here tonight." I stood up in my seat and opened my arms to the world. "Right here, y'all. Right here!"

The pit boss looked over. I hardly noticed. Nigel pulled me down and turned my head toward him. He looked intently in my eyes. "What the fuck has gotten into you?"

"Nothing. What do you mean?" I jerked out of his grasp.

"This is not like you, mate."

"Stop looking at me as if you're examining me. I'm fine. Christ, I'm better than fine. Better than James Brown! Just look at this stack. Look!" I stood up again. "I'm king of the world!"

As if to underscore that, I doubled down on an eight and three. I couldn't see straight, but I had down five hundred dollars. Now I had one thousand riding on one card. Dealer dealt it out. Fucking jack. Twenty-one. The table erupted. There were high fives and calls for more booze. Nigel looked concerned.

"You're a fucking killjoy, you are," I said and turned to Nigel, but he was no longer there.

It might have been a few seconds later. Or it might have been an hour. I couldn't be sure.

CHAPTER 26

An inmate sat across from me; I didn't recognize him. I looked down at his chart, but I couldn't read it. No matter how much I tried to focus, I couldn't make out the name or what the issues were. He kept pestering me. "Doc, you said you'd get me out of here. You said you'd get me out of here."

I stammered and stalled for time. The inmate got up, clearly exasperated by my incompetence. I looked around for a CO, but no one was there. I could see the whole unit. I sat in the interview room, but there were no walls, so I could see for a very long way. All was emptiness. The inmate made his way around the table and put me in a headlock. I pulled my chin and head free from his chokehold so I could read the chart. No matter how fucking hard I squinted, though, I couldn't make it out. "Just a minute. Give me a minute," I sputtered.

My neck pain grew. Why couldn't I read that goddamned chart?

Two burly, suited men half-carried, half-dragged me through the casino. One had his eighteen-inch bicep wrapped around my neck. So intense was my headache that the redness that passed through my eyelids caused my head to throb. Our footfalls went from the clacking of heels on tile to the muted thump of carpet. They dumped me off in a chair. I opened one eye a crack and took in my surroundings. Pretty big corner office with a nice view of the woods behind the casino. I opened the other eye a crack. Thick burgundy carpet, big oak desk, and a man in a two-thousand-dollar suit behind it. I didn't ask him for his membership in the Pequot tribe, but he appeared to be one of the natives, if you'll forgive the looseness of my language. He looked like George Hamilton. Just not as dark.

"Good morning, Dr. Black." He spoke in soft tones, but he might as well have yelled in my ear.

I thought my head would split open. I had no recollection of the previous night. That was disturbing.

"Where am I? Who the fuck are you, and why did your hired help man-handle me?"

"My name is Mr. Whitefoot, and it's curious you take that tone with me considering your behavior in our casino. We consider ourselves hospitable, but we do expect a minimum standard of decorum from our guests."

Flashes of said behavior came back to me. Lots of yelling, standing on chairs, and possibly the stripping of a shirt.

I offered a note of conciliation as I rubbed my temples. "I apologize for my exuberance. Why didn't you just simply escort me from your premises?"

"It's a bit more complicated than that, Dr. Black, considering your markers."

"What the hell are you talking about?"

"Are you trying to play dumb? Because that doesn't fly here," Whitefoot said.

I got defensive. "It's not feigning when I really don't know what you're talking about."

He picked up some documents and tossed them across the desk at me. He must have been a hell of a paper football player because they came as close to me as they could on that big oak desk without falling to the ground. I squinted at the writing. In a wave of emotion, my dream flooded back to me. This time I could easily make out the IOU with a number not to be believed.

I looked up. "What kind of shit is this? I don't remember taking out a marker."

"Spare me the routine. I've heard it all. Before you leave here, we have to come to some sort of arrangement. You have some sort of collateral?"

"You think I have fifty thousand dollars burning a hole in my pocket?"

Just saying the number caused me to get dizzy in the chair. In my career, I had interviewed hundreds of drunks who'd described their blackouts, but until this moment, I had never experienced one. Now I was in the middle of a blackout nightmare. A thought hit me.

"Where is my friend?" I asked.

"The gentleman you came in with left several hours ago. Now are you able to honor this marker?"

I fidgeted in my seat. Fucking Nigel. Gone when I needed him the most. How could he let this happen? Then I recalled flashes of Nigel trying to corral my behavior and some less-than-cordial responses from me. This all seemed strange. Completely out of character. I could be a prick, but I'd never been this irresponsible.

"This feels like a shakedown."

"Shakedown? You've been watching too many movies, Dr. Black. This isn't *Casino*, I'm not Robert De Niro, and we don't break kneecaps. Look at that bottom there. You see that signature? It's yours, correct?"

I looked from his face to the papers. My signature was in fact there. It was the illegible scrawl replete with my trademark loops on the J's.

"You're on the hook for the money. Because we run a respectable business, we simply hand this over to our attorneys, and they are extremely aggressive."

"What does that mean?"

"Well, for starters, we will report you to a collection agency. We will put the word out to all casinos in the country not to allow you to gamble there. Then we'll get started looking into all your finances and taking pieces where we can until you satisfy both the debt and the interest that continually accrues."

"What interest?"

"It earns 22 percent quarterly."

"That's highway fucking robbery. Usury, in fact."

"You forget that we are not subject to your federal laws. Makes it easier to recoup debts from deadbeats...er...gentlemen such as yourself."

Jesus, my head really ached. I picked up the papers. "Is this my copy?"

"Sure is."

"How much time till I have to make good on this?"

"The interest began the moment you took out the marker. We expect a minimum payment by Friday. That's five days. All the information is there in those documents."

"Can I go now? Or do you have the ability here to hold me against my will in some sort of prison tepee?"

"Oh, Dr. Black, that is an insensitive thing to say, isn't it? And quite shortsighted considering you've seen what my security people are like, and you're not on American soil."

I quieted in a hurry.

"You have a bit of a temper, don't you, Dr. Black? That's going to get you in trouble. Well, more trouble, I should say." Piece of shit actually smiled at his own joke.

"Can I go now?"

Mr. Whitefoot stood. "I suppose. After all, we know where you live."

I stood up and then sat back down heavily.

"Those free drinks don't seem to have agreed with you. If I were you, I would watch what I drank from now on."

"Thanks for the advice." I hobbled my way out of there, making adequate use of the walls.

I wondered how I would return to Boston on my own. I took out my wallet. They hadn't taken the emergency hundred I kept. I couldn't find my cellphone, though. I took a minute to try to remember the last time I'd had it. This was an exercise in futility.

Behemoth luxury buses were ubiquitous in the parking lot. They transported willing participants from everywhere to drop their cash. I hitched a ride on a bus populated by blue-hairs from Lynn. I had never seen so many canary cardigans in my life. They were more than delighted to have me aboard. I got a lot of "c'mon" looks for what I could only assume would be postmenopausal, K-Y-assisted intercourse. Jesus, I was an asshole. Here they gave me a lift, and I was full of venom. Probably due to the ice pick that had pierced the top of my cranium. That and the fifty-thousand-dollar marker in my pocket.

They dropped me off within two miles of home. I decided the walk would do me good. Help clear my head. I added the marker to a growing list of problems. Maddeningly, I recalled devising a plan of action in the car with Nigel, but for the life of me, I couldn't remember it—no matter how much I rattled my brain. Close to my apartment, I gave up and laughed out loud.

"Is crazy contagious?"

Lost in my thoughts, I hadn't noticed Hatchett walk up next to me.

"Always important to be aware of your surroundings, Dr. Black. Reverie is not a luxury you can afford. And laughing without a Bluetooth in your ear makes you look like a nut."

"Thanks for the tip, Officer Hatchett."

"I'm a marshal. Not an officer."

"Marshal, officer. You all meld together in my mind."

"Hey, don't lump me in with that corrupt statey. I'm on your side, remember? By the way, thanks for that tip. I got friends in the Bureau interested in what you told me."

"The Bureau? What? You're too busy to say Federal Bureau of Investigation or even FBI?"

"Testy today. What's eating you?"

"Rough night at the casino. I got bombed and apparently dropped fifty K on the tables, and I don't even remember."

He whistled. "That's a shitload."

"The worst part is I took out markers. That's not like me at all. I've never done anything like that. I've interviewed manic patients who acted like that." I sighed. "I'm on the hook for it all the same." I stopped suddenly. "Hey, you're a federal guy, right?" Hatchett nodded. "What do you know about the laws of money and interest as it relates to reservations?"

"Indian reservations?"

"Yeah, those kind. Not the McCormick & Schmick's kind."

"Don't be a wiseass. I don't know much about the legal ramifications of such a debt. You should probably contact a lawyer. Anyway, how did it go at the end of the week?"

I bristled at his lack of concern for my newfound financial woes. I said, "I don't know where you got your information, but Manson didn't ask me to help him escape."

"Did he ask you to do anything else?"

"He wanted me to banish some rival gang members from the unit."

"Reyes?"

"Yes. You know something about that?"

He stroked his day-old stubble. "Los Reyes coming to your facility. Some sort of big melee on the horizon. It's got everyone skittish. That's why I came to see you. Give you a heads-up. See what I could do to help you."

"The behind-the-scenes kind of help, huh?"

"What's that mean?"

I stopped and turned to face him. "You seem like a decent fellow, so don't take this the wrong way. But fuck off, all right? I'm in a world of shit. You come off as friendly and supportive, but we both know you've got an agenda, and my safety is low on your list of priorities. At the end of the day, I'm either going to lose my job or my life. In just the last two weeks, I've been assaulted by an irate boyfriend after finding out his hot girlfriend digs me and threatened by an incarcerated gang leader, his sidekick, his son, a crooked state trooper, and an Indian casino tribal leader. Who knows what might be in store for me in the next two weeks? On top of that, I feel as if my head is going to split open. So do me a favor. Let me be miserable in peace. OK?"

"You can feel sorry for yourself in a minute. For now I need you to focus. You have a role to play in the goings-on at Wampanoag. We need you."

"Holy shit. Do you actually think I'm going back to work? No fucking way."

"You're quitting?"

"I suppose my not going in forever will signify that at some point."

"Why would you quit?"

Pantomiming cataplexy and apoplexy at the same time is a feat, I can assure you. "I just spelled it out for you. I am not getting killed or thrown in prison over a job."

Hatchett's steadying hands gripped my shoulders. "Focus with me, Dr. Black. What laws have you broken up until now?"

"Well, no laws as of yet, but you're asking me to assist an inmate in an escape. I'm pretty sure they've got laws against that."

"But that hasn't happened yet."

"I manipulated my clinical thinking for Manson," I countered.

"Yeah, maybe that gets you fired. I don't know. But it isn't necessarily against the law. You could certainly claim duress. I'd attest to that. As far as getting hurt goes, up until now, it's been only threats, right? The only person who beat you up is the guy who caught you making out with his girlfriend. Can't blame a guy for that."

"No, you got me there. But I don't have the strength to face this shit anymore. I can't face the lying I've done. Mostly to Paul, my boss."

"Why not tell him what's been going on?" he offered.

"It felt as if I could keep it under control, you know? Like the situation would resolve and not get out of hand." I hunched over and put my head between my knees. "I'm such a fucking cliché. Tried like hell to avoid it, but looking at it objectively, I pulled the same stupidity. The illusion of control even as it spiraled around me." I stood and rubbed my temples.

Hatchett's face went from compassion to focus. "OK. Enough of the self-flagellation. That's a luxury you don't have. In the next few days, Manson is going to ask about the escape."

"How do you know?"

"Take my word for it. Oblige him. Help him get out of there."

"I don't want to, and even if I did, I wouldn't know how."

"Sure you do. What happens when someone needs more extensive medical care than what the prison infirmary provides?"

"We transfer that person to a general hospital the next town over."

The marshal held up his hands. "There you go. You arrange for him to require that treatment. En route, his people will try to break him free."

"It could work, I suppose, but I don't know what excuse I could come up with. Remember, I'm a psychiatrist, not a general internist. The internists make their own decisions."

"I leave that to you, Dr. Black. But he needs to get out of there."

"Why is it so important that he leave the state hospital?"

"There are people inside who will kill him," Hatchett said.

I threw my hands in the air. "So let them."

"He can't be killed inside by a rival gang. That would lead to a shitload of violence."

"Wait a fucking second. Armed with all this inside knowledge, why are you relying on me to do this? Use your own fucking people to take care of this."

"Things are more complicated than the little piece of the world you see. Gang politics are precarious. If things don't happen a certain way, it could spark violence that would tear this country apart."

"Aren't you laying it on a bit thick?"

He sighed. "Look, Jojo, you've come to this moment in time with an opportunity to do some real good. Take my word for it. You'd be doing good. Ever want to serve your country? This is your chance. Go to work tomorrow, and tell Paul everything. Get that off your chest. You'll feel better. Then give me a call, and we can plan out the rest."

"If I tell Paul, they'll can me."

"Take my word for it. That won't happen." Hatchett seemed so earnest.

The whole thing made me want to dig a hole right there and lie down in it for a year. Mental exhaustion. Hatchett registered that and took a merciful tone. "Go home. Get some rest."

I trudged homeward. The conversation with him rattled around my skull. I focused my thoughts on my bed and the question of how much Tylenol PM I could take and still wake up the next morning.

CHAPTER 27

I **woke up**, and my head was still banging to the rhythm of my pulse. I was more rested, but still in need of more time and perspective. I called Paul and told him I would be out a couple of days more due to illness, but he didn't sound as if he bought it.

There was only one place to go to reset. Sometime overnight my brain had decided to go home. I hated the idea; I knew my father would give me shit. I knew he would reduce my situation to black and white, right and wrong. And I wasn't ready to leave the grays. Or was I chickenshit and needed my father to do for me what I couldn't do for myself?

I packed a light bag and headed for my car. I tossed the bag on the passenger seat and stopped. I slammed the door shut, jogged to a convenience store at the bottom of my street, and bought a pack of cigarettes. I lit the first one and inhaled deeply; I realized the immature nature of this behavior. My father would surely smell the tobacco on me and get pissed off. Nothing to do about that now. I got in the driver's side, lowered the window, and began the trip to Long Island.

I spent the first few years of my life in Elmont, New York, on Long Island. That name might ring a bell. It boasts the third leg of the Triple Crown, the Belmont Stakes. It's a pretty modest little burgh. My father, a resident at Long Island Jewish Hospital, found it affordable. I'd describe my childhood as idyllic. Tight-knit neighborhood and good friends. We moved to better digs when my father began seeing some success as a surgeon - Oyster

Bay, known mostly for its most famous son, Billy Joel. It also boasted the likes of Theodore Roosevelt and John Gotti. That's one hell of a juxtaposition of famous New Yorkers. Anyway, we had a very nice house in the hamlet of Oyster Bay. I developed some nice friends there, but I always missed my guys from Elmont.

I drove down 95 and Rhode Island went by in a hurry my mind lost in thought. I lit each new cigarette from the butt of the previous one. I crossed into Connecticut, the land of the Indian casino, and felt perspiration bead on my forehead. I passed the time singing off-key to Led Zeppelin's *The Song Remains the Same*. I didn't feel bad about it. Shit. Who can sing like Robert Plant? Before *Houses of the Holy* finished, I approached New York City and ratcheted up my aggressive driving instincts. I skirted the worst traffic and traveled eastbound on Long Island toward my parents' house. The road clear, my mind turned to an unanswered question: How much should I share with my parents? Anything short of the absolute truth and they'd know it.

"Fuck it," I said aloud. "In for a penny, in for a pound. Might as well come clean so I can get real feedback."

The people in the adjacent car looked at me funny. I pretended to talk on the phone. Realizing how fucking stupid that was, I gunned the engine and left them behind—never to be seen again for the rest of my life.

"Hi, honey," my mom said when I arrived. "It's surprising to see you on such short notice."

"Hi, Mom. Nice to see you too." We hugged.

The house smell instantly flooded me with memories. Mostly good. A mixture of carpet cleaner, Zep, food, and perfume. My mother always smelled like flowers. I put my bag down.

"Where's Donny? Is he sleeping?"

"He's in his room, and he's awake. Dad's at the hospital, but he will be home for dinner. He isn't operating today."

Growing up, that had always been the key question: Would we see my father? Was he operating or not? If yes, he could be in the OR until midnight. If not, he usually came home for a late dinner.

"He excited to see me?" I asked.

"Dad or Donny?"

"Donny."

Mom offered a sad smile. "In his own way."

I ran up the stairs and knocked on his door. No answer. I tried the knob. Unlocked. I opened the door but felt resistance. I looked down and saw Donny had rolled a big towel and put it on the floor against the crack.

"Close the door please, and replace the towel."

Donny sat on the other side of the room. He was hunched over a desk and drawing. He spoke without looking up. His clothing looked rumpled— serving double duty for several days. The room was stuffy but not malodorous. I replaced the towel as he'd requested and walked over to the desk. I put a hand on his neck. "What's with the towel at the crack?"

"Mom uses that cleaner. The fumes mess with me."

Fair enough. "Other than that, how you holding up?"

He didn't answer but continued to draw. When he'd moved back home, we had held out hope he could be stabilized and possibly return to medical school. It had quickly become apparent that wouldn't be in the cards. The hopes had been replaced with the modest goal of engaging in any type of work. Alas, he couldn't cope with even the smallest amount of stress.

He immersed himself in drawing. Donny copied existing comic books and graphic novels. He did them freehand; they were frighteningly good. You would have a hard time determining the original. Of course, we fantasized that maybe he could get into doing it for a living, but he refused. He did it for himself. His walls were plastered with graphic depictions of Superman, the Dark Night, and Watchmen. Donny wasn't a fan of Marvel. Lord only knew why.

I sat at the edge of his bed. "Not doing so great myself, Donny. In a bit of a jam."

He stayed silent and maintained his intense focus.

"Got myself into a huge debt with a casino. And that's not even the biggest issue." With the silence and the heat of the room, my head began to swim. After a couple of minutes, Donny spoke. "What's the biggest issue?"

I smiled and stood. Looking over his shoulder, I said, "That's some amazing shit you got there. You could easily get a job drawing for Marvel."

That got his attention. He turned to me. "Don't say things you can't take back." He gave a smirk. "You didn't answer what the biggest issue is."

"True. I got myself in over my head at work. Don't worry, though. I'll manage."

Donny turned back to his work. "You are the consummate troublemaker, Jojo. It's who you are."

I gave him a kiss on the top of his head. "Thanks for the pick-me-up. I'm going downstairs to visit with Mom and wait for Dad."

Donny gave a big sigh and put his pencil down.

"What's the matter?" I said.

"I have to get up and put the towel back after you leave. I don't like the interruption."

I laughed. That was the thing with Donny. He hadn't seen me in a few months, but that paled in comparison to the hassle of replacing the towel.

My mother and I sat in the kitchen and drank from mugs of coffee. She loved the Torani flavors and had enough to make a Starbucks proud.

"You must be in some dire straits." She spoke softly over her mug.

"Why do you say that?"

"Because I know you, Jojo. Dad's concerned."

I put my coffee down hard. "He's always fucking concerned."

My mother was unruffled. "No need to use foul language. Tell me we've got nothing to be concerned about, and that will be the end of it."

"I'll tell you when Dad gets home."

"Well, you can start now. Here I am." My father stood in the doorway.

He was holding his leather bag—the same one he had carried to work daily since time out of mind. I had once asked him about its contents. He'd told me it contained spare body parts, and I wasn't to go snooping.

He looked tired. Then again, he always looked tired. Yet he was one of those people who required little actual sleep. Probably what made him a successful surgeon. I needed a good eight. That was how I knew I never would be like him. A man's got to know his limitations. Harry Callahan taught me that.

My father poured himself a coffee and sat down.

"This is an unexpected visit. Happy to see you, Jojo, but like Mom said, I'm a little worried. Is this about what you alluded to the other night?" He sneaked a glance at my mother. I saw he had made good on his word not to share it with her.

I let out a long sigh. "I got involved with a girl who works at the same prison as me. She came to me with a problem she had with an inmate. A dangerous inmate. I approached that inmate with the sole intention of helping her. Before I knew it, I became embroiled in a huge jam." My parents listened intently and dispassionately. I paused, and then I said rapidly, "To blow off some steam, I went to the casinos."

"Jesus, Jojo. How many fucking times did I warn you about gambling?" That broke the nonjudgmental spell.

"Language, Frank," my mother said.

"F that. I'm pissed." He stood and paced the kitchen.

"If you didn't want me to gamble, how come you raised me next to a racetrack?" He shot me a look. "Bad joke," I said and held up my hands in surrender. "Anyway, I'm into the casino for a fairly large amount of money."

"How much?" my mother asked.

"I'm too embarrassed to say. And I'm not here for money. I just need some clear heads to help me think this through."

"How come you didn't go to the authorities like we discussed? Huh? You're in way over your head. Just end it by turning yourself in and taking whatever punishment is merited."

"It's not that simple, Dad. There are people threatening me on all sides."

My father sat back down. He wrung his hands and tried to calm himself. "You want to explain it then, in all its complexity? Because it's hard for me to know why you don't release the potential energy of all this."

My father had hammered that theme all my life. The physics of a glass on a ledge applied to all life. A glass perched on a table had all the energy of its distance from the ground. Placing it on the ground removed the potential energy of its destruction. He infused his explanation with a twist of Occam's razor. The simplest way to remove the difficulty of a situation, he said, was to identify what you were avoiding and face it. To wit, if you've been in agony because you're cheating on your wife or your taxes, come clean, and the internal conflict will be eliminated. We never discussed how to deal with the inevitable consequences of coming clean. Probably because he was a straight arrow and never had to deal with any.

He'd posed the key question. Why didn't I just turn myself in? Place myself in the hands of the authorities—come what may? *Because I can't,* I thought. *I won't.*

"It's…I, uh…" I sighed and looked away. "I can't. I just can't, Dad. I'm sorry. Maybe it seems like the right thing, but it doesn't feel right to me. That said, I do need your help, and I realize how shitty it is for me to ask for it without divulging all the information."

He looked really worried now. My mother did too. It was harder for me to tolerate seeing that concern etched on their faces than the situation itself. Especially my mother's. I wasn't protected in a cocoon of anger toward her like I was with my father. She sat quietly. He said, "How serious are we talking? Bodily harm? Prison? What?"

"Threats of bodily harm. Prison, I don't know. I haven't done anything really wrong as of yet. But I'm being squeezed. That's why I came here. For a timeout."

"Jojo, there's nothing else for you to do but go to the authorities and face the music."

"Which authorities? That's one of the problems," I said.

"What the hell do you mean?"

"Never mind, Dad. How about Jerry? Can we talk to him?"

Jerry Rosenblum, a high-powered attorney. Became a good friend of my father's after a surgery to relieve severe back pain. My father was the sixth surgeon he had approached. The others had turned him down because he was a lawyer. Grateful, he'd been a powerful friend of my father's since.

My father shook his head. "No. If you get arrested, maybe I'll talk to him. But you don't run to a lawyer when you haven't faced the music yourself. Shit, Jojo, what are you doing up there in Boston? You forget how to be a man, or what?"

"Frank, how is that kind of question going to help, huh?" My mother put her hand on mine. "But I agree with your father. If you won't tell us specifics, the general approach is for you to go back there and do the right thing. Take the consequences, whatever they are, and face up to your responsibilities. If they end up being legal, we'll certainly help any way we can."

I sat back in my chair. I don't suppose I'd expected anything different. But I felt comforted knowing I wasn't alone in this. Now going back was not a question. It was about choosing my path—passively or with head held high.

CHAPTER 28

Fifteen minutes elapsed, and I remained in the parking space outside my apartment. I repeatedly commanded those parts of my body responsible for operating a car to do their jobs. They rebelled. My foot declined to apply pressure to the clutch. My hand refused to turn the key.

On the ride back to Cambridge, I'd ruminated on my predicament objectively. I'd gone to bed resolved to put an end to this situation. In the morning, the shower had eroded my determination. Back and forth it went. The cons section of the debate was pretty solidified. The pros were a loose confederation of factors. Strong dollop of morbid curiosity for how things would turn out mixed with a splash of doing the right thing. Like a well-made martini, with just a hint of vermouth.

The gentle rat-a-tat at my passenger window startled me into action. Wilson, the state trooper, pantomimed a request to get in the car. I was fucked evermore. I unlocked the doors. He smiled and sat down. "I'm sure you've got quite the dilemma going on. You've been sitting here for near a half an hour."

"Can you do me favor? Cut the bullshit. Just tell me what the fucking threat is so I can go about my day," I said.

"Have it your way. You're being suckered, and you don't even realize it."

"What are you talking about?"

"You're being manipulated by that fuck Hatchett. He's happy to see you do his dirty work and get thrown in prison for your troubles."

BUGHOUSE

"Who's Hatchett?" I said in my most nonchalant tone.

"Didn't you just ask me to cut the bullshit? Door has got to swing both ways. I know Hatchett's been buzzing in your ear. You can't trust him. He's dirty, and he'd love to use you. I'm going to take him down, and if you're with him, you're going down too."

"Hatchett is crooked? Is that what you're telling me?"

"Dirty as a cheap hooker. Bought and paid for," Wilson said.

"By whom?"

"You let me worry about that. He don't live here. He's a resident of no-where. I live here in Boston. Like you."

"Actually, I live in Cambridge."

"Shut the fuck up." The statey looked pissed.

If you've never seen a state trooper pissed off, it's a hell of a sight. Crew cut and flushed face. Scary. Got my attention.

"I'm trying to help you out. I thought I made it clear to you that you needed to remove yourself from this situation. Quite clear."

"You threatened me, if that's what you mean." I gripped the steering wheel tighter.

"I thought a bright guy like you would understand the threat was a means of scaring you enough to do the right thing." I grinned. He didn't like that. "Why the fuck are you smiling?"

"You reminded me of Scooby-Doo. 'Those meddling kids.' The bad guy uses shitty props to scare away the Mystery Machine gang."

He smiled evilly. It was scarier than when he looked pissed. "You need to smarten up. Use your head." As if to underscore his point, he pointed at his own. "Without all the layers of bullshit, what does your head tell you about aiding a convicted felon? Huh?"

Good point.

"I'm going to assume you'll do the right thing. Manson can threaten all he wants, but he's on the inside." Wilson leaned in menacingly. "I'm out here, and I can put you down if you choose to help that scumbag."

He took a last look at me and got out of the car. I watched him stalk away, making certain he didn't come back. Well, now the parking spot seemed less hospitable. My body parts miraculously sprang into action. I started the car up and pulled out.

I arrived at the treatment team office, and it buzzed like a hive. Paul was conspicuously absent. I asked Rose, the secretary, where he was. She handed me a note and answered my question. "He's onsite. Been at administration all morning. He asked that you guys divide up the patients yourselves."

The note was from the COs. Manson was requesting to be seen right away. *Here we go,* I thought.

Before I even sat down, Manson said, "I am going to need you to help me get the hell out of here."

"You get straight to the point, don't you?"

"No use beating around the bush. Besides, I've laid the groundwork with you."

I sat down and dropped the chart on the desk with a bang.

"I'm aware of what you are capable of doing to me," I said.

Manson switched gears on me. "You know, Dr. Black, you're not looking so hot this morning. Have a rough couple of days?"

"Let's talk about your request."

He ignored me. "You look like hell. What happened? Have one too many?"

"What are you driving at?" I asked.

Manson sported a peculiar grin. "These days, a man's got to be careful who he accepts his drinks from."

Revelation washed over me. I recalled the grittiness of the drink at the casino. After that, everything had gone hazy. Manson smiled like a kid burning an ant with a magnifying glass. Something I don't doubt he did. "What'd you think of our new concoction? It's something we've been working on. Trying to perfect it. Not easy when you have to work under the conditions my guy does, but he's a genius. Was a high-level chemist for DuPont, if memory serves. That was before a nasty meth habit got the best of him, though."

"You had someone slip me a mickey?"

"Nice, Dr. Black. I love the fifties noir reference. Yes. That is just what happened. We've been working on an amphetamine and sedative combination.

Kind of an ecstasy-slash-Xanax type of feel. Makes you feel mellow and jazzed at the same time. So tell me. Was it a good high?"

I rubbed my temples. "You really are a miserable piece of shit."

"That's not the kind of market research I'm looking for. I must say, though, you're a lot ballsier than you were before. Was it good?"

"More ballsy, huh? That's probably because I don't have that much to lose anymore. Or maybe that shit you slipped me is giving me a false sense of confidence. As for how good it was, I had a headache for thirty-six hours."

"Yeah, we've had a bitch of a time getting rid of that. Even thought about adding some aspirin, but that made the chemistry complicated. I hope you enjoyed it before the headache. You interested in buying more of it?" I gave him a blank stare. "That aside," Manson said, "you owe me fifty thousand after your weekend of overindulgence."

"What the hell do you mean?"

He laughed. It was not a "bad guy sitting behind his big desk in a wing-back chair with a purring cat in hands" laugh but a real belly-buster. "Man, you've got to catch up. A casino that exists outside federal laws is a business made for me, so I bought a piece of that place. Ergo, I own your marker. Now, Dr. Black, let's talk turkey 'cause I really need your help."

"I don't get it. Why would you bother putting me in a fifty-thousand-dollar hole when you've already threatened me six ways from Sunday?"

"Hey, I didn't put you in the hole. You did that all by yourself. As to why I was glad to buy up your debt, in my experience, threats only go so far. The quality of work suffers. Guy gets nervous. More likely to fuck up or sabotage. I like to throw in the carrot alongside the stick, you know? Give the person an incentive, if you will." He tilted his chair and rocked back and forth. "You help me get out of here, and I'll forgive your fifty-thousand-dollar debt."

"You're real magnanimous. Your fucking drug caused that debt."

"Tsk, tsk, tsk. You're going to blame me for your gambling? You took out those markers. You could have quit at any time. From what I heard, your friend tried to get you to stop, and you weren't having any of that. Can't blame others for your own actions."

"I'm getting mental health advice from a psychopathic bigot."

"Bigot? Why am I a bigot?"

"It comes as a shock to you to be called a racist?"

He tilted his chair back and stayed there. "Racist? What are you talking about?"

"White Dawn? You're the leader of a white-supremacist gang."

Manson chuckled. "You are a naïve young man, you know that? Take things too literally." He leaned in and gestured for me to come closer. "I've got a secret to tell you. Come closer." I complied just a little. He whispered, "I don't hate blacks. Don't tell anybody."

"So why the skinhead facade?"

"You find a better way to motivate men, and I'll be all ears. You can intimidate, threaten, incentivize, hope, and pray, but you've got to have something. For centuries it's been known that hate mobilizes in a most powerful way. It's the 'us versus them' phenomenon. I use it to my advantage, but I assure you my business is drugs, territory, and influence. I don't hate blacks. Shit, I love basketball, jazz, and rap music."

"And Jews?"

"Jews? Look at the disproportionate contribution they have made to a wide variety of fields. And their acumen in business. I'd like to think I have some Jew in me."

"So you tolerate the rah-rah, heil-Hitler bullshit just to manipulate others? Is that what you're telling me?"

"Yes. But, Dr. Black, as much as I'm loving this banter, I must insist we get down to business. Time is running out. Either you get me out of here, or I'm going to be killed. Believe me, you don't want that. I'm infinitely more stable than what awaits the world if I suffer an untimely end. Los Reyes? They're animals. No credo. No honor. For them, it's all machismo shit. They kill indiscriminately. It's better with me around to balance things out. Take my word for it. If I'm taken out, it will be chaos."

"So you're a real humanitarian. Doing society a service."

Manson looked hurt. Almost human. It lasted a second, and then his face returned to its usual hardness. "Don't fuck with me, Black. You might think me vulnerable, but don't forget my ability to cause you grievous harm."

I sat back, and we settled into silence. Strangely, I no longer felt scared. Just exhausted.

A loud ruckus outside drew both our attentions. We made for the door and I hustled down the hall. COs surrounded an overflowing dayroom where several inmates hovered over someone I couldn't see. I feared the long-awaited gang melee. The COs pulled people off one at a time like officials in a football scrum after a fumble while the alarm sounded overhead. At the bottom of the pile lay Cecil Goldberg; inmates stood around and rained curses on him.

"That piece of shit. I'll kill him."

"Nah, because I'm gonna kill him first."

"Pipe down. All of you!" the sergeant yelled.

I sidled up to CO Johnson. "What's going on?"

He looked over at me. "Oh, hey, Jojo. It's nothing. Fucking Cecil took a shit in one of his socks and put it in with all the laundry. Pissed everyone off."

"What happens when you put a piece of shit in the laundry?" I asked.

"What the fuck do you think happens?" He chuckled. "You get a lot of dirty and smelly clothes and a lot of pissed off inmates. And yesterday he shit in the shower, making it unusable for the rest of the unit. You should do something about him, Doc."

Something about Cecil's scatological assault hit my funny bone, and a laugh welled up from deep down. It wouldn't stop. Each time I thought I had it under control, it bubbled back up and rendered me speechless. In the process I experienced an intense catharsis. My way forward coalesced in front of me. I gestured to Manson to follow me back to the interview room and I closed the door behind us.

"I'll do it," I said.

"Great."

"For one hundred thousand." I thought it would make him angry, but he smiled.

"I knew you'd come around. See? I got a feel for people. As for the money, what makes you think I'm going to give you shit?"

"Like you said, you want motivated people. The money assures you that my interest will be in getting you out rather than ratting you out."

JOSEPH H BASKIN

We stood and stared at each other. "A hundred seems steep," he said.

"You leave me no choice. I won't be able to stay here after this goes down. So I'll have to pay off my marker and have some seed money until I get a new job."

"So the hundred K includes the marker? Or are you asking for one fifty?"

"Just one hundred. And I want half now."

He snorted. "What the fuck are you talking about? No fucking way to the upfront money. How I can I trust you won't run off with the fifty?"

"How do I know you won't kill me as soon as you're free?"

Manson put a rough hand on my neck and applied a little pressure. "How do you know I won't kill you right now, you greedy bastard? Stop dicking me around. I'm in no mood to be fucked with." He pushed me down in the chair, walked around the table, and sat opposite me. "Tell me how you plan on getting me out of here."

I massaged my neck. "I figure you have some sort of arrangement once you're outside the fence. I will prescribe you a medication that can cause an adverse reaction. You act out that reaction and I transfer you to the infirmary and make a stink that you be sent out to the general hospital."

Manson shook his head emphatically. "No. No. I'm not doing any drugs."

"You will take this. It's called Mellazine; I'll give you a low dose. In rare instances, it can cause the throat to spasm, and that can be life threatening—"

"I ain't taking that shit."

"It's not going to happen to you. I'm just giving you pointers on how to act like you're in trouble medically."

He shook his head. "No pills."

"Well, you come up with something because that's all I've got. And it's a good idea, by the way. But you take your time and think it over while the Reyes plot your demise. Have a good rest of your life."

We stared at each other. He relented. "All right, Doc. We'll play it your way. But if something bad happens—"

"How many ways can you threaten me? Jesus. Just take the pill. Then, during lockdown, complain of feeling your throat closing up. Fake breathing

172

troubles. I'll take it from there. And don't be over the top. Just do enough to get attention, and I'll facilitate the transfer."

He laughed. "You're giving me advice on subtlety? Hilarious." He pointed at me. "You be subtle. In this world—my world—you're a fucking amateur. I see you for a thousand miles before you even think of your moves. Don't try to be too smart. Because—and I am not trying to threaten you now—our lives are on the line. You got that?"

I nodded. Manson had a way of acting like a mirror to me. Showing me I appeared different than I believed I did. I already hated him on an abstract level because of his criminality. I further despised him for what he'd done to Margot and me. But I reserved my worst loathing for his preternatural ability to see me for me.

We parted, him to the dayroom and me to the nurses' trap. That was the cagelike closet where the nurses kept and dispensed the medications. I placed the order for medication and stressed that Manson needed it right away.

I stopped at the officers' trap and spoke with Johnson. "That stunt Cecil pulled gave me a good laugh," I said to him.

"Me too, Doc."

"Things are pretty intense, huh?"

"Fuck yeah. The head of Los Reyes came here a few days ago. His name is Javier Cruz, and he's a bad man."

"Tell me."

"This guy fancies himself a Pablo Escobar type. But he's more like Muammar Gaddafi. One of these guys who really gets into the role of being El Jefe. You know, the position, the prestige, the glamour, if you can call it that. Way I hear it, the guy is so full of himself he's delusional."

"You sound like a psychiatrist."

"I've worked around you folks long enough I should receive an honorary degree." He then got very serious. "Jojo, you need to listen to me. Watch your ass, OK? What's going down here, it's no joke."

"I appreciate the concern. You take care of yourself too."

I walked down the hall to the office.

CHAPTER 29

This was how it all went down. I think it's important to start with one fact. During the rest of that day, my heart rate never went below a humming-bird's pace. I'd always read about the failure of the polygraph to pick up vibes from hard-core psychopaths. They were cool and collected under criminal conditions. Lying being second nature to them, they didn't experience the rise in heart rate, the galvanic skin response, or the breathing changes. Me? I was a fucking wreck. I was certain that at any moment one of the COs would correctly identify my nefarious intentions. I discovered a newfound respect for the criminal. I didn't have the chops for this kind of work.

Of course, none of the COs actually gave me a second glance. The unit went about its business without disturbance. The inmates were confined to their rooms for lockdown. I tried to concentrate on my notes.

"Dr. Black, the nurse is looking for you." I looked up at the CO who had walked out of the office to the officers' trap. I dropped my pen and caught up with him. "What's going on?"

"Oh, just some shit with Manson. Complaining about something. That fucking guy always has a gripe."

The nurses' trap was catercorner to the officers' trap. It was empty. I walked over to Manson's room, where COs huddled. Johnson was one, and he offered a wry smile and rolled his eyes. Manson writhed on his bed and clutched at his neck. I had to admit it was a good performance. Not too over the top.

"Good. Here's Dr. Black," the nurse told Manson.

It was unusual to see the nurse in the wild. Rarely did I see her venture outside her nicely locked cage, where she could safely dispense medications without having to interact too much with the inmates.

I did my best to exhibit calm and concern for Manson—just as I would have if I hadn't agreed to a harebrained scheme to bust said patient out of the joint. I checked his pulse and monitored his breathing. Manson looked up at me with panic in his eyes. He didn't look like faking was a stretch. I'd seen enough drug reactions. Mellazine was an older tranquilizer. Given to someone who wasn't psychotic, it could be incredibly sedating and disorienting.

Turning to the nurse, I said, "Did he take the Mellazine?" She nodded. "You did a mouth check?" She nodded again.

This was a necessity inside prison—having the patients open up and demonstrate they weren't cheeking the medication or otherwise faking the swallow to either store the pills up for sale or suicide.

"All right. Let's get another set of vital signs and move him over to the infirmary. He's having an adverse reaction to the medication."

The other CO started to help Manson up, and Johnson went to get a wheelchair. I walked briskly to the treatment team room to let Rose know I would be escorting an inmate to the infirmary and would return. The other inmates trickled out of their rooms. This signaled the end of lockdown. They shuffled into the dayroom. I caught up with Johnson in the yard. He was pushing Manson toward the infirmary.

"This feels like bullshit to me, Doc." Johnson didn't hide his opinion from Manson's ears.

"I can understand your skepticism given Mr. Manson and his reputation. In this instance, though, I did start him on a new medication. His reaction is fairly common."

We walked in silence. Manson continued to writhe, but he managed to stay in the chair. He looked pale and sweaty. I silently prayed the medication would take some of the edge off his aggression. We went through the doors to get into the infirmary. COs milled about. All looked on edge—especially when they saw our cargo. The internist and his nurse ate at his desk. He dropped his sandwich and stood. His nurse did likewise.

"What's going on?"

"Hi. I'm Dr. Black, one of the psychiatrists in the admissions unit."

"Dr. Singh." We shook hands.

"How you doing? I gave Mr. Manson here a dose of Mellazine, and he's having an allergic reaction. My concern is that his airway will be compromised."

The COs assisted Manson onto the exam table, and Dr. Singh immediately put his stethoscope to the supine inmate's chest. The nurse obtained vital signs. Dr. Singh took off his stethoscope and wrapped it around his neck. He nodded to me and stepped out of the room. I followed him to the hallway.

"I don't think he's in imminent danger."

"I would feel better if he could be transferred to the hospital."

"Why? This looks like a simple drug reaction."

I started to panic. "I think you're underestimating the potential for something bad to happen." I leaned in and whispered, "I think I fucked up. I missed that he had an allergy to the medication, and I don't want my fuckup to cost this man his life. If you don't mind erring on the side of caution, I would be eternally grateful."

Dr. Singh looked at me with compassion. "OK. I understand. No harm in making sure he's safe, right? Don't worry. This kind of thing happens to all of us."

I thanked him and walked out feeling like a bigger heel than I believed possible. What a nice guy the internist was. What a shit I was.

Despite my self-loathing, I felt relief that the plan was in motion. I walked back to the unit and basked in the glow of a possible light at the end of the tunnel. Alas, it was not to be. Midway through my return, the emergency siren went off and announced a wave of entropy within the previously ordered walls of the state hospital.

Chapter 30

I **sprinted back** to my unit, heedless of the yard CO. The loudspeakers blared, "Emergency, max units. Emergency, admissions unit. Emergency, max units. Emergency, admissions unit."

COs moved in every direction. I stopped short of the unit's doorway. The sliding door stood open; everything inside was chaotic. The dayroom resembled a run on a bank. Inmates scuffled with each other and COs. In the doorway of the dayroom, inmates pushed to exit, and three COs struggled to keep them in. Within the melee, some inmates caused general mayhem. They lit makeshift torches (T-shirts on toilet plungers). Officers pushed by me into the brouhaha to help their comrades. I caught a scent in the air. Panic. Glands in the body released a particular odor when in danger. The pungent, unpleasant smell clung to the officers desperately working to regain control.

"Get in the fucking office!" Sergeant O'Leary yelled.

With a push, he sent me down the hall. I stumbled into the office as the loudspeaker sounded out what would be the last overhead announcement that day. "Code violet. Code violet. All officers are to report to their designated locations."

I puzzled over that and looked around the room. A group huddled around Paul's desk. It included Rose and another social worker, Mariano Vega. He worked on the max units, but he had been helping out since Margot was fired. He'd been at this work for a long time, and it showed in his efficiency and deftness in handling difficult cases.

I sat heavily in one of the ancient wooden chairs. Paul spoke on the phone. I waited till he hung up. "Man, it is chaos out there. I can't get my heart to slow down, you know?"

He looked me over. "You're sweating like a whore in church. Did you see what happened?"

"No. I was halfway back from the infirmary when they called the emergency. The dayroom looked like it exploded. The COs are in a panic."

"Holy shit. Well, we knew it was coming."

"What's a code violet? I've never heard that before."

"Code violet means there are more emergencies in the hospital than can be managed at once. It usually means a riot."

"Shit."

"Oh yeah. You know, it's almost a relief that it finally happened." To underscore his point, he let out a sigh worthy of the stage. "Like when storm clouds roll in and threaten you with thunder and then finally release their torrents of rain."

I lowered my voice. "Paul, I need to talk to you."

"We could be in here for the long haul." Paul hadn't heard my request. I repeated it.

"What does 'long haul' mean?" Rose squeaked.

"Just what you think it means. There was a time we were in this office for, what, six, seven hours? You remember that riot in '92, Mariano? Christ, we thought we were going to have to shit in a corner it got so bad."

Mariano nodded his head solemnly. "A long time to be holed up in an office," he said with his Spanish accent. "I was over in the maxes, where the shit went down. We were scared. I tell you that."

Paul turned to me. "What'd you say?"

"I said I have things to tell you."

He gave me a knowing look just as the door flew open and gave us all a shock. O'Leary came in. He was breathing heavily. He closed and locked the door, and then he looked at each of us. "One, two, three, four. Where are the rest of you?"

Paul stood and came around his desk. "We're a little short on staff overall. This is who was in here when they called the emergency."

The sergeant ran a hand through his sweaty hair, put an arm around Paul, and tried to walk him to a corner.

Paul stopped. "Hey, man, you got something to say, we can all take it."

The big sergeant turned to the rest of us. "OK. Here's the deal. The captain's pulling all the COs out. It looks as if there's a hostage situation, and this is how they want to handle it."

"Fuck. Who's involved?" Paul asked.

"Pulling out? What do you mean?" Rose's voice reached a new pitch.

O'Leary ignored Rose and answered Paul. "We're not sure, but it's gotta be either Los Reyes or White Dawn, right?"

"Who's being held?"

"We're not sure of that either. But we haven't accounted for a couple of the COs, including Johnson."

I sucked in air. O'Leary looked over. "What?"

"We escorted Manson over to the infirmary."

"Why did you take Manson to the infirmary?" Paul asked.

"He had an allergic reaction to a medication I gave him."

The sergeant looked skeptical. "I heard that story from Johnson when he left the unit. Anything to do with Manson, you know, is automatically suspect. You had to be aware of that, Doc."

I didn't know what to say. I wasn't sure if he had just accused me of something nefarious or called me an idiot. Maybe he was just pissed off I had put one of his COs in harm's way. O'Leary breathed heavily. "Well, this is what we worried about. Right, Paul? So shit finally happened, and here we are."

Nobody seemed to know what to say to that.

Paul finally broke the silence. "What's going to happen now?"

The sergeant shrugged his shoulders. "You heard it. You know what it means. They're pulling us out."

"Pulling you out?"

Paul placed a reassuring hand on Rose's shoulder and gave O'Leary a questioning look. "I'm also confused by that order."

Still no answer from the sergeant.

"So what do we do now? Do we just stay in here?" I asked.

"You bet your ass. We sit tight; that's what we do," O'Leary said.

"We? You mean you're staying in here?"

"Fuck yeah. I got no control out there. Right now the inmates are somewhat confined, but that usually doesn't last. My guys are gone, so I can't guarantee your safety."

"I don't understand. What do you mean your guys are gone?"

"Doc, the captain called a code violet. They pulled everyone back. In a situation like this, where there's total chaos, the best option is to regroup, figure out where the problems are, and solve them. I understand why they do it, but I never like the idea myself. Leaving my clinical staff unprotected doesn't strike me as good policy—even if you can bunker down here behind a locked door. I sent my guys out, as per protocol, and I came in here to settle down with you folks."

"What's going to happen to us?" Rose pleaded. She looked like panic incarnate.

The sergeant put a meaty hand on Rose's other shoulder for reassurance. I had half a mind to add my hand to the mix. Like rubbing the Buddha for good luck.

"Nothing will happen to you. We're behind a strong door; we'll wait for the cavalry. Something you should know about inmates. A lot of them talk tough, but it's only a few who are really dangerous. Most of these guys don't want to get involved with something that's going to add a lot of years to their bids. The heavies, the violent ones, they've got beefs with the gangs—not with us. We stay in here. We'll be all right. Soon enough, they'll bring in the state troopers and get us out of here." He sat down and spoke in a quiet voice. "Sometimes you need to have these explosions. Like opening the valve on a steam pipe. You don't do it, and worse shit happens.

"All in all, Pat, it's mighty decent of you to stay with us," Paul said. "We appreciate the support you've always given us these many years."

"Thanks. You too, Paul. You too."

Paul nodded at the sergeant's hip belt. "I see you got your radio. Any chance of getting updates?"

O'Leary took the radio out of its holster and placed it on the desk. "Useless as teats on a slab of bacon. They went to radio silence in case an inmate gets hold of a CO's radio and listens in on our conversations."

Paul nodded and picked up the phone. "I'm going to try to see what's going on."

Rose still looked petrified.

"You OK, Rose? Rose?" She snapped to attention and looked at me. "I asked if you're OK."

"I don't like being trapped. I'm claustrophobic."

"It will be OK, Rose. *No te preocupes.* We're safe in here," Mariano said.

Paul got off the phone. "No info. They just said to sit tight."

"Oh shit. Oh shit. Oh shit." Rose rocked in her chair.

"Relax, Rose. Everything is going to be OK," Paul said.

Rose started to go off like a Roman candle. "I don't like that door locked. We are shut in. What if we run out of oxygen? What if I suffer a heart attack? Am I just going to die here?"

"Nobody's going to die. You're going to be fine. Right, Dr. Black?"

"That's right, Paul." I walked over to her. "Close your eyes. Take some deep breaths."

Rose made desperate attempts to breathe slowly. It would have been comical had it not been so pathetic. "Slow down. Slow down. I want you to visualize yourself in a great open field. Can you do that?"

She bobbed her head up and down. Her wide eyes searched my own for reassurance. It was ironic. Here was someone having a panic attack, and a psychiatrist was close at hand. Medications were just down the hall, but for all intents and purposes, they were a thousand miles away. I turned to Paul and made that point.

Rose looked sheepish.

"What is it, Rose?"

"I have some Xanax in my purse."

That was a big no-no. We were expressly told that if we brought in any drugs into the hospital, it warranted immediate job dismissal. In the present situation, I didn't think anyone would rat her out. Having her pleasantly sedated would also prove advantageous.

"We won't say anything if you take a pill. Right, Sergeant? Right, Paul?"

"Absolutely," both said, but O'Leary looked exasperated.

Rose got her purse, rooted through it, and pulled out a pill bottle. She wasn't even trying to hide it in her bag. She had a lot to learn about camouflaging contraband. I would have to arrange for a tutorial for her from one of the hardened cons when we got out of this. She took out a pill and dry swallowed it. Clearly she'd done that before.

"Better?"

Rose's head went up and down again. Her pupils were no longer dilated. *Got to love the placebo effect,* I thought. The real effect of the Xanax would put Rose in a pleasant fog for the duration of the lockdown. During that time, Mariano would handle it like the pro he was. For me, it turned out to be a time of reckoning and coming clean. My confessors would be Paul and O'Leary. Absolution was not necessarily in the offing.

Chapter 31

We sat in silence. The thick doors and walls blocked out the sounds beyond our refuge. Rose's rhythmic breathing kept time for us inside the make-shift bunker. Egocentricity kept me shrouded in a cocoon of self-absorption. I could only think of my own predicament. What had happened with Manson? What type of legal trouble could I be on the hook for?

I realize now just how oblivious I was to the dangers around me at that moment. For whatever reason—naïveté and stupidity, probably—it only occurred to me later that we sat on a razor's edge in that office. A wooden door built sometime in the forties was the only thing between us and the capricious whims of psychotics and psychopaths—a pack of wolves incarcerated because of moral laxness and, for others, distortions of reality. God looks after orphans and drunks, they say. I would add narcissistic, self-absorbed, naïve fucks like me.

Here's how we were arrayed in the room. Mind you, it was not a big room to begin with, and it grew even smaller quickly. Though one wall was lined with windows, those windows didn't offer much of a view. There's nothing like metal grating over glass to reinforce the message that there is nowhere for you to go. Paul, his long legs ever propped up on his desk, sat in his own swivel chair. I was opposite him in a straight-backed wooden job that made me think of hemorrhoid commercials and rectal discomfort. Mariano sat cat-ercorner to a dozing Rose. She was sprawled out face first on the desk in front of her. Finally, Sergeant O'Leary sat in the last corner. He had a swivel chair as well and leaned against the wall periodically. He extended his hands above his head and drummed a beat with the backs of his fingers. His presence, though welcome, dampened the discussion; it was unusual to have officers in the treatment team office. Paul broke the ice. "This is going to be a giant cluster."

O'Leary's head bobbed up and down. "Heads are going to roll. That's for sure."

"What do you think happened?"

The sergeant leaned forward in his chair. "We knew there would be trouble. I mean, shit, you put these gangs together in such small quarters. It should never have happened. No offense, Paul, but the powers that be never listen to us when it comes to the bughouse. They take their cues from the mental-health folks and send us guys who don't belong here. They just hope we sort it out."

Tension always existed between us and the COs. They thought we indulged the inmates too much. In their minds, all the inmates pulled the wool over our eyes. To them, there wasn't so much mental illness as degrees of faking. Anytime we advocated for someone, they thought we were idiots falling for a ruse.

"That's a little unfair, don't you think? Some of these inmates need to be here. The rest take sorting out. We do a pretty good job of that. Anyway, we don't go petitioning the supermax prisons to send us their shittiest customers."

"That's true. Maybe I spoke too quickly. You guys over here, especially on this unit, do a good job. But those knuckleheads in supermax, they want to unload their headaches. So they send them here, not realizing that security concerns aren't priority. I know you guys try to do good work here and aren't just fucking around, but you're trained to see things differently than us COs."

"We're part of an important process. Some of these guys don't belong in prison, and you know it."

I hadn't seen Paul show so much irritation before. It wasn't lost on O'Leary. The beefy CO held up his hand. "I know you're a good guy, Paul. Security is not your primary concern, and that's how it should be. But I got to be mindful of those issues. Sometimes the needs of the psych hospital make my job difficult."

Silence again.

"Did you think they would pull everybody with this code violet?" Paul asked.

"I suspected. Maybe not what I would have done, but we got a good union. They look to protect COs. In a riot, you can't ensure the safety of your own people. Why put them in harm's way?"

Paul paused. "This is all on Manson, isn't it?"

The big head bobbed. "Got to be. All his people coming here along with the Reyes boys. It was a disaster waiting to happen. I still don't know why you kept him here."

I had an idea about that. My heart anticipated spilling the beans and kicked into high gear. I opened my mouth to speak, but Paul beat me to it.

"We received pressure from above to keep him here and not send him back."

That was news to me. Hatchett and the US Marshals Service came to mind. It made sense they wouldn't just put their eggs in one basket—mine, as it were. I cleared my throat, and all eyes turned toward me. "I might know something about that."

Paul put his feet on the floor, folded his hands, and leaned forward. He wore a half smile. "Finally. Some disclosure. I wondered how long you could hold out."

I let out a combination of a sigh, a cry, and a whistle. It was spontaneous and the product of a shitload of built-up stress. "I am in a world of shit, Paul. You have no idea."

"Don't be so sure. I have some idea."

"I suppose you do."

Shouting in the hallway outside the door cut me off. We got deathly quiet. There were multiple voices and footsteps, and then the doorknob jiggled and pulled. The lock held, and the footsteps and voices faded. We collectively exhaled.

"You were saying?" Paul turned back to me.

"How much do you know?"

"What the fuck are you two talking about?" O'Leary chimed in.

Paul and I didn't break eye contact. He said, "I've been in this business a long time. As soon as you started acting funny, I knew he had something on you. I imagine it's to do with Margot, but I don't know specifics. I know you're tormented. It will help for you to unburden yourself."

"Keeping this from you has been the toughest part for me. I know that sounds like bullshit just to garner pity, but it's true."

"I believe you."

"Anyway, like you surmised, Manson used his leverage with Margot to get me to advocate keeping some of his cronies here," I said.

"You fucking didn't!" the sergeant yelled.

I ignored him and kept my eyes focused on Paul. "I'm not proud of it. I have professional integrity. It made me sick to do, but I couldn't let him do something to Margot. She's not a bad person. She trusts too much and got pulled in by a psychopathic piece of shit."

"You did too," Paul said. "Maybe you shouldn't be so hard on yourself."

"It gets worse. You remember how fucked up I was last week? I went to the casino to unwind, and I ended up getting into a fifty-thousand-dollar hole that Manson bought up. He put the screws on me to help."

I clammed up and looked over at O'Leary. This confession was not helping clinician-CO relations. He fumed in his corner.

Paul noticed O'Leary. "Pay no mind to the sergeant. He might look as if he's pissed off and has no compassion for what you went through. But he's been to Vegas. That is to say, he's been around. He knows damn well there's often a thin line between the fellows wearing the orange jumpsuits behind the bars and those wearing blue uniforms in front of them. In fact, there are guys here on both sides that were high-school classmates, and it was only the grace of God—or a drug bust—that sent one to prison and one to work for the prison. If the good sergeant is truly honest with himself—and I know him to be a good, honest man—he will remember, oh, fifteen years ago we had a CO who got himself in deep with an inmate. I recall that CO gave a uniform to the inmate and walked him out of here. Quite the scandal. In fact, it's often the COs who get in trouble, seeing as how they are in closer contact with the inmates."

It felt good hearing Paul say those things. O'Leary softened—or displayed what he was capable of showing as softening. "You might be right, Paul. But that don't excuse what this young fellow did. He put us all at risk."

"No. I mean, yes. He did fuck up. No question there. But you gotta take it in context. This guy, this Dr. Black, is a caring and compassionate guy. He might get his judgment clouded with pussy or money or gambling…" With those words, he shot me a glare. "But his heart is pure nonetheless."

I smiled. "Thanks, Paul. You're a gem of a man. I mean that from the bottom of my heart. No sarcasm."

"What did Manson want in exchange for forgiving the debt?" O'Leary irritably asked.

Looking back and forth between Paul and O'Leary, I waffled. My courage waned. I couldn't admit my role in this fiasco. The sound of the door being shaken in its frame broke the awkward silence.

"Open up in there! It's all over. You can come out now."

O'Leary stood, put a finger to his mouth, and shook his big head. Someone jiggled the doorknob roughly.

"Dr. Black, we know you're in there. We seen you running into the office. Come out. We don't want to hurt you."

I couldn't be sure, but it sounded like the big guy, Whitney. Manson's right-hand man.

It unnerved me to have someone just on the other side of the door. I shot a glance over at Rose and saw she still slept. At least that was good. She would have shit herself.

"I need your help, Dr. Black," he continued through the door.

The quiet between his yells was oppressive. My heartbeat pounded in my ears.

"Mr. Manson needs you. He ain't going to make it. Whatever shit you gave him left him defenseless." More banging on the door.

At that moment, on the other side of the room, shadows formed at the windows. Sparks flew outside the window on the far left. We were all startled. Assaulted from both ends.

"C'mon, Dr. Black. If I wanted to hurt you, I could easily do it. You come with me, and I will guarantee your safety."

The sparks stopped; black-glove-clad hands pulled the grate off. State troopers in full SWAT gear appeared in the window.

"Fucking finally." O'Leary stood and roused Rose.

They used a crowbar to open the final part of the window frame. The lead guy poked his head in. "All right, folks. Let's get you the hell out of here."

Behind him I saw an opening in the fencing. A squad of black-clad men with AR-15s at the ready surrounded it. O'Leary put one hand on the window frame and helped the groggy Rose up and out. He asked for a status update from the statey.

"What we know is there are several COs unaccounted for—some in the high-security unit and others either in the maximum units or the infirmary. We aren't completely sure. We've got a hostage negotiator here."

"We still don't know which COs are being held hostage, right?" I asked. Ever so slowly, I backed away from the window.

The statey turned to me. "I don't have their names."

Paul noticed my movement and shot me a funny look. He extended his hand. "You're next, Dr. Black. Up and out."

I retreated toward the door leading to the chaos. "I'm more capable as a hostage negotiator, don't you think? I know these guys. I know how to handle crazies."

"What the fuck are you talking about, Doc? You get your ass out with the rest of your team. Let the professionals do their jobs," O'Leary said.

Paul agreed with O'Leary. "Whatever you're thinking of doing—for redemption or some such fucked-up motivation—don't. You have to come with us right now."

I slowed, but I didn't stop.

"Holy fucking shit, Doc. You go out that door, you only give them another hostage. Use your fucking head," O'Leary said. His face was a deep shade of crimson.

The statey chimed in. "We've got to get moving now. I can't keep the window or the fence open any longer. I need you all to exit. Right now."

"I'm sorry, Paul." My hand reached the doorknob. "I haven't covered myself in any glory with this whole situation. Right now, I've got nothing to be rescued to. I'm looking at serious trouble for what I've done, and I won't be able to live with myself. Especially if I've caused harm to Johnson. He's a good and decent man."

The statey glanced at my hand on the knob; he raised his gun and pointed it at me. "Doc, or whoever the fuck you are, if you open that door, you'll be sorry."

My sphincter went lax. I'd seen a lot of movies, but until that point, I'd never had a gun pointed directly at me. Another first. Much more fun watching it from the comfort of a big theater bucket seat.

Paul put his hand out to calm the situation. "Whoa. Bring it down. There's no reason to make threats. We're on the same team here. Jojo, take your hand off the doorknob. That's a good boy. Now come here, and let's get the fuck out of this room."

Maybe it was the influence of the automatic rifle's business end pointed at my head, but in a way, my life flashed before me. It wasn't a replay of highlights. More a reckoning of everything I had accomplished, aspired to do, and failed to do. I felt empty and unfulfilled. In that moment, I made a split decision that was at once impulsive and reckless but also reasoned out—if that can be believed.

"Paul, I can't rely on extreme unction. I have to make things right myself."

His face registered alarm. "It's not redemption, man. It's suicide."

I lowered my head to Paul as if to say he was right. What was I thinking? I feinted a move forward in the direction of the hole and rescue. The statey lowered the muzzle and turned his attention back to the fence. In that moment, I opened the door and slipped through a crack barely wider than my profile. I slammed the door just as quickly and cut off Paul's shouts.

Chapter 32

I walked down the unit and looked around. The doors to the rooms were all open, and guys milled about. Some lounged in the dayroom. That included Thompson, who'd remained a poor study on faking mental illness. He pointed and called out. "Hey, Doc, whatcha doing here?"

He stood and jogged over to me. I tried to melt into the wall. Vulnerability, thy name is prison without any guards.

"Doc, you seen Lester? I know you left with him. Where's he now?"

"I'm not sure." I tried my best to keep things light. This was like being at the zoo with no fences or boundaries between you and the whims of feral animals. I forced my focus back to the infirmary. "Look, Thompson, I have to go. You make sure people are safe here, OK? I'm counting on you to do the right thing."

His hyena laugh suggested I had told him the funniest joke. Thompson slapped me on the back playfully. "You're a riot, Doc. I'll keep guard." He performed a half-assed salute. "Who's gonna look out for you, huh? You goin' into the yard like that?"

We both regarded my oxford shirt and tie. Thompson peered out into the yard. "Doc, in that outfit, you're like a neon sign advertising 'fuck me up.'"

He took off his white jumpsuit and looked at me expectantly. I complied by stripping off my shirt, tie, and pants.

"Why you doing this for me?" I asked him.

He looked me straight in the eyes. "I joke around, but I appreciate what you said to me. You didn't give me any bullshit. Told me like it is. You really

190

cared." Thompson blushed and looked down. "Believe it or not, Doc, I want more out of life than this." He spread his arms wide and indicated the unit.

That made me smile despite my circumstances. I fastened the jumpsuit's buttons from stem to stern. "How do I look?"

Thompson nodded his head appreciatively. "Like a doctor who's going to a Halloween party. But it beats the other outfit. Good luck."

We shook hands, and he sauntered back to the dayroom. He hooted it up as he modeled his new threads for the other cons.

I walked into the yard and found a study in surrealism. Instead of the accustomed order imposed on the yard, it was chaos on display. Inmates were everywhere. On the lawn, white jumpsuits mixed in with green, but it was more than that. Men had stripped to their waists, showing off every color of the human spectrum from Casper white to the deepest umber. I walked toward the infirmary, and several smells hit me at once. It was not just the dead smell of prison but weed and tobacco smoke and something more acrid.

I was flooded with memories of school during summer break. The grounds looked the same, but without the sense of authority, there was freedom to do what you wanted. The empty school dared you to act out against it. You strutted everywhere with impunity. Where discipline had once reigned, there was now a vacuum. Palpable. As if someone had released a giant pressure valve. The inmates were happy to be free of the constant order. I caught the fever and flitted on and off the grass.

Outside the minimums, inmates sunbathed. I moved through this throng unmolested. I recognized some of the genuine psychotics as they shuffled along the paths. What would become of them when they didn't get their meds? Things would get interesting then.

My path to the infirmary took a serpentine trek around various clusters of men. I kept my focus on my destination. A rising sound caught my attention. To my left, several inmates encircled an unfortunate smaller man. I couldn't see who, and I wasn't interested. Onward.

"Leave me alone! Somebody help."

Shit. I turned toward the recognized voice and caught sight of Anjelica, the makeup-wearing transgender inmate. I didn't recognize the inmates who tormented her. She kept shrieking. "Don't let them hurt me! Don't let them rape me!"

I came to a dead halt. A detour, to be sure, but could I live with myself if I didn't intervene?

I jogged toward the circle as an impromptu plan formed in my head. I drew near and pulled inmates away like a blooming onion. I relied on the element of surprise, my jumpsuit, and general chaos to help me. In the center, two inmates sported the tattooed insignia of Los Reyes on their biceps. They pushed Anjelica down and pulled at her jumpsuit.

"Let's see if he's got a pussy, courtesy of the good old Massachusetts Department of Corrections."

Anjelica looked in near shock. I grabbed her arm and yelled at the top of my lungs. "Honey, how could you? After all we've been through."

I pulled with all my strength. The two gang members stood stunned. I dragged a stumbling Anjelica and dodged in and out of the crowd. I crouched low and pulled her down with me as she hastily pulled her jumpsuit up. We watched the two assailants scan the grounds for us.

"I'm OK, I'm OK. Leave me alone." She ripped her arm free.

I stopped and faced her. "Anjelica, it's me. Dr. Black."

She offered a big grin when she recognized me. "I knew you were a kind man."

"That's great, Anjelica. Come with me."

"Where you going?"

"Does it matter? It's away from those two."

I did my best to walk nonchalantly and scan the masses. The crowd thinned around the maxes. Made sense. The gangs were concentrated in those buildings. Two stacks of burning mattresses ten feet high stood sentry at the entrance. That explained the caustic smell. We both felt the bad juju and Anjelica said, "Let's get the hell away from here."

We cut a path straight across the grass to reach the infirmary. I held her back and peeked in. There were more Reyes inside. I turned to Anjelica.

"Go to the administration building and see if you can hide in there. I don't think you'll be safe out here." I pointed with my head inside. "More gang members."

She shook my hand appreciately. "You be careful, too, Doc. They don't like your kind, either."

"Thanks, Anjelica."

She gave me a puzzled look.

"What is it you're doing here anyway?"

"I have to see if I can help Johnson in any way." I replied.

"Oh, he always treated me nicely. Good luck." With that, she was off.

I paused to come up with a plan. Nothing. Oh well. By now I was one with improvisation. It seemed a reasonable strategy, owing to the fact my mind was maddeningly blank save one intention. Redemption at all cost.

I inhaled deeply and entered the building. Several inmates sat around the infirmary's half-door and smoked cigarettes. To the left, two inmates banged on the Shoe's heavy metal door and yelled into the camera mounted above it.

"Come out of there, you motherfuckers. Face the music. You can't stay in there forever."

The inmate stopped banging just long enough to notice me. "What the fuck?"

I backed away slowly, but another inmate grabbed me roughly. "Who the fuck're you?"

"I'm nobody. Leave me alone."

"Nobody? Except you wearing motherfucking Cole Haan shoes and try-ing to pass off as another con."

The door-banger looked me over. "I know who this is. Hey, Javier! You gotta see who we got. One of the fucking doctors!"

That didn't sound good.

"Fellas, what are you doing?"

"Shut the fuck up. Javi, we got something good for you."

A third inmate came out of the infirmary. Powerfully built, he carried himself like a boxer. To add to the effect, he cocked his chin with his fist and cracked his neck.

"You in a world of shit, Doc. This ain't no place for someone like you. Seems to me you're engaged in some sort of spy shit if you wearing that white jumpsuit."

"I just wanted to check to make sure there isn't someone hurt who I can help."

The inmates holding me chuckled.

"What's funny?" I said and looked at them.

The door-banger spoke. "What the fuck is a psychologist going to do, huh?"

"That's a common mistake. I'm a psychiatrist. That means I went to medical school. I did an internship in general medicine. I can help."

"Good for you, George Clooney. Why don't you shut the fuck up? I don't give a shit if you can do brain surgery. You shouldn't be here. This is the cons' prison now. And you ain't no con," Javier said.

With my hands in the air, I spoke with an even voice. "Look. I'm not here as an agent of the DOC. I'm here as a goodwill gesture to see if I can help. That's why I work at a place like this. It's not for the money. That's for sure."

"Guys like you work here 'cause you can't hack it in the real world. Don't try to bullshit me."

"That's not fair. I work—"

He held up his hand. "Shut the fuck up." He nodded to the two guys holding me. "Bring him in here. We can add him to the other two."

They pushed me into the infirmary's treatment room. Two COs sat on the ground, leaning against the wall. Johnson looked bloodied but not too bad off. He looked at me with intense eyes, but he didn't speak. The other CO appeared to be in worse shape. His uniform was sodden with a mixture of sweat and blood. He drew shallow breaths. Broken ribs likely. Not a good sign.

"Look what we brought you, pigs. Don't be fooled by his outfit. That's one of the docs."

Johnson spoke up. "Let him go, man. He's a civilian."

An inmate delivered a sharp kick to Johnson's midsection. "We'll fucking decide who's a civilian and who ain't one. This guy's a shrink. He's just like you—far as we concerned."

"There's no reason to kick him," I said, and I made a move to help Johnson.

Everything went black. I came to on the ground, and my head ached.

"You want another, Doc?"

I shook my head and crawled up against the wall next to Johnson. The inmates gathered at the entrance to the infirmary. The room stopped spinning, and I took the opportunity to whisper to Johnson. "How you doing?"

"I'll survive," he said, and then he cocked his head to the other CO. "I'm not so sure about Franklin. They beat him bad. Payback. He had a cruel streak."

"Where's Manson?"

"In the Shoe. Why you think they're pissed?"

"The boxer-looking dude. That Javier Cruz, the Reyes leader?"

"That's him. In all his glory."

The ringing in my head intensified until I realized a phone was ringing. Cruz walked over and picked it up. We watched him pace back and forth the length of the phone's cord.

"You figure it's the hostage negotiator?"

Johnson nodded and gave me a reassuring pat on my thigh. "Just sit tight here. We'll be OK. The cavalry will come for us soon."

Cruz yelled into the phone. "Fuck with me, and see what happens. I got nothing to lose and would love to add a couple of your COs to my to-do list." He slammed down the phone and pointed at another inmate. "Get me Manson. Now."

We watched Cruz fume. I shook my head. "So that's what they want, huh? That's why they staged this riot?"

"Pretty much. But you gotta know that cons don't need much of a reason to riot. Some of them are looking at life sentences. Nothing to lose, you dig?"

"I got you. Maybe I can do something."

I prepared to stand. He shot his hand across my abdomen and bore holes into my head with his piercing eyes.

"What the fuck you think you're going to do besides get yourself beat to death?"

"I have a plan. Officer Johnson, I have to make this right."

Still applying pressure, he said, "Phil. No need for formalities." He offered a wan smile. "Look, man. This is an extremely dangerous situation. You be a wiseass with these guys—or confuse them—they will kill you and not even bat an eyelash."

"I'm willing to take that chance. I put you in this situation. Not to mention what I did to Manson."

"That miserable fuck? You're worried about him? You crazy."

"I've got to try to make it right. I mean, I appreciate your concern and all, but I couldn't live with myself if I didn't try," I said.

Cruz paced angrily. "How is it you fuckers can't get in the Shoe? There has to be an emergency way in. Like when the electricity goes out."

His guys responded with sheepish looks. The door-banger said, "Sorry, Javi, man. They don't buzz us in, I don't see how we can get through there. Bars everywhere. Thick metal. You know. You been in there."

I decided the time to act was now. Inching up the wall, I stood. They noticed.

"You best sit down 'less you want another shot to your head."

Still hunched over, I held up my hand. "Hold on, Mr. Cruz. Just give me a moment."

"OK, motherfucker. What do you want to say before you get beat down?"

"Maybe I can help you."

He cocked his head and cracked his neck. But he didn't hit me. "How?"

"It's Manson you want, right? I can get him out of the Shoe for you."

"You full of shit. He ain't coming out for nobody," Cruz said.

"He'll come out for me. He's hurt, and I know what will make him better. Once I'm inside, I can convince him to leave."

He squinted his eyes and looked at me sideways. "Why would I trust you? Out here, you're a trading card. I can use you to make my life easier when all this shit is over."

"Wouldn't it be worth the risk to have Manson, though? A worthwhile trade?"

The door banger nudged Cruz. "He's right. We got these other two COs, and we getting supermax after this anyway. Might as well make it worth it."

Cruz turned slowly to the door-banger. "Luis, you make a good point, but shut the fuck up, will you? I'll decide this without you."

I made a mental note that door-banger was Luis.

Javier turned back toward me. "What's in it for you? Why you want to give me Manson?"

"Two reasons. First, that piece of shit got one of my coworkers fired and made my life miserable." That sure as shit was true. "But second, I want something in return."

Luis snorted. "I can't wait to hear this."

Cruz maintained his eyes on me, but he pointed at Luis. "Did I not just tell you to shut your fucking trap?"

You would have thought someone emptied all of Luis's blood how white he went. *This Cruz must be a ruthless mofo,* I thought.

"What do you want, Doc?"

I took a deep breath. "In exchange for Manson, I want to walk out of the infirmary with the COs."

He shook his head. "No fucking way."

"How about one then? You keep one for your bargaining chip."

"Which one you want?"

"The more injured one. Franklin."

There was a pause like a collective deep breath. Everyone in the room waited for his response. Cruz shook his head again. "Fuck that. You take the brother."

I suppressed a smile. I had counted on the oppositional part of Cruz, and he hadn't disappointed. "Does that mean we have a deal?"

"A deal, motherfucker? You deliver, and then we'll talk. I'll believe it when I see Manson."

He took my arm and began walking me toward the door of the infirmary. "You orchestrated all this just to get to Manson?"

"You bet. You want to get to the top, you gotta eliminate all competition."

"I'm just amazed you were able to overcome the prison security."

"Just like Tet, man," Cruz said smugly. "Enough spontaneous, over-whelming force, you can overrun any organized system. You just gotta know how many are needed and where. Then you apply the right amount of pressure."

I have to say, he impressed me. He was a thug, to be sure, but one that quoted military history.

He walked me to the door of the Shoe.

"Just remember, Doc, you will deliver on your promise. I won't hesitate to bury you out back if you piss me off."

The hairs on the back of my neck went up. I didn't see this as an idle threat. I swallowed hard, but I couldn't find my voice. He couldn't have cared less. Cruz let go of my arm and retreated to the infirmary. I pushed the intercom while looking up at the camera. It was quiet for what seemed an eternity while I contemplated my next move. The door buzz shook me from my thoughts. I pulled on the handle and entered the first sally port of the Shoe.

Chapter 33

The door behind me closed and the second door buzzed. I opened it and an unexpected voice greeted me. "How the hell are you, Doc? Great to see you."

Cecil walked toward me followed by a skinny inmate with a lot of tattoos. I addressed Cecil.

"I knew you weren't crazy."

Tattoos patted Cecil's shoulder. "Don't let him fool you. This is one crazy-ass fucker. He's just not crazy like you think. You must be the doc. We're glad to see you 'cause the boss ain't doing well."

We walked toward the officers' trap at the end of the long hall. Seclusion rooms were on either side. A few had their doors open. Others, I could see, still housed inmates. Among them were some of the more psychotic cons. I was glad to see Manson was smart enough to know who not to fuck with. We walked to the alcove room at the end of the hall. Manson lay in the bed. It was like the first time I met him, but he wasn't strapped down. He was curled up in a strange position. His head and neck were contorted, a look of suffering etched on his face. I immediately recognized his predicament.

"He needs some Cogentin," I said. "Right away."

I walked to the open nurses' cage. Looking through the various drawers, I got what I needed: syringe, medicine, and alcohol swab. I drew up a cocktail of Cogentin and Ativan. Back to the alcove.

"Hold him down."

Tattoo called over to another guy who loitered in the officers' trap. "Jimmy, get over here. The doc needs you."

Jimmy turned out to be a mountain of a man. Lots of tattoos as well. You could put the whole fucking atlas on his back and have room to spare. "What you got, Sally?"

I looked up at Tattoo. "Sally?"

"Don't get smart, Doc. It's short for Salvatore. Just do what you got to."

"Jimmy, hold his legs, if you don't mind. Sally, up top. Keep his torso from bucking."

I pulled his pants down to expose his upper buttocks.

"What the fuck are you doing, Doc?" Jimmy yelled.

"Shit, Jimmy, you ain't never gotten a shot before?" Sally chided him.

I imagined it would take an army of COs to hold Jimmy down, so maybe he hadn't. I swabbed the area and jabbed in the needle. Making sure I wasn't in a vessel, I pushed the plunger in. We all stepped back. Manson continued his writhing. I pulled a chair near the bed but not close enough to get kicked.

Jimmy stood over his boss. Real concern was in his eyes. Cecil hovered in the hallway. Sally pulled up a chair next to mine.

"What happened, Doc? How come he's like this?"

"I gave him a drug to get him to the infirmary. Part of the plan we devised to get him out of the prison and away from danger. He had a bad reaction. Ironic."

"Why's that ironic?" he asked.

"Well, before I gave him the drug, he was just fine. He was supposed to feign symptoms in order to get to the infirmary. But what I gave him actually caused him a serious complication, making the transfer necessary. Just ironic is all."

"I get it. So what did you just give him?"

"The antidote."

"How come he's still fucked up then?" Jimmy asked.

"It takes a couple of minutes."

We sat there. Sure enough, in a few minutes, Manson stopped writhing. His neck loosened up.

"There we are, Boss. There we are. Take it easy." Jimmy helped Manson into a sitting position.

Manson's jumpsuit sported sweat rings under the arms and at the neck.

"Fucking A, Doc," he said slowly. "What the fuck did you do to me? You were only supposed to get me transferred to the infirmary. Not turn me into a pretzel longing for death."

"Sorry about that. An unintended side effect. It certainly wasn't on purpose."

He looked at me intensely and then turned to Sally. "What the fuck is going on? Catch me up."

"Boss, the whole place got a royal fucking. Reyes started a riot. COs hauled ass out of here. I mean, just fucking scattered. When the shit started going down and they cleared out of the Shoe, Joe rescued you from the infirmary and brought you in here."

Joe Whitney. The other big guy. I had wondered where he was. Seemed I wasn't alone in that thought.

"Where the hell is Joe now? And how did Joe get in here to bring me?"

"Beats me. But he overcame the COs in here, tied 'em up in their trap, and released Jimmy and me. Then he went to get the doc. Joe saved your ass. Reyes didn't know you were in the infirmary. They only got here after we had it locked down. Banging and yelling, but no way to get in. I think we're safe in here for now."

Manson massaged his neck and turned to me. "Is there going to be any permanent damage?"

"Not likely."

"Not likely? Not likely? What the fuck kind of answer is that?"

"Hey, I'm not Carnac the Magnificent." Staying up late to watch Carson was one of the only things I shared with my father growing up.

"Who the fuck—"

"I just mean I'm not clairvoyant. You'll be fine. It's a habit I have not to make predictions. You know, you tell a patient something will never happen, and the next day it happens. So I avoid it. But you'll be fine."

"Just covering your ass. I get it, Doc." He stood, stretched, and slowly paced the room.

Sally stood too. "What are we going to do, Boss?"

"I need time to think."

I also needed to think. How was I going to get out of the infirmary with Manson and Johnson? Also Franklin, the critically injured CO, if I could manage it. Then all of us out of the prison, ideally with the integrity of my body. That would be nice.

An idea presented itself, and I cleared my throat. Everyone turned. "I came from the infirmary. Javier Cruz is there with some of his guys. They know you're in here and want you bad."

"Cruz is there? Fuck."

"Shut up, Sally. We need to think this through. Go on, Doc."

"I promised you to Cruz in exchange for the safety of one of the COs."

"You did what?" Sally spat.

"Which CO?" Manson asked.

That puzzled me. "Why does that matter?"

"Just tell me which one."

"Johnson."

He nodded. "OK. He's one of the decent ones. I see why you made that deal. Just one question, though. Why the fuck you telling me? You could have ambushed me."

"True. But I have no interest in seeing you killed by Cruz."

"What do you propose?"

The phone rang in the officers' trap. We listened to it ring four times and then stop.

"It's the DOC. They keep calling to negotiate," Sally said.

"I have a way to make this work." I stood and pulled at the bed. It was bolted. I looked around. "Is there a bed that's portable? Or a gurney?"

We left the alcove and looked around. In the nurses' cage we found a plastic bodyboard for emergencies. "OK. I've got an idea." I turned to Sally. "The next time the COs call, you pick up. I'll talk to them."

"What's the fucking idea?" Manson was irritable.

"Sorry. The plan is this. We put you on this gurney and cover you with a blanket so Cruz thinks you're injured. That's what I told them. Anyway, Jimmy and Sally come out carrying you, and then—"

"And then what? We fight through a hoard of Reyes? That's your plan? It's pure shit."

Sally spoke up. "Wait a minute, Boss. It ain't all bad. In the trap there are some of those green jumpsuits of the cadre workers. Jimmy and me put them on, and they won't immediately know who we are. It's a good bet they don't even know we're here. We've only been in Wampanoag a couple of days. We tell them we're just bringing you out and want nothing to do with any bad blood. The element of surprise has some advantages."

Manson didn't look persuaded. "I'm stuck between a rock and a hard place. But in here, for now, I'm protected. I don't see a percentage in leaving the safety of the Shoe."

"You think they're going to stop trying to kill you?" I chimed in. "You stay in here when the riot ends. Then what? Even if you go back to supermax, you won't be safe."

While Manson thought that over, another voice piped up. "What if I was the one on the gurney?"

We all looked up. Cecil had all of our attention.

"The fuck?"

"Hear me out. Lester, you've always looked out for me. I owe you for the many times you saved my ass. I propose you all put on those green jumpsuits. Except you, Doc. You have me on the gurney with the blanket over my head. Maybe, Lester, you should shave your head or do something to change your appearance. The three of you come out carrying me. When they peel back the blanket, they'll know they've been had, but you'll have a good jump on them. We can grab some pipes and shit and really fuck them up."

"I knew you weren't crazy. All along I knew it."

"Good for you, Doc. You're brilliant," Manson said. He turned to Cecil. "Shave my head? What the fuck are you talking about? You see a fucking barber here? I mean, I appreciate the gesture, Cecil. I just don't think it will make a difference. What do we do once we're outside the safety of the Shoe, huh? Lots of Reyes out there. We get through the first wave. Maybe. But you know Cruz is a badass."

"What am I? Chopped fucking liver?" Jimmy actually looked hurt.

"No offense intended, Jimmy. Lord knows you're a bull. But even if we get past them, what happens then? We're still outnumbered."

"Not exactly," I said. "Psychologically, expectations are everything. I will set it up to them that you're on a gurney being brought out by cadre workers. Cruz's attention will be on the gurney. He won't expect any trouble from the cadre workers. They're a docile bunch just interested in finishing out their bids. It'll be like a good magician's sleight of hand. Once you get the jump on them, we rush out of the infirmary and into the yard. I'll arrange for an exit out of the prison for you and the COs."

"Just how you going to do that?" He remained skeptical.

"You leave that to me. I can make that happen."

"You're asking for a lot of trust, Doc. I don't think I can muster that kind of faith in anyone."

"What other choice do you have? Ultimately, you want out of this prison, right? You stay in the Shoe, yeah, you'll survive this riot. But they'll get to you, and you know it. This is your chance."

Sally agreed. "Boss, how much have these guys really seen you? It's not as if they got a mugshot of you. The doc has a point about the element of surprise. I like the idea."

Manson turned back to me. "Why would you help me? What's in it for you?"

I laughed. "How the fuck do you think I'm getting out of here without getting killed by Cruz? This plan is as much for me as it is for you. Besides, if I can get Johnson out, I will feel a small amount of redemption. Bringing you along allows me to do that."

Manson's eyes narrowed. I doubled down. "Look. Like you said, if I had wanted to fuck you over, there were easier ways to do it. I could have injected you just now with something to make matters worse. Clearly I didn't. Besides, I couldn't have planned this if I tried. My part was to get you to the infirmary. I mean, how the hell could I know that Cecil would even be here? Or two of your henchmen for that matter?"

"Henchmen?" Sally said. "What the fuck century are you in?"

"Quiet, Sal. I need to think." Manson stood and scratched his head. "You know what? Next time the phone rings, you talk to the DOC. Then we'll see how we proceed."

"Deal."

We walked over to the officers' trap. I opened the door to the little bathroom and found two COs. They were unharmed. They regarded me but said nothing. I closed the door. Sally asked me how many Reyes there were in the infirmary.

"Besides Cruz, there were two guys I assume were his. He might have summoned more over in the meantime. I don't know."

Manson shook his head. "That wouldn't be like Cruz. I know something about him. As strong and violent as he is, he's also arrogant. He won't think there's anything in here he can't handle—least of all me."

We sat in silence for a few minutes in the officers' trap. The phone rang again. I let it go for a couple of rings, and then I picked it up. "Hello."

"This is Captain Reynolds. With whom am I speaking?"

Impressive. Even in a crisis, he avoided ending the question with a preposition. "This is Dr. Black."

Silence. Heavy breathing. "Dr. Black, do you have any idea how much trouble you have caused us? It's most unfortunate you failed to follow the order to evacuate. Now they have another hostage. One who has more value to them than the COs because you're a civilian. We've had to delay an assault on the prison until we knew where you were. When we get you out—and we will get you out safely—I'm going to make sure you get charged with obstruction of justice. The marshals and the state troopers are here, and they are equally angry."

"Jesus fucking Christ, Captain Reynolds. Is now the time to chew my ass out? You can do that as soon as I am in your custody. Right now I need to talk to you about more important shit."

"You've got some nerve, young man." More heavy breathing. "OK, who's there? Where are they, and what are their statuses?"

"Two COs in the Shoe. Good condition. Didn't catch their names. In the infirmary, two more COs. Johnson and Franklin. Johnson is awake and mildly hurt; Franklin looks more serious. Maybe some broken ribs. Possible developing pneumothorax. Life-threatening. It is my intention to bring the two injured COs to safety."

"What the hell are you talking about? You sit tight there. Wait for the state troopers to come in there and liberate the prison."

Liberate the prison? I couldn't wrap my mind around that concept. "I'm telling you it's my medical opinion that Franklin won't be able to wait. He needs to come out now."

"How do you propose to exit the prison?"

"The same way my colleagues did."

Silence. "Negative. You stay in the Shoe and wait for the cavalry. If you try to be a hero, you'll just add yourself to the list of casualties. You are to sit tight and let the professionals do their jobs. You understand me, Dr. Black? You are already in trouble. Don't make it worse."

Raising my voice, I said, "I'm coming out, Captain, and I don't want any fucking helter-skelter clusterfuck COs who couldn't hack it as real police officers getting in my way."

"Now you listen to me—"

I slammed the phone down. The three guys looked at me. I shook from the confrontation, but I collected myself and spoke to Manson. "All right. Here's how it will go. I'll exit first and tell Cruz the cadre workers are bringing you out. You'll need to have one of you man the cameras. I'll signal to you to come out. Oh, and I'll put up my hand with fingers to indicate how many are out there. You got all that?"

Manson smiled wryly. "Look who grew a pair of leader balls, huh? I knew I had the right guy when I pegged you for this job."

"Good for you, Lester. You're brilliant."

Manson appreciated me throwing his wiseass phraseology back at him. The plan set, we all stood, and the three White Dawn members changed into the green jumpsuits.

CHAPTER 34

Man, my heart pounded so much I thought it would explode. They buzzed me through the two doors back into the hallway outside the Shoe. My fear and sweating were good props for my next acting role. Looking scared would work in my favor. Besides being true, it would make me less suspicious. Cruz and the other two Reyes sat by the infirmary door. Cruz stood as I approached.

"So, Mr. Psychology, where the fuck is Manson?"

"He's hurt but conscious. I told him you sent me in there to negotiate a truce. That you were scared of retribution and wanted to cool things off before things got out of hand."

He nodded his head. "That was good, Doc. Smart."

"Anyway, all I have to do is signal, and the cadre workers can bring him out."

"What do you mean 'bring him out'?"

"I mean he's seriously injured. He's on a gurney."

"A what?"

"A bodyboard." Puzzlement was still on his face. "The kind of thing they carry the injured out from battle." Nothing. "Anyway," I continued, "if you don't mind, can you give safe passage to the cadre workers? They got caught in there and are nervous they could get mixed up in this. They're close to the ends of their bids, you know, so they just want to avoid any trouble."

"Sure. I got no beef with them. You signal whatever you're supposed to, and we'll take care of the rest."

I walked up to the camera to give the signal. Before I did, two more guys entered the building. I didn't ask for their Reyes membership cards, but I had a good goddamned idea whom they were with. With one shaky open hand, I signaled that five guys were outside. The inside door buzzed. The Reyes positioned themselves in a semicircle around the Shoe's door. I focused on how to get myself out of the way without appearing to do so. And without soiling myself.

The outer door buzzed. Then it opened, and the first thing that showed was the back of a green jumpsuit. It wasn't obvious to me who it was. The semicircle closed in and then blocked my view. As planned, all eyes focused on the figure covered by a sheet—not the three would-be orderlies who carried it. They'd covered Cecil's turned head with the blanket and done a good job of it. The Reyes didn't suspect an ambush.

Cruz directed traffic. "Put him down in the infirmary."

They put the bodyboard down and slowly backed away. Manson cleverly timed his retreat with that of Jimmy's. He was, after all, big enough to block out the sun—let alone a man of Manson's proportions.

Cruz regarded the figure on the gurney and kicked at it lightly. "I heard you was injured. I'm here to tell you I don't give a shit. You still going to die."

He produced a blade from inside his sleeve, kneeled down, and peeled back the blanket. Cecil turned his head, flashed a king-sized shit-eating grin, and said, "Hey, baby. Where you been all my life?"

Before anybody could react, Jimmy took two of the Reyes and knocked their heads together like two coconuts. He stepped through their falling bodies and bulled his way toward Cruz. He danced like Sugar Ray. Sally went after another Reyes. Manson engaged in a wrestling match with the fifth. I froze with fascination until a random elbow glanced off my shoulder. I ducked down and crawled toward the COs on the ground. Johnson dragged Franklin away from the scrum. The latter had labored breathing, and his face was ashen.

"Good to see you again, Doc. This working out like you expected?" Johnson said.

I grabbed a hold of Franklin's collar and helped pull him. I put my fingers on his neck and felt for a pulse. Weak and thread, but there.

I turned my attention back to the fight. Jimmy was something to behold. My karmic opposite, he was in his element in a fight. For such a big man, his actions held a mesmerizing economy of motion. The White Dawn crew controlled four of the Reyes. Cruz was the last man standing. He squared off with Jimmy, who didn't seem winded at all. Sally and Manson, sporting minor bruises, sat down heavily against the wall near the subdued Reyes and settled in to watch this last contest between the two gangs.

Cruz bobbed and weaved around Jimmy, holding the blade and throwing some test jabs that didn't land. Jimmy held the same spot, pivoting and turning to face the fluid Cruz. The big man had his guard up, but he had thrown no punches yet. Cruz feinted with a bladed jab and brought his other arm around in a controlled haymaker. At the last second, Jimmy saw it coming and blocked it with his arm. Cruz retreated.

"C'mon, Jimmy. Stop playing with him. Put him on the ground," Manson said.

"It's the blade I'm watching," Jimmy said between breaths.

"*Jefe*, tear that big *cabrón* a new asshole."

"Shut your fucking trap, you spic fuck." Manson smacked the fallen gang member's head against the hard floor.

Jimmy looked relaxed and focused. He bobbed his head with Cruz's bouncing and dancing.

"I gonna fuck you up, big man. Don't you worry. I gonna *fuck* you up."

Cruz threw another couple of jabs that didn't land. Then he settled back and coiled. In a flash, like a cobra rising, he threw another haymaker. With incredible alacrity, Jimmy turned his body away from the blow, held up his left arm to deflect it, and threw an uppercut with his right. It connected with his opponent's abdomen. Cruz's grunt reverberated through the room, and he flew back four feet and fell to the floor. The blade clacked on the cement. Jimmy walked over to Cruz. He held his collar and lifted the smaller man up just enough to rain rapid blows on Cruz's upturned face. It quickly grew bloodied, and Cruz lost consciousness.

"Jesus, Jimmy. Can you throw some fucking fists or what?" Cecil had materialized.

I hadn't seen where he'd disappeared to. This was the second confirmation he didn't have a crazy bone in his body; he'd had enough sense to vanish when the shit went down. "I mean, fuck. You don't look it, but you are fast as shit through a goose."

Jimmy walked over to Manson and helped him up. "You OK, Boss?"

"Good job, Jimmy. Yeah, I'll make it. Let's get the fuck out of here. Doc, you're on."

I turned to Johnson and said softly, "Can you walk out on your own?"

"What do you have in mind?"

"I have a way out of here. I spoke with the captain. We just have to get to the admissions unit. If you stay here, I don't think you'll make it. I know Franklin won't."

Manson walked up to us. "What are you plotting over here, huh? None of this whispering bullshit, or I'm going to think you're looking to double-cross me. And then, who knows? Maybe I think it's worth killing all of you."

Manson looked every bit the gang leader in that moment.

"Relax. The deal remains the same. I was just seeing if Officer Johnson could walk."

"I can walk and carry Franklin here."

"You don't look up to it," I said.

"I don't give a fuck who you carry. Just do it now. I don't like sitting here," Manson said.

Johnson lifted Franklin up, but Manson put out a hand to stop him. He looked me over. "Seeing you in that white jumpsuit, I just thought of something." He turned back to Johnson and motioned at Franklin. "Put him down." Manson began taking off his green jumpsuit. "Take his uniform off."

"What the fuck are you talking about?" Johnson said.

"Jimmy, come over here."

That was all Johnson needed to hear. He eased Franklin back to the floor and began removing the bloodied top.

"See? This is a better way for me, Doc. You were right to put on that outfit. That bloody uniform will be great camouflage." He smiled and looked down at my loafers. "I won't make the same mistake about the shoes." Manson kicked off the prison-issued canvas sneakers.

Everyone's a critic, I thought. As he stripped Franklin, I crouched and explored the CO's injuries. His trachea was moving away from the injured side. A very bad sign.

"Hey, Quincy, MD, enough of that. We gotta move."

Manson stood decked out in a CO's uniform complete with the boots. We propped Franklin between Johnson and me. Sally did recon and looked out the door. "We're clear. Let's move."

The six of us stumbled out of the infirmary into the yard. The distance from the infirmary to the admissions unit was maybe the length of two football fields, but at that moment, it looked like a thousand miles. Especially hauling the unconscious body of Franklin. We started the trek. About halfway through, we heard shouting in Spanish. I turned my head as best I could and saw one of the beaten Reyes standing in the doorway. He was yelling to the maxes. I didn't catch every word, but my rudimentary Spanish figured he was calling for his amigos to avenge their beaten leader. Right the *chingada* now.

Johnson and I lost our grip on Franklin, and he dropped. We stopped to pick him up. I chanced a glance upward at the tower, and I glimpsed the unmistakable outline of a rifle and a scope.

"Let's fucking move!" I shouted.

We broke into a run. The deadweight of Franklin made us gallop like a horse with a broken leg. The three White Dawn members made it to the unit first and disappeared inside. Streaks came into my vision from the left. Black-clad, heavily armed figures stormed the yard from the main building and fanned out. Johnson didn't notice; he dragged me along with Franklin into the admissions unit.

"To the right. Go to the right to the treatment team office," I yelled at Manson.

Inmates sitting in the dayroom stood and pointed at the scene we made hobbling down the hall. The door to the treatment team room was locked. I didn't have a fucking key. As I began to panic, Johnson put Franklin down and fished the key out of his pocket. I let out a big sigh.

He opened it, and we all tumbled in. The door slammed behind us. I collapsed on the floor to catch my breath. A barrage of banging and Spanish curses from behind the door serenaded me.

I looked over at the window and confirmed the stateys had kept it open. I tugged on Manson's sleeve and nodded toward the hole. "We don't have much time; we've got to move. I think the stateys are storming the prison."

Sally and Jimmy huddled around Manson. He offered them a blank look. "No, boys. I'm sorry, but you all have to stay here."

"What do you mean, Boss?" Sally looked pissed.

"Use your head, man. When they see cons outside the fence, you know what they do? They shoot 'em on sight. No discussion. No Miranda shit. Just blow you away. You can't take that risk. I got the uniform. I'll make it. But don't think I'm going to forget what you did here. You will be rewarded."

That seemed to mollify them.

"I'm not going either, Doc," Johnson said. That didn't come as a surprise. "I'll wait on the stateys here with Franklin. We'll be safe."

"How are you going to explain how you got here?" I asked.

"Don't worry, Jojo. We'll tell them how you rescued us from the Reyes."

"Shit. You wouldn't be in this predicament if it wasn't for me."

"Nah, don't say that. I saw how much you risked to get me safe. That's the story I'm going to tell." God bless him, he still wore the same smile on his face. I shook his hand.

"Looks as if it's just you and me, Doc. Show me the way to get out of here." Manson said.

"Hey, Boss," Sally said. "What are you going to do once you're outside the wire?"

Good question. I'd wondered that myself.

"My son is waiting for me," he replied.

I led the way to the window and waited while Manson climbed up first. As I clambered through that hole, I turned back to the room. Jimmy and Sally sat on the ground next to Johnson. They lay Franklin across their laps with his head on Johnson. As long as I live, I could never see a sight more incongruent. In that moment, the four of them, two hardened cons and two corrections officers, were thrown together in a way that could never happen again in a thousand lifetimes. Life can be strange.

We jumped down and found the cut area in the first fence. Then we crawled through and stopped between the fences. There were no shouts, no blinding lights, and no guns firing. To our left, maybe a hundred yards, there were a lot of cars and trucks near the entrance of the prison. In our area, though, it was eerily quiet. Twilight made it difficult to make out details in front of us; we silently scanned the outer fence for a throughway. I felt tension coiled inside me like never before. At that moment, if Manson had farted, I would have jumped the ten-foot fence. He seemed calm, but I sensed intense anticipation emanating from him in waves.

"I'm so close. So close," he whispered.

Then we spotted it at the same time—a breach in the fence. Beyond that was open land. I made a move forward, and Manson shot out his arm and grabbed mine.

"One second. I gotta signal my son."

He pulled a small flashlight out of his pants, flashed three short bursts with it, and then pushed me down.

"We wait."

Crouched in no-man's-land. Every second felt like an eternity, and the silence weighed on me. I mumbled my confession in low, rapid tones—an impromptu tribute to extreme unction. It grated on Manson's nerves. He quivered like a leopard waiting to pounce. "Fuck it. Action is better than doing nothing," Manson finally said.

Suddenly a return signal of three quick flashes of light pierced the growing darkness.

"Hot shit. OK, Doc. Let's go."

He led the way. That was fine by me.

I pulled the metal fencing back to allow Manson to pass through. He got on all fours and wriggled through. Once out, he got in a crouch and pulled the fence from the other direction and allowed me passage. I got on my hands and knees to do the shimmy through the hole.

"Jojo, get down!"

The shout rent the air, and I shut my eyes. I let my body go limp. Muzzle flashes turned my eyelids bright red, and I heard popping sounds. Three rapid shots followed by a heavy thud. I opened my eyes a crack. Manson lay fallen right in front of me, a tight cluster of three bloody holes in his chest. His face registered a look of complete surprise. That held true for the both of us. I dropped my head on the grass and breathed in the dirt.

Chapter 35

was in a state of shock—something I'd witnessed but never experienced. All around me there was activity. Bright lights and sounds. But I processed none of it. At that moment, I was more vulnerable than I'd ever been in my life.

Hatchett picked me up and walked me off the grass. I caught flashes of officers swarming us and trying to pry me from his arms. In my mind, I saw a lioness on the savanna after an exhausting and successful hunt of a wildebeest. Hyenas, witnesses to the kill, descended in numbers to take the corpse from her. Hatchett proved a strong lioness, though. He pulled me with one arm and held up his badge with the other.

"He's mine. Fuck off. US Marshals Service. Federal fucking government. Take it up with the president of the United States if you don't like it."

Hatchett guided me to a car in the lot and deposited me in the back seat.

"Hey, do me a favor. Look after the good doctor for a few minutes while I detail the body of that scumbag Manson," Hatchett said to the driver.

"Sure thing, Tommy."

Steve Gomes turned around to face me and switched on the car's interior light. "Hey, Doc. You made it. I'm really glad."

"Steve, what the fuck?" I mumbled.

"I'm going to let Hatchett fill you in on all the details. Suffice it to say, we're very happy how things turned out. You did well, my man. You did very well."

I sat in silence and breathed deeply. I was trying like hell to get enough air. Hatchett returned to the car, and Steve started it up and pulled out. The marshal threw his arm over the headrest to face me. A huge grin was on his face. "Wow, Jojo. You really pissed off the corrections brass with that phone call."

"You were listening, then," I said, the strength returning to my voice. "I hoped as much."

"You know it. It was clever of you."

"I had to put on that asshole act to say what needed to be said."

He held up a hand. "No need to tell me. That helter-skelter comment was perfect."

"So nobody else suspected?"

"Nah. They just thought you were a snotty, stuck-up doctor prick. They were fucking pissed when you ran back into the fray. I mean, they went to some great lengths to rescue you folks, and you just flipped them off and ran back in. Hoo, boy, they were hopping mad. Talked about letting you fucking rot with the cons. Of course, we're glad you did what you did." He pointed to himself and Steve. "Run back in, that is. Not rot with the cons."

I looked at Gomes in the rearview mirror. "Who the hell are you?"

"Perimeter security at your service. But that's only part of the job. See, back ten, twelve years, I was a regular CO who caught wind of a drug-selling scheme involving inmates and a few rotten COs. I infiltrated that scheme and brought it down. It got me a reputation as someone who couldn't be trusted by other COs, but it also caught the attention of my superiors. They put me on perimeter security as a cover. You know, to be seen by all. But then they gave me internal security. Liaising with marshals and state troopers to keep the peace on the inside."

"This guy's being modest. He's got a pipeline to almost every nook and cranny in the entire Massachusetts Department of Corrections," Hatchett said.

"Anyway, Doc," Steve continued, "I knew you were getting into heavier shit than you could handle. That's why I kept the information lines open with you."

I leaned forward. "Were you working out just to keep tabs on me?"

He laughed. "Shit, look at this physique. I'm a gym rat. I wasn't even involved with you until you did that thing for my mother." His face got serious. "I ain't never gonna forget that. Just so you know. Anyway, Tommy and I began trading notes, and we put the puzzle together—with Paul filling in the holes."

Hatchett patted my shoulder. "You're a good guy, Jojo. Everyone saw you as someone who could be expected to do the right thing in the end."

"How's delivering Manson to you and letting you shoot him the right thing?"

"You upset about that?"

"I guess I am. Cruz looked as if he could kill me and not think twice about it. Whatever Manson was, he stayed true to his word to get me away from the Reyes. I feel as if I betrayed him."

"That's because guys like Manson are skilled at getting people's heads all twisted around. Let me remind you, Jojo, Manson got you involved in all this. Would you ever on your own do something as unethical and illegal as what he made you do?"

I hesitated. My confidence in myself was shaky.

"On your own, Jojo. Without prodding."

"No. I guess I wouldn't."

"Of course you wouldn't," Hatchett said. "You don't have the conniving nature—or the street smarts, for that matter—to pull shit like that off. No offense. You're book smart. Just not savvy about crime. That's why a guy like Manson targets you. And then he fucks your mind up so much he has you thinking he's doing you the favors." He shook his head. "You listen to me because I know these guys. He would have bled you dry, and when you no longer proved useful, he probably would have killed you. You did the right thing."

"What happens to me now?"

"Here's how it's going to work. I'm going to say you were cooperating with my office all along. Every act you made was in direct consultation with the US Marshals Service, and you served admirably. In fact, I'm going to put you up for a citizen's commendation. It might not save your job, though. I mean, telling a captain to go fuck himself, that's not going to go over well anywhere."

"I never said that."

"You might as well have," Steve chimed in.

Hatchett nodded. "I can guarantee you, though, you will not be prosecuted for anything."

"What about Margot? What happens to her job?"

"Nothing. We can't help that one; it was an internal thing. But she won't be prosecuted for anything either, if that makes you feel any better."

We rode in silence on the highway. Then something dawned on me. "How long have you been planning this whole thing out?"

"What do you mean?"

"Well, you coming along and propping me up when everything turned to shit. Were you just using me to get to Manson?"

"I'm sorry, Jojo. I know this thing was tough for you. Remember who the enemy is. It ain't me or Steve. It might not feel we were with you, but believe me, we had a handle on this thing from the moment you came to Steve and asked about Manson."

I knocked my head against the window repeatedly. Hatchett leaned over and pulled my arm so my head no longer reached the window. "Take it easy, Jojo. Take it easy."

"I don't know how you can say you were on top of this. I never felt more alone in my life."

"We had to keep our distance. But we had people on the inside helping us out," Steve said.

"Like who?"

Hatchett nodded his head to Gomes. "You can tell him. We picked everyone up tonight."

Steve spoke. "Whitney's been working with us for some time now."

"You're shitting me. Manson's right-hand man? That asshole who threatened to beat me was on my side?"

"He played his part well. For a long time, he's wanted out of the gang life. We think he got wind of Manson handing things over to his own kid, and that was it for him. He approached us months ago and fed us info. He's going to be relocated to another state to serve out his sentence."

That explained where Whitney had disappeared to after getting me to the infirmary.

"Does this mean Manson's son is going to take over?"

Hatchett smiled. "Nah. He suffers from delusions of grandeur. We picked him up on a small beef and insinuated we had him on a murder rap. He ratted out his old man to stay out of prison. That's how we knew about the light signal from Manson."

I had only one more question. "How about the state trooper who threatened to kill me? Wilson. Was he in on this, too?"

"No. He's just corrupt. Which reminds me." He picked up the radio handheld. "That's a go on Trooper Wilson's arrest."

The receiver squawked back, "Roger that."

"How can a marshal arrest a state trooper?" I asked.

"I *also* work for the marshals. Like Steve, my talents have me doing some unusual work with several agencies. You helped us cement a case against that statey piece of shit. He won't be bothering anyone else. I can assure you of that."

I pulled free of Hatchett's grip and resumed banging my head against the window. "I can't believe this. I must have aged fifty years in the past few weeks, and you knew about all this. You led me through it like a rat in a maze."

Steve smiled. "I also want to tell you that Paul's been looking out for you. He reached out to you, didn't he?"

"He did. Repeatedly. You know how much guilt I've lived with the past couple of weeks? And to know that everyone else was in on this but me— that's goddamned humiliating."

"Jesus, Doc. Don't be so hard on yourself. All in all, you handled yourself well," Steve said.

"Can I go home?"

"No," Hatchett answered. "I've got to take you to be debriefed. It might take some time, but I'll take you home afterward. Unless you want to get a drink after we're done."

"Speaking for the future me, I'll be in need of a big fucking drink."

CHAPTER 36

Holy shit did my ass hurt from bouncing up and down, almost falling with every goddamned trot. I was barely in control of my fate. How did people once use these things as a means of conveyance? My only experience with horsepower came in the form of a spec on my vehicle. I wouldn't have been able to get around in the days before cars. Just being on this equine hemorrhoid machine for the first (and last) time was enough to convince me of that. On the other hand, it was beautiful country—the foliage turning colors and all that New England crap. A good time to reflect.

I had been thrown a curveball. No doubt about that. Paul had been kind to defend me to O'Leary when we were trapped together. Hatchett and Steve were also generous. I saw the sum of my behavior differently. All my life, I had envisioned myself in dangerous scenarios, and in them, I rose to the occasion. I was, you know, a hero in my own mind. In real life, when I came face-to-face with a challenging situation, I'd acted like a complete asshole. To Margot. To Paul. Thinking I'd outsmarted everyone, when in reality I was the one with the least information.

I was proud of one thing, though. In the end, I had assisted in helping Johnson escape without further injury. And he turned out OK. The other CO, Franklin, survived, but he would probably go on permanent leave and would never be the same. Steve told me not to feel too bad about that one; Franklin had been a notorious shit to the inmates.

As for me, for all my transgressions, I only ended up losing my job. I wasn't even fired. After all the shit that went down, the Massachusetts Department of Corrections decided they no longer wanted to be affiliated with the university. The state hospital went with a private contractor, and that contractor brought on a new medical director. They called me on the telephone and informed me my employment was "no longer needed." That was how they put it. They weren't firing me. I just wasn't part of their future plans.

Hatchett made good on his word. He arranged all the reporting to reflect my cooperation with his agency. The way Hatchett made it look, I'd handed them Manson. "Without Dr. Black's help, we wouldn't have been able to blah, blah, blah." They gave me an official commendation that went into a drawer after I thought briefly of putting it in the trash out of anger at myself. My narcissism wasn't to be placated that easily.

Hatchett filled me in on what had happened back at Wampanoag after we drove away. State troopers and FBI agents came in droves and flooded the prison. Jimmy had beaten Cruz within an inch of his life. Last I heard, he remained in a coma. Fucking Jimmy was a bull. We all saw that.

With Manson getting killed the way he did, looking as if he was trying to escape, the beef on the streets between the White Dawn and Los Reyes died down. Hatchett's plan had worked, so the crisis was averted for the time being. It seemed everyone was content with the outcome.

A few days after the riot, I got enough nerve to call Paul. I could actually hear his head shaking as he listened to my explanation for the incredibly stupid things I did when I eschewed rescue. He couldn't believe I had survived my own stupidity, and he told me that if I didn't play the lottery, I was truly an idiot. Surely my luck was otherworldly, and in addition to protecting me from psychopathic criminals, it should spell instant riches. He got serious and told me he really liked me and valued our friendship. I reciprocated. The company who bought the DOC contract had asked him to stay on at the state hospital in a new role as head administrator. I congratulated him, and we vowed to stay in touch.

Shortly after the prison riot, Nigel treated me to a steak at Morton's. I harbored some resentment that he had left me behind at the casino. He told me that agents of the casino separated him from me and forced him to leave. Nigel had worried and called several times, but because I had lost my phone, I didn't see the messages. He even came to my empty apartment looking for me when I was in Long Island. When he saw the news of the riot, he was convinced I was killed. Over a filet and a good scotch, I filled him in on all the details. He cheered me up as only Nigel could do. I was to join him in a private-practice venture: Thomas & Black, purveyors of the finest psychotropic pharmaceuticals in the greater Boston area. He wouldn't take no for an answer.

So after all the shit I went through, all the fear and pants-shitting, in the end, the only punishment was the termination of my services at the Wampanoag State Hospital, a hard job with more inherent danger that paid less than most other places. I missed it already. I knew I would be chasing that job for the rest of my life. No other place would be quite as fulfilling or energizing on a day-to-day basis.

As for my father, one day I would muster the courage to tell him what went down. For now, I knew what he'd say: that I'd not really learned anything from this because the consequences weren't dire enough. He might have had a point.

I dreamed about Manson. Mixed-up scenes that made little sense. I didn't share my innermost thoughts about him or the events that transpired with anyone because I doubted anyone could understand the complicated feelings I experienced. Manson could be a miserable piece of shit, but he'd taught me a lot about myself and people. It would take me years to sort all that out. As he'd bought up my markers and was now dead, I was debt-free. Seemed fitting, but I stayed away from that casino just the same.

That left me the one loose end I was here to tie and brings me back to my sore ass. Finally, after the thousandth slap of my coccyx on the saddle, I spotted her performing the kind of jumps she'd described oh so long ago. She looked good in her riding outfit. Tight tan pants and leather boots. Hair tied back with the black riding hat on top of her head. I rode up to the fence and waited. Images of that riding crop danced in my head. Margot spotted me and reined in her horse. She trotted over to me. A blank look was on her face. "I don't imagine this is a coincidence."

"No, it isn't. I sacrificed my comfort to find you and apologize."

That seemed to take her aback. "What exactly are you apologizing for?"

"Well, to put it succinctly and in a terse way—and without preamble—I acted like a schmuck."

"When specifically?" The hint of a smile emerged. "I heard about the riot. I was glad to hear you were OK."

"Thanks. Look, Margot, a lot happened to us because of Manson, and I didn't have a handbook telling me how to handle extortion from jailed psychopaths to guide me along. So I took some of it out on you. Acted like a complete asshole. And for that, I'm sorry."

"Just for the record, Jojo, I didn't sleep with you in a manipulative attempt to get you to do what I wanted. Though, I will say in hindsight it was poor timing on my part. I felt very vulnerable and wanted to share space with the one person who could know what I was going through."

"I know. I know. I panicked and acted like a jerk. What you don't know is that I also didn't stick up for you with the administration. For that, I am sorry as well. That bit of weaselly behavior is going to stick with me for a long time."

"I knew about that too. But it's nice you're coming clean."

I thought for a minute. "Oh. Paul told you. I guess I deserve that. Just so you know, I don't work there anymore."

"Really?"

"Yeah. They went with another vendor of mental health services, and my contract was not renewed. 'Your services are no longer required.' I think I would have preferred some sort of Costanza blaze-of-glory firing, but what can you do?"

"I heard some stuff from Paul, but I didn't hear all the details," Margot said.

"I would love to tell you all about it. How about over dinner after my ass recovers from riding this horse?"

"I don't know. Maybe what we went through is too much to get over. Like we had our time, and it's over between us." Margot's horse grew restless.

"Like I told you before, Margot. I don't meet a lot of women who really interest me. I like you, and I don't want to lose that due to some piece of shit who took advantage of our good natures and tried to ruin our lives. Let's give it another chance and see where it goes. What do you say?"

She cocked her head to one side. It was a nice move augmented by the black riding hat. I found her irresistible in that moment. If the saddle hadn't been cutting off the circulation to my nether regions, I would have become even more uncomfortable. "Good nature?" she asked. "Who said you have a good nature? Certainly not me."

"Does that mean we're on for dinner?"

"Why don't you bring that horse around, and I'll show you some jumps. Maybe you'll even do some yourself."

I grieved over my aching pelvis, pulled the reins to the right and made my way to Margot.

ABOUT THE AUTHOR

 Joseph H Baskin lives with his wife and children in Cleveland. *Bughouse* is his first novel.

in the USA
nardino, CA
ober 2016